A CHINESE WINTER'S TALE

A CHINESE WINTER'S TALE

An Autobiographical Fragment

by

YU LUOJIN

translated by Rachel May and Zhu Zhiyu

A *RENDITIONS* Paperback

Renditions Paperbacks
are published by
The Research Centre for Translation,
The Chinese University of Hong Kong

General Editors
John Minford   T.L. Tsim

Printed in Hong Kong.

Contents

等我想过味儿来，他全身的重量已压在了我的身上，两只粗硬的大手将我的头紧紧把住，我闭了眼，哎呀，他那粘乎乎的舌头正拼命往我嘴里塞呢！天哪……我拼命地想别转脸去，可是怎样也无法躲过这"爱的深情"，而下身的意外疼痛，又使我仿佛挨了猛然的一击……这无法形容的难受，大约只有一分多钟，他便突然地松开了双手，瘫软地扒在枕上喘气去了。呵，我用力挣开他，浑身难受地坐了起来。只是探着身子，朝地上连连吐着口水——我的嘴里真有说不出的脏呵！我想穿上裤子下地去漱漱口、洗一洗，忽然发现了褥子上那块尚湿的血迹，不由得楞住了。

"这是怎么啦？"我惊讶地轻轻叫道。

志国抬起了头，倦滞的眼睛望见了它，忽地迸出喜色道：

"你真不明白？"不知他哪里来的一股子兴奋，一把将我紧紧搂住，按倒在炕上，对我耳语道："这叫'金针刺破桃花蕊，未敢高声暗皱眉'呀！嘻嘻！"

话犹未住，那舌头又伸凑过来，天呐，我不由使出浑身的力气，将他猛然一推，一翻身下了炕。

"你……"我急赤白脸地往地上吐着口水说道："说的什么话呀！你脏死了，脏死了！"

我用热水洗呀、洗呀，找出干净的贴衣裤换上。而当我做这一切时，志国一直半张着嘴，惊呆地望着我。我一眼也不想看他，仿佛多看他一眼，连眼珠也要变脏、变瞎似的。

Author's manuscript note to galley-proof of Chapter 7 (see Introduction, pp. xvi-xvii).

Introduction

Yu Luojin is undoubtedly the most notorious woman writer to have emerged in China since the death of Mao and the end of the Cultural Revolution.[1] She has never been recognized as an "official" writer; she has never been a state-subsidized member of the national Writers' Association, only an "amateur" member of its Peking Branch. This amateur status has meant that she has had to work full time in order to support herself. She began by designing toys, and later did art work for a publishing house. But despite this, since the early 1980s her name has become more widely known to the Chinese reading public than that of almost any other woman writer of her generation. She has simultaneously offended and fascinated.

There have been two things that have focussed public attention on her. The first was her elder brother Yu Luoke, who was shot in 1970 as a counter-revolutionary, but was later hailed as a martyr and as one of the few voices of sanity amidst the early excesses of the Cultural Revolution. Liu Qing, one of the leading figures of the Democracy Movement, now serving a long prison sentence, paid tribute to him in his Prison Diary:

> When others were trembling with fear, or raving with hysteria, Yu Luoke had courage and wisdom. He spoke for the whole of society, and he paid for his words with his life. History has proved him right... He is gone; he has been gone for many years. His grave is deserted, there are no fresh flowers, there is no green grass there; only a solitary wild goose occasionally cries as it flies past in the sky.[2]

The poet Bei Dao, spokesman for the conscience of a whole generation whose idealism had been betrayed by the Cultural Revolution, dedicated one of his early poems "An End or a Beginning" to "the martyr Yu Luoke":

> *Here stand I*
> *In place of another, who has been murdered*
> *So that each time the sun rises*
> *A heavy shadow, like a road*
> *Shall run across the land . . .*

In a note to the poem, Bei Dao wrote:

> Some good friends of mine fought side by side with Yu Luoke, and two of them were thrown into prison where they languished for years. This poem records our tragic and indignant protest in that tragic and indignant period.[3]

Yu Luojin was devoted to her elder brother, and has dedicated herself to the task of keeping his memory alive.

The other thing about Yu Luojin that has caught the public eye is her impulsive personality, which manifests itself as much in her tempestuous personal life as in her spontaneous and vivid style of writing. She is an uninhibited defender of the rights of women, denouncing the immorality of loveless marriage and arguing that divorce should be made more easily available. She has taken this stand in a country where, despite claims to the contrary, women are still oppressed by a deeply structured feudal approach to marital relationships. For this she has won quite a following, and at the same time made many enemies. She has been attacked by the Party authorities as a "fallen woman", and as a "handmaiden of the bourgeoisie".[4] As Sun Longji has observed in his book *The Deep Structure of Chinese Culture*:

> Many people—often women—publicly distanced themselves from Yu

Luojin, in order to prove that they did not belong in the same category as she did... In this society of stereotypes, people who take a single step off the track are branded for the rest of their life. They will have no position in society, let alone any right to love or marriage... Naturally the "well-behaved" and "obedient" majority has to draw a clear line of demarcation between itself and such people...[5]

The tragic fate of her brother and its disastrous consequences for her entire family, and her own individual search for love and dignity, are the two themes of Yu Luojin's first and most successful work, *A Chinese Winter's Tale*. In this and in all her subsequent writing, she is intensely engaged on a quest for truth. Indeed, Yu Luojin herself calls what she writes neither fiction, nor autobiography, nor "reportage" (a thinly fictionalized form of documentary writing popular in China), but a "literature of truth". She has tried to be honest about subjects such as love and sex, marriage and divorce, violence and cruelty, deceit and weakness, in a culture that has always cultivated hypocritical face-saving in relationships. While some of her bolder contemporaries have dared to expose social darkness, "the voyage Yu Luojin takes us on is a more revealing one, one which penetrates into the interior of her own private life."[6]

We can see this search for truth in Chapter 8, for example, when she writes of her "extramarital" romance with Wei Ying and the rediscovery of feeling:

I seemed to have been born again. For the first time I felt alive, for the first time I felt like a human being of flesh and blood and emotion. The youthful gaiety of my art school days was rekindled. No, I was much happier now because *then* I'd always been suppressing my feelings, hiding behind a mask of indifference. When I looked back on it, it all seemed so stupid and foolish! What need was there for pretence? People should just be true to themselves! My heart was like a torrent bursting through the gates of a lock...

In Chapter 7, she denounces the sexual ignorance that has been such a

handicap to the psychological maturity not only of herself but of all her
fellow Chinese women:

We learned nothing about sex, either from our parents or from our
schools. The very word was something shameful and immoral, to mention
it was almost a crime. And yet all of us women would have to experience
that night. So why should any understanding of it be kept hidden and
secret from us? Why should a motley collection of men be left to initiate us
instead, each in his own particular fashion?

Since Liberation, there'd been no ''sex education'' whatsoever in
China—we'd not even had enough of the most ordinary education, enough
food for our most basic spiritual needs as human beings...

...I realized that my longing for a life of the spirit could not be denied.

Yu Luojin is not afraid of confrontation. She believes in trying to
show things the way they are. For this many condemn her. They don't
want these ugly issues raised, and certainly not by a woman. The
Chinese male establishment the world over, Communist, Capitalist,
Nationalist, Confucian or Middle-American, has a profound suspicion
(and fear) of any woman who dares to stand up and speak her mind in
this way. And anyway, they say defensively, these threatened ''men of
letters'', she'd better go away and practise being a ''proper'' writer
first.

But Yu Luojin's reply to that is: Truth must come before Beauty.
So many of China's so-called ''proper'' writers and critics are just
playing elaborate games, the better ones among them writing reams of
palatable rubbish to placate the Party, in order to be able to slip in the
occasional sentence of ''truth''. The trouble is that having once sold
their souls in this fashion, they can only play with controversiality and
toy with modernism; they have lost their integrity, they are no longer
capable of confronting the real issues. And yet what they do for a living
passes for literature. Yu Luojin has preferred to persist in her lonely
search for truth. She has a passionate vision of the writer's calling:

Ah, this is the stuff of life! This is what writers should be writing about!
This is real and alive! We shouldn't allow our literature to be cluttered up

with garbage, with people writing just for the money and not even themselves believing the things they write! We should be telling people how to live. We should be telling them how beautiful, how precious, and how sacred this rich land of ours is! Then they will toil and sweat to create, they will yearn and aspire, they will live real lives, they will struggle—then there will be real progress!

Yu Luojin questions, without tact, the very basis of personal and sexual relationships, the very fabric of a society that brings such pressure to bear on people in their emotional and spiritual lives. It is a painful process of examination and self-examination. At the same time the act of writing has become for her a way of transcending the limitations of feminine respectability.

*

Yu Luojin's life has gone through many further upheavals since *Winter's Tale* was first published in China in 1980.

Since I was five years old, every political campaign has directly affected my family and myself. It has been a rough road. Every step has left its mark . . . Each move we have tried to make has been met head on by the authorities, and has drawn curses from the empty-headed public swayed by the official line. I could have managed all right if I'd been willing to learn how to lick the boots of the high and mighty Krats[7] concerned, and "write to order". But I could never do that.

In the midst of all this endless aggression and insult, I have never been able to convince myself of the existence of such a thing as a Rule of Law in China! What is the function of our so-called legal system? How much longer will it remain a meaningless ornament? When have humanity and human rights ever been respected in our country?[8]

These strong words were written in Germany in April 1986, as part of an interview with a popular Hong Kong magazine. A month or two earlier, Yu Luojin had shocked her friends and readers by suddenly, during the course of a limited tourist visit, asking for political asylum in West Germany, the first Chinese writer of any significance to take such a step. *Winter's Tale* had been published six years earlier, long before the thought of going abroad (let alone seeking asylum) can have occurred to Yu Luojin. But the fact that its first English translation is appearing in the Western world at this point in her own life inevitably leads us to read it in a different light, and to ask certain questions.

What was it that led Yu Luojin to take the step of seeking asylum, at a time when so many observers are being cautiously optimistic about reform in China? Some have interpreted it as an act of childishness, a rash and foolish move. She was enjoying her stay in Bonn, she could not get an extension through the normal bureaucratic channels, so she decided to use asylum as a desperate way of getting a visa. The truth must surely be very different. Even a woman as impulsive as Yu Luojin would hardly take such a step without having weighed up the consequences very carefully. She must have realized that she would in one blow be cutting herself off from her one and only reading public. She must have known that the Western academic community would do its best to ostracize her too (in order to placate the Chinese cultural apparatchiks). She knows (as yet) no foreign language, though she has read foreign literature in translation. The decision cannot have been taken lightly. The pressures leading up to it must have been immense, as were the pressures that led her to seek refuge in a loveless marriage to a stranger in the Great Northern Wilderness—the story we have before us in *Winter's Tale*.

What does she herself have to say about seeking asylum? First, let us hear her on foreign perceptions of "progress" in China:

I very much doubt if these people (Westerners who visit China and sing its praises) have gone there at their own expense. The Chinese government always treats its own officially invited guests with great lavishness and warmth, smiling all the way from arrival to departure. It puts them up at the most expensive hotels (which are not open to ordinary Chinese), and keeps them very busy. Lots of smiling faces and prosperous scenes are carefully laid on. These visitors know absolutely nothing about the tens of thousands of families like mine! They never spend a single day with people like us, they never have a chance to get to know our true feelings, or to listen to what we really think! Not one single day! So how can they possibly understand China? In Western society, ''insiders'' and ''outsiders'' are treated the same. There's no need to fake things. But in China, there's always been this double standard: one China for foreigners and Overseas Chinese, and one for the locals. This is something any child in China knows. But some foreigners are totally ignorant of it.

Then, on the pressures that ultimately drove her to this step:

Thirty-nine years of political purges have left me frightened, disillusioned and sad. I can never think of that lawless country of ours without being seized with terror...

I don't want to be a victim of the ''second Cultural Revolution''. Nobody can guarantee that it won't happen again. Look at the Campaign against Spiritual Pollution [an aborted purge of liberals in the winter of 1983-4]. All those Krats went leaping into action, hacking off high heels, cutting off long hair... It was well under way, and would have taken off properly, if the Party hadn't changed its mind at the last minute... Purges like that get started so easily, because there are always people wanting to climb up, and they know they can use a purge to put paid to others. They've seen that the persecutors of the past have never really been punished. So long as this is the case, so long as the persecutors are left unpunished, there will be more purges: to promise otherwise is futile...

Seeking political asylum is a way of protesting against China's policies, not just for myself, but on behalf of the thousands of educated people who have suffered persecution...

In China policies change three times a day. If one day they allow you to go abroad, you'd better jump. Because you never know when the next directive is going to arrive, telling you you can't go after all. It might be the very next day. I virtually fled from China.

These are not sentiments that go down very well nowadays. For a while, after the Cultural Revolution, it became fashionable for people in the West to think bad thoughts about China. But that quickly passed, with the coming of tourism and joint-ventures and Special Economic Zones, and the signing of the Sino-British Declaration on Hong

Kong, and the formulation of the ''super-idea'' of One Country/Two Systems—and all the other things that are generally supposed to constitute ''the opening up of China''. ''The Dragon Awakes!'', as our forefathers were being told in the late nineteenth century.

The extent of misinformation in the West is as great as Yu Luojin herself suggests. It is hardly surprising, considering how little the Chinese themselves are prepared to talk or write about such subjects as their own police state. In this respect Yu Luojin is an outstanding exception. She does not baulk at describing the machinery of Proledic, the ''Dictatorship of the Proletariat''. Indeed, as she writes in Chapter 4 of *Winter's Tale*, she sees it as being part of her duty as a writer:

> If I were ever to write a book, and wanted to give in it a true account of daily life under Proledic, then my experience [in the labour camps] was a necessary prerequisite. The truth is that places like the one I was in are absolutely out of bounds. No writer, however famous, is ever allowed in, to taste what life is really like on the inside. And a person without firsthand experience of Proledic can never have a full understanding of our society.

It is only to be regretted that she did not go further and provide a more detailed account of her stay in the camps. For she is one of the few who know and are able to tell. Another one who knows is the Democracy Movement leader, Wei Jingsheng, or what's left of him after all the ''psychiatric care'' the State has lavished on him, mouldering away in some labour camp in remote Qinghai Province.

There are many wishful thinkers in China, as Yu Luojin has pointed out:

> A good number of Voicers, back in positions of power after twenty-two years of forced labour, are now shouting from the rooftops: ''The Party is our Mother! If a mother has punished her children, they should bear her no grudge. So let us forget the past!''[9]
>
> How pitiable these people are! How did they manage to get back from their camps in the first place?
>
> I personally know three such Voicers now occupying very high positions again. Originally they were all three of them writers of one kind or another. Twenty-two years of hard labour in camp nearly killed them...

In order to get back to civilisation, they had to visit their former persecutors (for the very people who had once persecuted them were still in charge of their former work-units). They had to pay their respects again and again, bringing with them expensive presents bought with borrowed money, trying their best to look friendly and compliant. Anyone refusing to go through this humiliating ritual stood no chance whatsoever of being "rehabilitated" and getting his original job back.

So if like those people we refuse to speak honestly, if we force ourselves to enjoy our punishment, if we insist that this country of ours, which is capable at any time of wantonly killing its own people, must be obeyed like a mother, then, I think, a second Cultural Revolution is on its way...

Yu Luojin's great strength is her passionate refusal to forget, to deny the reality of the suffering she has experienced herself and witnessed in others. After two loveless marriages of convenience, the first described in *A Chinese Winter's Tale*, the second a cause célèbre in China during 1980-1, she married for the third time in July 1982:

My third husband was Capped as a Voicer in 1957, when he was still a twenty-two year old student at the Peking Institute of Metallurgy. He had been too bold and honest in the suggestions he offered the Party. After that, whether he was eating, walking or sleeping, he was hemmed in by a crowd of so-called "progressive" students. They wouldn't leave him alone. They denounced him in public, they roughed him up. The Institute Party Committee made an example of him. They deprived him of the right to study. Instead they made him stoke the boilers, carry bags of cement and perform all sorts of hard labour under Masswatch for years. He got twelve *kuai* a month (it was raised to eighteen later on), hardly enough for food, let alone clothing and other necessities. This lasted for twenty-two years! Twenty-two years! How many twenty-two years are there in a life-time? You can count the years, but can you count the suffering and the despair he went through, the endless boredom and depression that ate away at his soul?

*

A Chinese Winter's Tale was first drafted in 1974—the date at which the events described in the book itself end. It was eventually published in August 1980, in the major Peking bimonthly magazine *Dangdai*. But the editors made enormous excisions, for a variety of reasons—political, prudish, "literary". Rather than elaborate here on the nature of their censorship, we have indicated directly in this English version, which is translated from the author's complete text, those passages that were removed in the *Dangdai* edition. For this purpose we have used a single pointed bracket (thus— ⟨...⟩). Some five years after this heavily expurgated first edition (which was reprinted in other journals), as Yu Luojin was preparing to travel to Germany on the trip that eventually led to her seeking political asylum, the People's Literature Publishing House in Peking brought out a fuller version of *Winter's Tale*. But still there were several major omissions (amounting to nearly one hundred lines of Chinese text), especially in the key seventh chapter, where Yu Luojin tries to tell the "truth" of her first wedding night. Earlier she had protested in vain to her publisher about this particular chapter:

> If you must insist on removing this passage, I would rather the book was not published at all. *You* have all read it with the greatest of interest and not been poisoned, so why are you worried about the ordinary reader being "polluted"? You insist on editing my work, blurring its original intent, and making it ambiguous, thus forcing the reader off onto flights of fancy of his own. This is the real poison, the "poison" created by your feudal mistrust of other human beings! It's people like you who have really filthy minds! Authors should be allowed to bear the responsibility for their work. If anyone is poisoned by reading my book, and wishes to rebuke me, then by all means let him go ahead. We can hold a public debate. We can ask the question, should the book have been written this way in the first place? They can state exactly in what way they have been poisoned. And at the same time we should give those other readers who have *not* been poisoned a chance to speak out too.
>
> It is truly tragic when an author's rights are not respected. If there is no respect for the author, how can we possibly talk about respecting the reader?
>
> I beg you not to remove a single word from this passage... I bear sole responsibility for it. The editors of *Dangdai* removed the whole thing, and it made me very angry. If *they* can read it without being "poisoned", what possible justification can they have for saying that the average reader is in

peril? Handbooks like *Physiological Hygiene* go into far greater "detail" than I do, yet they are used as textbooks in schools. What I want to know is, where is the "poison" you are all talking about?[10]

Those passages that were still not reinstated in the 1985 edition are indicated in this English translation by double pointed brackets (thus— 《...》). The entire unexpurgated Chinese text is simultaneously being issued by the Research Centre for Translation of the Chinese University of Hong Kong, in a limited edition.

*

The style of this translation represents something of a new departure, and readers are directed to the Glossary at the end of the book, where the terms and the thinking behind them are carefully explained. The determination, and nearly all of the ideas incorporated in this embryonic English form of Maospeak, were Rachel May's. The Translation Centre provided a useful testing ground for some of the new terms: we tried them out, and found that after a while some of them stuck... We hope that other translators will continue where this book has left off.

Winter's Tale has recently been rewritten by Yu Luojin and incorporated into a long autobiographical work (three quarters of a million words), which includes most of her other writing to date. The complete book was to have been published, both in China and in Hong Kong,[11] but since her request for asylum and the ostracism that followed it, these plans have been dropped. Now the only place that seems willing to publish her work—and not necessarily for reasons that would please her—is Taiwan. She is an exile like Heine, her favourite German poet, after whose "Germany: A Winter's Tale" she named her book. She has joined the sad ranks of the Chinese diaspora.

*

I'm not intellectually minded. I'm not one for theories. I live by intuition—I'm like that now, I always have been, I always will be! I always rely on first impressions to understand life and society.

This statement very much sums up the character of the author and the tone of *Winter's Tale*. It is heady stuff, and some readers may find its romantic fervour altogether too much for their palate. Her purple passages may not be to their taste:

> The universe was still. Countless stars glinted their mystic light in the dark blue sea of the night. The gentle moon shone tenderly down on us, sometimes hiding itself behind the lotus-flower clouds as if afraid of disturbing our lovers' tryst...

But to have removed such passages, or watered them down, would have been wrong. It is our firm belief that this is an important and authentic personal testimony of an era that is already in too great danger of being forgotten.

John Minford

Hong Kong, November 1986

NOTES:

1. For the basic facts about Yu Luojin and Yu Luoke, their life and family background, see the Biographical Notes at the back of this book.
2. See Liu Qing, *Yuzhong shouji*, Hong Kong 1981, p. 72. The translation is adapted from the version in *Chinese Sociology and Anthropology*, 1982/3, vol. XV.
3. See *Notes from the City of the Sun*, Poems by Bei Dao, edited and translated by Bonnie S. McDougall, Cornell University China-Japan Program, 1984, pp. 58-60.
4. See *Zhengming* no. 42 (April 1981), and Cai Yungui writing in *Huacheng* (1982:3).
5. Sun Longji, *The Deep Structure of Chinese Society*, Hong Kong 1983, pp. 292-3.
6. See the introduction by Huang San and Miguel Mandarès to their French

translation of *A Chinese Winter's Tale, Le Nouveau Conte d'Hiver*, Bourgois, Paris 1982, p. 27.

7. For this, and other newly-coined expressions (Proledic, Voicer etc.) see the Glossary at the back of the book.

8. From *Zhengming*, no. 103, (May 1986). Subsequent quotations are translated from this same interview, unless otherwise specified.

9. As George Santayana said, "Those who forget the past, are condemned to relive it." These words, which hang above the entrance to the Dachau Concentration Camp Museum on the outskirts of Munich, were also placed by William Shirer at the front of his *Rise and Fall of the Third Reich*, and later by the Chinese poet Sun Jingxuan, at the beginning of his poem "The Spectre" (1980), a powerful evocation of the ghost of the Cultural Revolution, and of the forces of feudalism. For a translation of Sun's poem, see the anthology *Seeds of Fire*, edited by Geremie Barmé and John Minford, Hong Kong, Far Eastern Economic Review, 1986.

10. See the facsimile of this manuscript note, p. vi.

11. The Lijiang Press in Guilin in fact had the whole book typeset and printed earlier this year (1986), but did not dare to proceed with publication when the first rumours of Yu Luojin's "defection" reached them (officially the Chinese press has still not reported her action). Lijiang Press has lost RMB 150,000 (c. US$45,000) as a result.

IN MEMORIAM

Y.L.K.

I have written this true story

in memory of my brother

Yu Luoke

1. First Acquaintance

Suddenly, the outer door opened. It was strange that our white dog wasn't barking, considering the reputation he had in the village for fierceness.

I pushed back the small stool and stood up from my bowl of washing; and looking out through the window, I saw our white dog in the yard, facing the outer door and wagging his tail.

Two men came in, and close on their heels the snowflakes, driven in by the biting north wind. From the kind of padded coats they wore, of a faded blue cotton, you could tell that they were Urblings* from some neighbouring village.

"Is this where Zhao Zhiguo lives?" asked the young man in front. He had quite a dark complexion, large darting eyes like a goldfish, and a thick top lip which curved up at the corners in a smile. The other man, whose face was hidden from view by his yellow padded hat, was stamping his feet to get the snow off his shoes.

"Yes, it is. Please come in," I called out to them.

They came on into the room, bringing with them a rush of cold air.

"It's nice and warm in here," said the young man with the dark complexion. He took off his padded hat, walked up to the *kang**, and sat down. He took a look around the room and went on: "We just about froze to death on our way here! And then half-way we ran into this blizzard!"

The other young man, as soon as he'd come in, had grabbed an old copy of the *Reference News** which was lying on the *kang*, and sat down and started reading it without looking up, totally forgetting that he hadn't even taken off his hat.

"Would you like some water?" I put a thermos flask and two glasses on the small table between them on the *kang*, and then took a handful of fruit-drops out of the cupboard. "Have some sweets."

Urblings had the habit of constantly dropping in on one another, so there was no need to stand on ceremony; I sat down and carried on doing my washing, chatting to them at the same time.

"Where's Zhao Zhiguo?" asked the dark young man.

"He's been away now for a couple of weeks." I thought for a little while: "It's the fourth of January today, isn't it? He went back to Peking as soon as we'd been paid for the year."

"Oh, did he? Then aren't *you* going back this year?"

"Us married people are not as free as you are! If I don't stay and look after things here, how do you suppose we'll manage this coming year? Anyway, which village are you from? And what brings you here?"

"We're from West River. We just came out for the walk," the young man said. "Do you know who we are?"

"Mm, let me think, West River. . ." I put down my washing for a moment. "All the people there have been round to see us, except the Wei brothers."

"That's us! Got any tobacco?"

I handed him Zhiguo's tobacco pouch. He took a small piece of crumpled paper out of his pocket and began skilfully rolling a cigarette. Soon he was breathing out a pale cloud of smoke with the relish of a seasoned smoker: "I'm Wei Li. And he's my elder brother, Wei Ying."

"Wei Li and Wei Ying?" As I scrubbed at the clothes, I thought to myself what a lovely ring the names had. "They're nice-sounding names."

The man who had been reading the newspaper suddenly looked up as though something had caught his attention, and gave me an apologetic smile, kind and slightly rueful. It struck me how soft and intelligent his face was, and how calm he seemed. Seeing his face was like suddenly pushing open the window of a smoke-filled room and catching sight of a silver crescent-moon hanging in the clear dark-blue canopy of the heavens. It was like a gust of cool refreshing air.

Something about him reminded me of my elder brother, Luoke. Was it the oval shape of his face and his glasses with their clear plastic frames? Or was it his fair skin, his gentle features and quiet manner? It was hard to say...

"Actually," he took a close look at me and smiled shyly, "we first heard about you a long time ago."

"When?" I looked at him with great curiosity.

"In '66." His voice was so pleasant, so like my brother's.

"Do you still remember Wei Lan?" he asked.

"Wei Lan? Yes, I do!"

"She's my elder sister."

"Really?"

He smiled, and then lowered his head bashfully. My brother was never so shy.

"Wei Li and I already knew about you then."

"But that's eight years ago!" I put down my washing for a moment and turned to him: "What did she say about me, your sister?"

"She told us that you once wrote her a poem singing her praises, and she said it made her feel so proud! And she gave us quite a detailed description of what you looked like." He smiled kindly.

"Oh yes," Wei Li laughed. "So you see, we're really old friends!"

"How extraordinary!" I remembered her quite vividly. She had always stood out from the others. I could picture her clearly in my mind's eye. She had just graduated from university when I came to know her. It was '66, just at the beginning of the Cultrev*, and she had been sent to our toy factory as a member of a Squad*. I had graduated from art school in '65 and was then working as a trainee at this factory, and Wei Lan was put in charge of our carpentry workshop. All the other workers in my section were old men, and none of them ever said a word at meetings. I was the one who took the minutes, and since I was the only other young person there, Wei Lan was always trying to encourage me to speak up. Her efforts were in vain (after all, what could anyone find to say about the Kroads*), but I came to like her a lot all the same. We mostly just chatted about very ordinary things. She was interested in hearing about my family, and I told her a lot about what had happened to them all. She seemed to like me. In fact, I thought how nice it would be if my brother could get to know her, because he never had any girl-friends. She too had the same kind of glasses as Luoke, with clear plastic frames. She often wore a black and white checked silk blouse with short sleeves, and she had short hair; she was attractive though, not at all ordinary-looking. But her Squad left our factory soon afterwards, and I never saw her again. The mention of her name made it seem as though there was an invisible thread joining my fate to Wei Ying's, something very intimate and natural, something almost sweet.

"What did I write in that poem?" I asked, still trying to think. "I've quite forgotten."

"You compared my sister to the sun." Wei Li drank some water, and laughed. "Once my brother went to your factory to take her some clothes. When he came home he was so disappointed he hadn't managed to see you."

"Is that true?" I was very flattered. But Wei Ying was embarrassed and looked down.

"How the time has flown!" Wei Ying finally took off his padded hat. His forehead had an intelligent look about it and his hair was soft and black. "Those eight years have gone by in a flash. Such great changes..."

Yes, the changes had certainly been great. Seeing Wei Ying today, I began to feel very nostalgic. But what was the good? I was no longer a little girl. His sister might not even *like* me now, if she were ever to see me again...

I rubbed at the clothes, trying to banish these gloomy thoughts. I looked up at them both and asked, "Are you really brothers?"

"Yes."

"But you don't look like you are."

"That's what everybody says," Wei Ying laughed.

"I'm the big, black oaf of the family, and he's the pale-faced scholar. Is that what you mean?" Wei Li's words made us all laugh.

*

In the Great Northern Wilderness*, the winter days are short. And at that season of the year, when farming was slack, people usually only ate two meals a day. As it was now time for the afternoon meal, I asked them to stay and eat. They accepted without any feeling of awkwardness, and in no time at all, I brought out the steaming rice and a couple of dishes to go with it.

"Mm! You eat pretty well here!" Wei Li picked up his chopsticks with obvious pleasure.

"Maybe a bit better than you do." It was not the first time I'd received this compliment.

"Better than us? What do you know about the way we live?" He almost seemed to be disagreeing with me. But he was gulping down his food all the same.

We sat around the small table on the warm *kang*, eating the good rice which had been distributed by our work-team*. It was that time of winter when every family had just killed its pig—so we had shredded meat with our pickled vegetable, and sliced meat with our potato; and we also had a soup made from turnip and shredded dried bean curd. The room was filled with these mouth-watering smells; and the good food made us more talkative and relaxed. The golden lamplight seemed to bring us closer together.

"How much has your work-team been giving you for a day's work over this past year?" asked Wei Li, chewing loudly. Even in his way of eating, Wei Ying was the exact opposite of his brother, and chewed slowly and carefully without making any noise.

"Less than the year before," I said. "One *kuai** seventy."

"About the same as us."

"How much did you get this year, the two of you put together?" I wasn't expecting the embarrassed smile they gave me.

"Fifty *kuai* or so," said Wei Li with a shrug.

"Why so little?"

"We didn't get back from Peking until July," Wei Li explained. "We've only been working for the last few months. Besides, if you include our ration of six hundred pounds of grain, plus a summer's supply of muskmelon and watermelon, plus firewood and oil and so on, we were lucky to get fifty *kuai*."

"Aren't you going back to Peking this winter?" I asked.

"Yes, we are," Wei Li said cheerfully. "I'm leaving the day after tomorrow. He'll follow later. My mother's been wanting us to go back for ages."

"This place of yours is so out of the way!" Wei Ying had finished eating and put down his bowl. He leaned over and melted a little of the ice on the window-pane with his breath, then craned his neck to look out at the pitch black yard. "It's such heavy snow, still hasn't stopped yet! There must be three *mu** of land round the house. Are those trees yours as well?"

"Yes, they are." When Wei Li had also had enough to eat, I got up off the *kang* to clear away the dishes. "It *is* very out of the way here. That's why we got it so cheap. And I suppose that's how come the three people who lived here before were murdered by that Drossnik*."

"You've really got guts living here! When that story reached our village, everybody was scared stiff." Wei Li grimaced, shaking his head. "All by yourself in this lonely place—aren't you afraid? Nobody would even hear you screaming! No wonder they'd already been dead three days before the villagers knew anything about it!"

"We've nothing to be afraid of. She was loose, the woman who lived here before—that's how that Drossnik got away with it."

"But your Domper's* with the First Team, isn't it?" Wei Ying asked. "That's more than half a mile away from here. So why did you buy a house here in the Second Team?"

"Our old house was so dilapidated. We were just thinking about building another when this murder happened here; nobody dared buy the place. Zhiguo and I came to have a look. It's got two big rooms—both facing south—and a storeroom, and three *mu* of land with more than a hundred young willow trees all round it, which we thought would provide plenty of osiers for making baskets... and then there's a walled yard with sixteen crab-apple trees and a wild cherry, and there's a river running in front of the house. Of course, it is right at the edge of the village, and a little bit out of the way; but still, at two hundred *kuai* it was cheap. And anyway, Zhiguo's got a bicycle so it isn't too inconvenient for him to ride to the fields. It's only half a mile."

"Is that land round the house counted as Ownplot*," asked Wei Ying, "or have you got other land as well?"

"They didn't count it last year, but this year they probably will. There's a new policy, isn't there?"

"You've got enough land here to keep you occupied the whole year round." Wei Li leant against the wall and breathed out a mouthful of smoke from his comfortable position on the warm *kang*. "How much did you make last year out of the produce?"

"We planted sixteen hundred tobacco plants and three thousand sunflower plants, and we sold them to the State for more than nine hundred *kuai*. And then we've got a small Ownplot for our family of three over in the First Team, one and a half *mu*, where we grow potatoes and pumpkins to sell; and we harvested two large sacks of crab-apples—too much for us to eat by ourselves, so we sold them as well. Oh yes, why don't I cook us some melon-seeds."

When the melon-seeds were done, Wei Li put out his cigarette. The three of us took off our shoes, settled ourselves on the warm *kang* and started cracking the seeds with our teeth while we carried on chatting—for those of us who had enough to eat and warm clothes to wear, the slack winter season was really a pleasant time of year.

We talked at length about what was happening in the rest of the country, swopping bits of news we'd picked up from other Urblings who'd been to Peking. We talked about how the fanatics in power had managed to bring poverty even to those parts of the country which had no cause to be so poor, forcing peasants from south of the Pass* to brave the journey up to the Northeast in increasing numbers every year. We talked about the Floater* settlements ("Floaters" was how the government described the itinerant peasants) and the terrible hardships these people had to endure when they first arrived. And we discussed how they were still up against the tyranny of Class Pedigree* (which prevailed throughout the country—in the comparatively rich Northeast no less than in the poorer provinces), making it just as hard as before for the children of former landlords and Kulaks* to find a marriage partner and even harder to join the Party or Youth League*. This artificially induced class struggle had not abated even in the fertile

Great Northern Wilderness. We went on to talk about the overthrow of Lin Biao*, his sudden transformation from close comrade-in-arms to Class Enemy* Number One—a reversal of fortune which perplexed even the most ignorant old peasant woman...

The furious north wind roared, hurling itself against the window-panes, making the room seem snugger than ever. Wei Ying involuntarily looked at his watch.

"Are you leaving?" I asked softly.

He shrugged and smiled. "It's about seven miles!"

"This damned weather!" said Wei Li, pressing against the glass at the bottom of the window. "The snow's already a foot deep, and it's still not stopping."

"Why don't you stay?" I urged. "You can't possibly get back in weather like this. You might run into wolves."

They looked about the room, apparently embarrassed.

"Oh, that's all right. There's a little room in there which I can sleep in." I got down onto the floor and raised the curtain which hung across the opening in the paper partition-wall. "See. I'll sleep here."

"Well..." They thought about it for a while and eventually seemed glad to accept.

"All right?" I sat down on the *kang* and declared, "It's settled then. Good, now we can talk some more." So I asked them cheerfully: "What's life like for you?"

"Us?" Wei Li smiled. "Our group of Urblings broke up ages ago. Now we all fend for ourselves. The two of us bought a small lean-to and set up on our own. You must come and see our place sometime. Zhiguo came a long time ago."

"I heard that you were managing quite well. But I didn't know then that you were Wei Lan's brothers, so it didn't really mean much to me at the time."

"Could you tell me something..." Wei Ying hesitated, "...something about your brother?" Seeing how I carried on cracking melon-seeds and didn't answer his question, he smiled wryly and added, "You know, ever since '66 when I first saw a duplicated version of "On Class Background"* posted on the wall, I wanted to meet the author so much. And then later, when the printed version came out in the *High School Cultrev Post**, everyone wanted to know who had written it. I really wanted to meet this person—whoever he was! I only found out that he was your brother after we came here...but...aah!'' He was too distressed to go on.

Wei Li looked up slowly from his reverie. There was an intense expression on his face. ''He was a martyr!'' He repeated the words as if to himself, but with great emphasis: ''A martyr!''

I was just wondering what to say when Wei Ying suddenly changed the subject. ''I hear that your father and two brothers live up here as well?''

''Yes, in the village.'' That was my reply, but inwardly I smiled. What a kind-hearted man you must be! I couldn't help noticing the expression in your eyes! You thought that maybe you'd upset me by mentioning my brother; and maybe you regretted bringing up the subject. But I'm not a sentimental kind of person! On the contrary, I'd like to tell the whole world about my brother!

''There really are so many things I want to ask you about.'' Wei Li was not as sensitive and tactful as his brother. ''I have one question in particular,'' he said excitedly, ''but I don't know if it's proper to ask.''

''So, what is it?''

''Well, you see...'' He hesitated and smiled awkwardly. ''We don't understand why you married a man like Zhao Zhiguo?''

''Like Zhiguo?'' I didn't care for the way he put it. I noticed that Wei Ying was staring at me too. From the expectant look in his eyes, he seemed even more interested in my answer than Wei Li was.

''Ah!'' I pretended a sigh of indifference. ''It's a long story. Let's save it for tomorrow.''

*

That night I slept on the wooden bed in the little inner room. So many feelings came flooding into my mind...

A joy and excitement welled up in my heart such as I had never experienced before. What could it be? Was it the whole effect Wei

Ying had had on me—his gentle face; his sensitivity and his open disposition, which reminded me of my brother; his generous spirit and kindness; or his voice, which had a restful quality like soft music? Or was it because of some feeling he had kept for me from eight years before?... How I wished that we had met earlier! I thought with regret that if I'd only met him in October 1970 when I was on my way to the Great Northern Wilderness for the first time, and we'd had a chance to talk a little, then perhaps I would never have married Zhiguo. But I had no right to think in this way. I must never forget that I was now a mother! I was not entitled to such thoughts. They were wrong! And besides, I hardly even knew him. Supposing I did like him, then the most I could hope for was that we could be friends. True friends, close friends even, but nothing more than that. Yes, when Zhiguo came back I'd be really happy to tell him that I'd made the acquaintance of Wei Ying and that I'd like them to be friends as well; maybe Zhiguo would be as pleased as I was, and then the three of us would get along just fine... Thinking of it like this set my mind more at ease. I put on the light, turned over quietly in bed and took up the notebook and pen which lay beside my pillow. The notebook had a sky-blue plastic cover, inscribed in gold with the words: "The World is Wide, and there is Much to be Accomplished."* It was a gift given to all Urblings the previous year by a group sent from Peking to convey "greetings and solicitude". It was quite extraordinary that someone like me, someone with "reactionary ideas" who'd already been in a camp for a term of Labour Cure*, should now have become an Urbling here in the Northeast. When had the change come about? Who had been responsible for it? It was hard to say. All I knew was that I was now treated exactly like all the other Urblings. Nobody bothered to delve too deeply into the past. That was what I liked about the Great Northern Wilderness!

Whenever I held that black fountain pen of mine, it always seemed to weigh a ton. My brother was executed on March 5, 1970, and my mother and father had brought it back from the prison. I had kept it, determined to use it to try and complete my brother's mission. I would use it to recreate his spirit, even if it took me ten years to do so.

I carried on writing down my memories of Luoke in my notebook and didn't go to sleep until about two o'clock in the morning.

The next morning, I got up quietly. Lifting the door curtain, I saw the two of them still sound asleep. Wei Li was snoring softly with his mouth half open; and Wei Ying was lying flat on his back under his quilt—from the neatness of the quilt and from his peaceful way of sleeping, it looked as if he hadn't moved the whole night. What a strange sight!—he was so still, almost as if he had given up the ghost!

I went into the outer room to boil water for washing and for breakfast, trying to make as little noise as possible. But when I turned round, Wei Ying was standing behind me, looking very pensive. I couldn't tell how long he'd been there.

"You're up so early," he said gently.

"Yes, I always am; but it's not really all that early now," I replied, carrying on cutting up the vegetables.

"Last night you were really burning the midnight oil, weren't you?" he said in a soft voice.

"When did you go to sleep then?"

He smiled shyly and said nothing more.

This silent response seemed louder than words. It gave me a slightly uneasy feeling.

After breakfast, they were in no hurry to leave, and we sat around the small table on the warm *kang*, like we had the night before, chatting and cracking melon-seeds. I started talking about my brother.

*

...I spoke for a while, and then the three of us fell silent.

"He was truly a martyr!" Wei Li murmured, his intense expression betraying the indignation he felt in his heart.

"You know," said Wei Ying, looking up with staring, thoughtful eyes, and with that same wry smile: "A young man in our neighbourhood was given eight years in prison just for putting up a poster saying 'Long Live the Author of "On Class Background"'!"

I breathed a deep sigh. "My brother's case involved a lot of people.

They dug up the addresses of anyone who'd asked for a copy of the *High School Cultrev Post*, and all of them got into trouble. So did the editors of the paper, of course.''

"Your family must have suffered terribly...." Wei Ying sighed a melancholy sigh.

"It goes without saying. What about yours?"

"Ours?" answered Wei Li, without giving Wei Ying a chance to speak. "My father was executed in 1950, when my brother was three and I was only two. My mother was a primary school teacher, she taught first year children. She's been a widow ever since, with three children to support. My sister was a star pupil at high school—she did well in class and got excellent reports for general conduct; but she only managed to get into the Youth League in her last year of senior school. She had to wait six years! She really had a hard time getting into teachers' college too. And then she wanted to join the Party, but no matter how hard she tried, she was always turned down because of her class background. She was really upset about it at the time, and later she gave up hope altogether. She once had a boy-friend but his class background wasn't too good. Mother was set against the match and found her a man from a worker's family instead.''

"How did they get along together?" I felt really sorry for her.

"Not too badly. They've got a child now."

"Do you remember anything about your father?"

"No," said Wei Li, breathing out a puff of smoke. "In fact, we all hate him," he went on at once, "especially my mother. He gave us nothing but misery."

I didn't quite understand, so I said nothing. And Wei Ying just hung his head silently as if something was on his mind.

"Did you have a hard time then, during the Cultrev?" I asked after a little while.

"Of course." Wei Li followed the smoke rings with his eyes.

"For a whole month," said Wei Ying, raising his head, "we all had to sleep in the railway station...."

He didn't finish, and I didn't feel like asking any further questions. No one wanted to talk about the sorrows of the past any more. They'd almost become too commonplace.

"Well, I really wish you'd tell us..." Wei Li looked at me searchingly as if he'd remembered something and said, "You know...what I asked you yesterday?"

"You'll be coming again, won't you?" I stalled. "Let's talk about it another time. If I finish the whole story *this* time, we'll have nothing left to talk about!"

Perhaps it was the way I said it that made them both laugh. After a little more conversation, they stood up and said good-bye. It had already stopped snowing.

I walked with them to the edge of the village and gazed after them until they vanished into the distance. Wei Ying turned round and looked back, and again...

I walked home slowly on my own, uncertain whether I was happy or sad. I don't know how it happened, but as I gazed out over the white expanse of snow, I started making up a poem in my head:

> Is this love, I cannot tell—
> That gentle voice
> Like mild sunshine.
> Is this love, I cannot tell—
> That tender heart
> Plucking mine.
> The song of the sea
> Never moved me like this.
> The murmuring pines
> Never touched me like this.
> A heart so open and pure,
> Soft as spring wind.
> A spirit bright and kind,
> Crystal-clear.
> In the ocean of friendship,
> I will seek the source of strength!

*

That night, I slept so soundly and had such a wonderful dream.

The next morning, I woke up before it was light. Looking at the beautiful patterns the ice had formed on the window-panes, I wondered to myself whether Wei Ying would come again. No, he would probably not come. He was too sensitive not to notice that I liked him. And he was rational. Even if he liked me too, he still wouldn't allow himself to be swayed by his emotions—I was married, and I had a child.

Ah, if only husband and wife loved each other so deeply that no matter whom they encountered in their lives, they could always look into their hearts and say, "But I love my husband (or wife) better." Perhaps Marx and his Jenny felt like that about each other! But few of the married people I knew loved in this way. It was so sad to think that Wei Ying would never be coming again, that our first meeting would be our last!

I was convinced he would never come again. I sighed a sad sigh to myself, and felt much better for it.

That whole day, I sat at the small table on the *kang*, and continued to write down my memories of my brother.

*

The next morning, I was carrying on with my writing when suddenly the outer door was quietly pushed open and there was Wei Ying standing in front of me, smiling.

"Wei Ying?" I called out in happy astonishment. "What a surprise!"

"A surprise?" he smiled shyly.

"Why didn't our dog bark? You must have thrown him something good to eat!"

"Of course not," he smiled. "It's because there's a bond, between me and anything connected with dogs."

"Do you mean me?" I laughed. "I was born in the Year of the Dog."

"No." He lowered his head in shy amusement and explained, "No, I didn't mean you. I didn't know in fact... What I said is true though, the dogs in our village very seldom snap at me, however fierce they are."

"Maybe you've got some kind of magic," I joked.

"What are you writing?" He leaned over to take a look at my book.

"Me? Just scribbling something to while away the time." I closed the book and got down from the *kang* to pour him a glass of hot water with some sugar in it. "I thought you wouldn't come again."

"Why?"

How could I say why? So I just smiled instead.

"I know what you were thinking!" he said with a quiet, sensitive smile.

"Then it saves me the trouble of telling you!" I feigned an air of nonchalance.

"I don't know why it is, but I haven't been able to stop thinking about coming here to see you."

Goodness, that he should make this confession of his own accord! He was faltering, he seemed to be trying to pluck up his courage.

"Did you...did you come without any hesitation, or did it take you a long time to make up your mind?"

"I hesitated. You're a good guesser!" He laughed happily.

We were silent for a while, lost in our own thought...

So it was love at first sight! For both of us! Who would have believed it possible! It so seldom happened! And yet, however close the bond between us was, we could never be more than friends...

He looked up at me and then lowered his eyes. "You know, it does puzzle us—me, Wei Li, and many of our friends—how you came to marry Zhiguo," he said to me softly. "Can you tell me?" He looked at me intensely, as if beseeching me for a reply.

Surely he hadn't come here today to ask me this? I wasn't interested in talking about myself if it was just to satisfy an idle curiosity of his. But his earnest, pained expression made it hard to refuse him. I was moved by his concern. What harm was there in his wanting to know me better, to be my true friend? He deserved my trust!

"You really want to know?" We sat facing one another, each leaning against a wall to make ourselves more comfortable. He looked at me attentively, as if preparing himself for a lecture by some distinguished professor. Slowly, I began my story.

2. Memories: The Diary

It all started with the diary...

What a fool I was! To manage to lose my own diaries, and the one my brother entrusted to me! How could I have done such a foolish thing? It was like betraying him! The memory of it still fills me with such remorse...

It was midday, August 28, 1966. I was sitting in our room when suddenly I heard my brother calling me from the door of his small room.

"Luojin!"

Straightaway I went to his room. He had a strange look in his eyes, as if he'd just made some very important decision. I began to feel nervous.

"They're really on the rampage now. They're Raiding* one house after another." My brother stood at his table looking at me seriously. "I don't want to cause any unnecessary trouble, so I've decided to burn everything—all my diaries, manuscripts, letters, and notes. I don't really need to keep them. You'd better do the same if you've got any diaries *you* don't need. But before I do burn them, I want someone to read what I've written, to share my thoughts. I've thought about it a great deal and you're the only person. So why don't you just sit down here and read them! When you've finished, I'll burn the lot."

I could only answer him with silence. It felt as if death itself had entered my being—because for us, a diary was like a heart, or a soul!

"Except for this one..." He took up a notebook from the table, with "Peking Diary" printed on its blue cover, and went on: "This one contains the things I've been thinking about during the past year. The ideas in it are more developed, they're worth remembering. I just can't bring myself to burn this one. Can you help me hide it somewhere, in a safe place? You can give it back to me when all this trouble has died down.''

''Yes, I will!'' I took the notebook without hesitation in both hands, and hugged it to my chest. He looked at me closely, and seemed to have complete trust in me.

''Now you can start reading.'' And with these words, he stood facing the closed door with his hands behind his back, gazing into the sky through the glass in the upper half of the door. I walked silently over to the small bed which was piled with his diaries, manuscripts, letters, and reading-notes. They all seemed to be staring up at me, weeping sadly. When I said, ''I've finished,'' they would be consumed in a sea of flames.

As I read them, the whole course of my brother's life and the growth of his personality, from when he first became a Young Pioneer* right up to the present, passed before my eyes like a series of pictures in an exhibition. It flashed through my mind, like a film in fast motion. . .

I can remember every detail. I can picture him now, a little boy standing beside the standard-bearer under a bright blue sky, the waving flag of the Young Pioneers caressing his face; giving his first reverent salute to Teacher Wang, who had just presented him with a red scarf.

I can remember him in one of the early purges of the fifties, the Three-Antis campaign*, having the courage to report our parents for sacking a worker named Yan, whose fingers had been mangled in a machine; afterwards, the city's Youth League Committee commended him for it, and the school held a special meeting to praise him for what he had done.

Then, at his last primary school speech-day, he was chosen to speak first on behalf of the pupils who were leaving, and his speech was so beautifully delivered, it touched the hearts of everyone present.

When he was twelve and had just started high school, he applied for membership of the Youth League. His results in school had always been excellent. And his chances of being accepted would have been even higher if he'd mentioned the stand he had taken in '56 when he'd tried to persuade my parents to hand over all their property to the State. But he chose not to mention it, and the League turned him down.

In '57 our parents were Capped* as Voicers*, and from then on he only got a "C" every year at school for general conduct; but he still kept trying his hardest to get into the Youth League, and often encouraged me to do likewise.

From his first year in senior high school onwards, the lamp in that small room of his never went out before midnight. He was studying day and night, all kinds of books—literature, philosophy, history, geography—turning his mind into a repository of knowledge, in the pursuit of irrefutable Truth.

When his political aspirations seemed doomed to failure, he transferred all of his energies to his studies in the hope of getting into the prospecting department of the Institute of Geology. To the same end, he did his physical exercises every morning without fail.

He wasn't accepted. But when even this last ambition of his was denied, he didn't lose heart. He signed up for work in the country, and tried a second time for university entrance in the summer of 1962, only to be rejected yet again.

And then there were all his short stories and film-reviews, published in the *Peking Evening News* and *People's Cinema*; and his Plum Blossom Drumsong* praising the glorious deeds of Jiao Yulu*, which was performed by the Peking Folk Arts Troupe; and his fearless article, exposing Yao Wenyuan* as a contemptible clown.

Life was never easy for him, either in the country, or in the city, where he had a series of temporary jobs. He worked as a messenger for the neighbourhood Telephone Service; as a library assistant at the Peking Library; as a research assistant in the Institute of Scientific and Technological Information; as a temporary primary school teacher; and later on, as a factory-worker in the People's Machinery Plant. He always worked conscientiously and well. It was this rich variety of experience that informed the spirit of his essay "On Class Background".

. . . Oh my brother, my beloved and revered brother!

Those diaries in which he so mercilessly examined his innermost thoughts, those courageous and outspoken articles, and those letters in which he and his friends offered each other such moral support, surely they were not all to perish? They were the poetry of youth, the flame of life! Reading his diaries that day I discovered for the first time how fearlessly he had been "dissecting" himself!

Since senior high school, when he'd first become a committed communist and had come to believe that dialectical materialism was the only correct way to understand the world, he'd embarked upon a daily examination of his own faults, relentlessly castigating in his diary every one of his words and actions that was not for the good of the people; he wrote a short summary every week, a longer one every month, and a comprehensive summary every year. He rigorously cultivated in himself many virtues—frugality, diligence, breadth of knowledge, self-discipline, lenience towards others, a resolute stand against misguided words or deeds, and an ability to get along with people. Whenever he was confused about anything, he referred to books or practical experience and sorted it out. Whenever he thought something to be right, he would stick to it with perseverance—he always had an accurate yardstick with which to measure right and wrong: dialectical materialism and the good of the people.

There were plenty of others who believed in dialectical materialism, but they lacked the courage to perform this kind of self-analysis, to overcome their own self-interest; they didn't dare to make themselves the first target of their own attack, it always had to be someone else. But my brother looked upon the overcoming of his own self-interest as a duty, and a pleasure. How bright the world would be if everybody could be like my brother! How much less hypocrisy, deceit and weakness there would be!

I turned the pages of the diaries one after another; the rustling they made was the only sound to be heard in the room. Every rustling sound, every turn of the page, made my heart shrink—another tiny fragment of life, another leaf of living history propelled towards its death. How I wanted to get down on my knees and beg my brother for mercy on their behalf. But there he was, standing in front of the door with his hands behind his back, staring into the sky, motionless. What was he thinking? I raised my head silently and looked at him, with pain in my heart. The small room was so chill and cold, but the look in his eyes was colder; they were sombre and pale, he stood there like a statue... In the next-door compound, the Red Guards* were on the rampage. We could hear it quite clearly, the hitting, smashing and angry swearing mingled with the pitiful sounds of weeping and wailing. Through the back window, smoke could be seen rising up from behind the neighbouring wall: they were burning something too. If thoughts had to be rooted out of the mind and the body humiliated in this fashion, what did a human being have left to call his own?

*

That night, Mother did not come home. She was detained in her factory along with anyone else categorized as Black*, to be given a dose of Proledic*. The next morning, I slipped the diary my brother had entrusted to me among twenty diaries of my own and placed them all in a printed cotton bag. I took it with me to the homes of any of my friends that could be trusted; but every family was burning things, there was a general state of panic. Without exception they all exclaimed:

"Why on earth haven't you burned them? And what are you doing wearing a skirt at a time like this?"

Nobody dared hide the diaries for me; and they were surprised that I should still want to keep them. I was exhausted from all the walking. Maybe I could hide them in the park, I thought to myself, underneath some rocks or in a little grotto. But the park had been closed for days, and the park-gate was pasted all over with Wallscreeds*. What was I to do? I walked to the Culture Palace and went inside, because I needed to go to the toilet. Inside the toilets it was unusually quiet, and clean and bright. I often used these toilets when I was sketching in the park. The row of cubicles opposite where I was squatting always had a piece of rope strung through the doors to show that they were not to be used. Today it was exactly the same: the

tall white painted doors stood there silently like a row of guards.
Suddenly my heart gave a thump... I knew it would be too dangerous
to take the diaries back home, because the Red Guards might come and
ransack our things: why not put the bag behind one of those doors, and
think of a better place in the morning? Yes, that was the only way! So,
making sure that nobody was around, I put the bag of diaries down
onto the white tiled floor and pushed it under one of the doors. Then I
bent over to take a look: good, nothing could be seen from outside. I
didn't think there would be any problem, just for one night; anyway,
this was a safer place than at home. Then I looked out of the window to
check that there wasn't anybody there, and washed my hands and
walked away, my mind more at ease.

By the following dawn, the whole city was sealed off. Chairman Mao
was going to receive thousands of Red Guards that morning. Even
bicycles weren't being allowed through. My whole plan was ruined! I
was very worried... The streets finally opened to traffic at two o'clock
in the afternoon, and I hurried to the hiding-place. When I stepped
inside, I got the shock of my life—both rows of cubicle doors were wide
open, and there was no sign of the bag. The floor which had been so
clean the day before was now covered with spit, scraps of toilet-paper,
and dirty footprints going in all directions. A woman was just coming
in to clean up. I asked her anxiously about the bag, but she only cast
me a sidelong glance and then lowered her eyelids and said sullenly:
''Haven't seen it.'' After that, I couldn't get another word out of her.

I left her, full of misgivings, and asked another woman who was
sweeping outside. I got the same look and the same response:
''Haven't seen it.''

It was gone! All was lost!

I was overwhelmed with shame and remorse. How I cursed myself!
My own diaries were of no significance—if I'd lost them, I'd lost them.
But what about my brother's? I had betrayed his trust! Two days
before, I'd read all his other diaries; but I hadn't read this one, because
he hadn't wanted me to. Who knows *what* he had written in it! He had
far more original ideas in his head than I had in mine. If he'd written
anything subversive, then it would be me who'd betrayed him. What a
fool I was! Was there another such fool in the whole world? I don't

know how I got home, I was like a sleep-walker. I was too sick at heart to go to work, and certainly couldn't bring myself to eat; I could only sit on the wooden planks of the big bed, staring at the wall and wiping away my tears. I had never believed in God, but now I prayed with an anguished heart. Please God, protect my brother, don't let him come to any harm. . .

Father reproved me. "You stupid girl! How could anyone be so stupid? How could you go and hide it in a place like that? Dear oh dear!"

I cried and cried. I knew it didn't help, but I couldn't do anything except cry. . . Where else could I have hidden it? In the straw roof of the shed? They could poke through and find it. In one of the walls? They could chisel it out. Bury it in the ground? But there were five other families sharing our small courtyard, and what if by some chance I'd been seen or heard? Children of neighbourhood Beavers* played in the courtyard all day long. . . My brother had probably looked high and low without managing to find a satisfactory hiding-place before entrusting the diary to me. Oh, how I'd let him down!

My brother was stunned when he first heard the terrible news: he didn't say a single word. Father asked him:

"Is there anything in it that could cause trouble?"

He replied as if in a trance, "Some criticisms of Chen Boda* and Yao Wenyuan."

"Oh you stupid girl!" Father glared at me angrily. "How could you be so foolish? And Luoke, how could *you* be so foolish?—you should have burnt the thing, not given it to this stupid girl."

I couldn't raise my head for shame, I was weeping bitterly. My brother soon recovered himself:

"Luojin, I'm not going to blame you for this." And so saying, he went into his small room.

I shall never forget those words of love and forgiveness! For the rest of my life I shall feel sorry for the wrong I've done him! I betrayed the great trust he placed in me!

I let him down! Not only in this instance, but afterwards, when I showed such weakness. . . when I went down on my knees. I was forced, against my will, to get down on my knees!

3. Memories: The Raid

It was the day after I'd lost the diaries, and exceptionally sultry, without the slightest breath of wind. The setting sun was disappearing among a rapidly gathering mass of dark clouds. There was a deafening jangling of bicycle-bells as people came back from work; buses hurried by crowded with passengers—the streets suddenly seemed to have become a lot narrower. After work, I rode my bike quickly home, worried that I might be caught in the coming storm.

My brother got back from his factory just before I did; my two younger brothers had been hanging about the house all day, because as Black children, they weren't allowed to "make revolution"; my grandmother was convalescing at my aunt's place; my mother had been detained in her factory for all of that week. My father was putting the dinner on the table, when a boy who lived in our compound came running in, puffing and panting....

"Uncle Yu! Aunty Yu's coming! The Red Guards are bringing her home! They're already at Money and Grain Lane! She's had her hair shaved off!" He ran out again at once.

We were all aghast.

"Be off with you, children, quick!" said Father hurriedly. "I'll deal with this on my own. I knew it would happen sooner or later! Go on, go!"

The three neighbouring families who were having their supper in the courtyard scuttled with their dinner tables back to their rooms in alarm. The other two families who lived in our courtyard had already escaped back to their home villages a few days before, to keep out of the way of the Red Guards.

My brother snatched up his beige raincoat saying, "Dad, I'm going to the State Council to have a look at the Wallscreeds. I'll stay out as late as I can." He wheeled out his bicycle and went off without looking back.

"I'll spend the night at school, Dad." The elder of my two younger brothers also hurried off.

My youngest brother made the same decision: "I'm going to school too."

"Take plenty of clothes with you!" Father flung him an old jacket.

"Why don't *you* get going too? Quickly!" My father stamped his foot impatiently.

I grabbed my violin down from the wall and ran out.

I caught up with my little brother at the entrance to the lane. Big raindrops pelted mercilessly down on our faces.

"Hurry up and run!" I clutched his sleeve and we bounded across the street and dived into the post-office.

The heavy rain came pouring down; the window-panes were shedding endless tears. We looked out through the glass—from time to time a cyclist emerged from the deluge, frantically searching for shelter. Lots of people were sheltering under the eaves of shops. The post-office began to fill up.

A white curtain of rain and mist blotted out the sky and the earth; everything was drowned in the furious roaring of the rain. It was a rain cantata, the God of the Heavens giving vent to his righteous indignation. And my mother was out there in the streets, being drenched with the merciless tears of this God!

What crime had we committed, that we couldn't go back to our own home? Was it simply our class!... A cold wind came blasting in from under the door, and blew against my skirt; a shiver ran all over my body. I glanced at my little brother, standing there, staring silently out of the window...

The roar of the rain gradually subsided, and the sound of the door constantly being pushed open interrupted my train of thought. In the streets, the furious jangle of bicycle-bells rang out once more. The light in the post-office was dazzlingly bright, while outside was now a stretch of clear, dark-blue evening sky.

My little brother and I stood in the open space in front of the post-office. The last few drops of rain were still pattering down. I took a deep breath of cool air—what a sparkling dark-blue night it was!

The stars winked at each other mysteriously and mischievously, as if gloating over the misfortune of the humans below who were too intent on killing each other to want to explore the astral secrets above them. Ah! We both instinctively looked towards the entrance of our small lane. Nothing seemed out of the ordinary; people were coming and going as normal, calm and indifferent, as though there wasn't anything strange or painful taking place.

"Luojin, let's go."

I grunted my assent.

Yes, hanging about there for too long might attract attention. We walked towards the cross-road ahead of us.

"Do you think it's OK for you to go to school?" I asked.

"Yes, lots of kids from school have been Raided—and they all spend the night there."

"Where do they sleep?"

"On the desks."

"Isn't it cold?" What a stupid question!

"They say it isn't too cold. Some of them have brought towelling covers with them, and maybe someone can share with me. Besides, Dad's given me this old jacket."

I sighed sadly.

"Luojin, one of the Red Guard leaders said yesterday that they're going to organize Prolethought Classes* in every school for Black children, and soon there will be one in *our* school. You haven't got one at the factory, have you?"

"It probably won't be long coming."

"Where are you going to stay the night?"

That really made me stop and think—where *should* I go?

"I think I'll go to Aunty's place," I decided. "I'd like to see Grandma. She's been ill for two months and we haven't had any news of her."

"Do you think that'll be OK?"

"Why not? They're not in any kind of trouble, are they?"

"All right, go there then."

I watched my brother cross the street with his little bundle of clothes, and disappear into the dark night.

*

The old black gate was ajar.

I pushed it open lightly and tiptoed into the small quiet courtyard. A pale yellow light could be seen through the curtain of my aunt's room. I held my breath and listened outside the window for a few seconds, but could hear only my aunt's violent coughing and my uncle's deep muffled sighs.

I tapped lightly on the window-pane.

"Who is it?"

A corner of the curtain was lifted up, and I saw my uncle squinting out anxiously with one eye.

"It's me."

"Why, it's Luojin! Come on in!"

The door was opened half-way, and I squeezed past. My uncle shut the door firmly behind us.

I said hello to them—my aunt and my grandmother were sitting on the bed, my aunt purple in the face from coughing, and sallow-faced Grandma tenderly patting her on the back.

"What are you doing here at this hour of the day?"

My uncle stood in the middle of the room, eyeing me suspiciously, with his thin eyebrows knitted together. It made my heart sink to see his panic-stricken expression—where was that warm-hearted uncle of mine who always talked and laughed so openly? Had he been possessed by some evil spirit?

"I've come to see how Grandma is," I said, trying to sound casual. "But it sounds as if you've got *your* old illness back again, Aunty."

I rested my violin against the wall and sat down on a stool.

"Why the violin?" My uncle stood there, still suspicious, examining my face very closely. "Are you sure nothing's happened at home?"

"Of course not! I've just been to my friend's house to practise the violin, and I thought I'd drop in to say hello."

"Then . . . I don't suppose you've had your dinner yet?" My uncle still didn't quite believe me, and was trying to catch me out somehow.

"Oh yes, I'm full up!" I said, patting my stomach.

"Hmm . . ." He walked to the table frowning pensively and sat down, not totally convinced. After puffing at his dying pipe, he asked me in a whisper, "How's your mother? Still going to work?"

"Yes, she is."

"Not been Raided?"

"No."

"It will come sooner or later, you'd better be prepared. It's already happened to us once."

"To you?" I looked around the room in stunned surprise, and noticed what a mess it was in compared to normal. "What have they got against *you*?"

My uncle didn't answer immediately, but only sighed.

My aunt had another coughing fit and Grandma gently pummelled her on the back with the sides of her hands, while asking me all sorts of questions about the family. I tried to make out that everything was fine.

"It's not something I like talking about, my dear!" My uncle tapped the bowl of his pipe and shook his head dejectedly. "You have no idea how miserably your aunt and I have suffered!" He stood up to reach for an old blue cotton jacket of my aunt's which was hanging on the door, and thrust it in front of my face saying, "Look at this."

The jacket had a rectangular patch of black cloth stitched on it, embroidered clearly in white thread with the words, "Black Wife".

"You a Black?" I looked at him in disbelief.

He heaved a deep sigh and hung the jacket back in its place, unable to conceal his emotion.

"All because I was once with the traffic police, just for six months!"

"But I thought you pulled a rickshaw for years and years? I never knew you were a traffic policeman too."

"You wouldn't understand! In those days life was very hard, and I had to take a job with the traffic police just to make ends meet. Six months later they cut down on staff and I was fired. That's when I had to pull a rickshaw. I had no choice then either. Later, I managed to find a job as an accountant and I've been doing that ever since. I never thought that six months with the traffic police would bring me such a lot of trouble. What sense does it make? Surely before Liberation there still had to be order in the streets? We still had to keep down the number of traffic accidents, didn't we? But they won't listen to reason! And in every political campaign since Liberation, I've come forward and freely admitted it, but fat lot of good it's done me! Now I'm a Class Enemy, and every day they give me Strife* along with all the other Kroads! They sent me off to a forge to work as a blacksmith. That's OK, I don't mind a bit of hardship. But what about your aunt, what's she ever done? She's just a plain honest housewife, she never sets foot outside the house. Why, she doesn't even know what's going on out there. All she wants is to get her health back, and they won't even let her do that. Now she's a Black Wife and she has to sweep the streets every morning before dawn. Look at her, look at the state she's in! If she doesn't sweep properly, she'll get beaten! What on earth have we done to deserve this?''

. . . So, I had to leave—how could I add still more fear and anguish to the suffering they already had to bear?

I went out by the half-opened gate, sighing heavily. I distinctly heard my stomach rumbling in the pitch-dark night. My uncle's parting words of exhortation were still ringing in my ears:

''It's better if we don't have too much to do with each other at the moment, my dear. Still wearing a skirt? Playing the violin? Even my Chinese fiddle was smashed to pieces!''

The night wind was bitterly cold, it made me shiver. My skirt conspired with the chilly wind, they both kept stroking my legs mischievously. I tucked the violin under my arm, hunched up my shoulders, and hugged my elbows with both hands. I started walking in the direction of home, very slowly. . .

The thing I was most concerned about was the diaries—my brother's and mine. In fact, as I later found out, at that very moment my diaries were lying in the security office at my factory, the whole bag full of them; and my brother's one surviving book had already been sent on to his factory. . . What a fool I'd been!

The mouth of the dark and narrow lane gaped in front of me like a monster; I gripped my violin tensely, and then walked on in, full of apprehension.

Suddenly, a head ducked down behind the wall. Trouble! I turned and started running, hearing a loud shout from behind:

"Stop her! Don't let her get away!"

The cry scratched across the silent night sky. In the distance, two passers-by hastily dived into the shadows. Several large hands caught me in a tight grip.

"You little bitch! Running away, are you? We've been waiting for you for ages! Get going!"

The violin had long since disappeared. They twisted my arms behind my back and started pushing me towards my home.

The lights were all out in the small courtyard, but that certainly didn't mean everyone was asleep. The only door open was the one to our room; the fluorescent light was blindingly bright. Mother must have already been taken away, after showing them the way there. A pile of our old things had been dragged out and dumped near the door. Father was kneeling in the middle of it, his bald head shining under the fluorescent light.

A Red Guard suddenly shoved me forward and shouted: "Let her have it!" They went for me with their dummy rifles and leather belts, and I heard them shouting: "On your knees!"

"What right have you got to beat me?" I struggled to cry out.

"Because you're a little bitch!"

"Look at your skirt! You're asking for it!"

"And hair-slides too! Hit her!"

"Are you going to kneel or not?"

For the first time, the thought of saving my skin cut into my heart like a knife, and with a thump, I fell to my knees.

"Get your head down!" They were still not satisfied and gave me another vicious beating. I hardly even dared to breathe.

"Get your head down!" Now they were whipping my father, who kept his head bowed low without uttering a sound.

"You bastard, you know you're guilty, don't you?"

"I know."

"Guilty of what?" They had turned and put this question to me.

"My mother is a capitalist, and both my parents are Voicers."

"So, you should grovel and confess your guilt before the people, shouldn't you!"

"Yes, I should."

"Why are you wearing a skirt? It's against our Order No—."

"And the other mangy dogs from your kennel, where have they got to?" another Red Guard asked... They whipped me now and then, as they barked out their questions.

Suddenly, the door was thrown open with a bang, and everyone in the room looked round in astonishment—my brother's pale face, so stern and calm, was silhouetted against the dark-blue night sky. His ice-cold, penetrating gaze seared through the stunned group before him like lightning; their souls quaked at the sight of his tightly closed, resolute lips, his straight nose, and the cold glint of his glasses.

He stood at the door motionless, surveying them in an imposing manner. Then the Red Guards, suddenly waking as if from a trance, bounded towards him, and completely surrounded him. But he stood there like a bronze pagoda, his piercing gaze so fearful to look upon that still no one dared touch him.

Kneeling there on the floor, timid and ashamed, I glanced up at him. I could see in his stern eyes the pain that Father and I were causing him! I had neither the heart to look at him, nor the courage to get up.

"I agree wholeheartedly with what you're doing for the revolution!" Not waiting for them to speak, my brother went on resolutely, "And if you hadn't come, I'd have invited you myself! But..."

"Are you Yu Luoke?"

"...but the Sixteen Point Circular* says that the struggle must be waged with words, not blows. The newspapers are always stressing this. Blows only touch the flesh, they can't reach the soul..."

"On your knees!" One of the "heroes" struck him a violent blow on the back of his neck.

"You dare to raise your hand against me?" My brother spun round, his face deathly pale, his fiery eyes burning into the eyes of the "hero". There was something awesome about my brother's presence, something almost inviolable. The Red Guard withdrew his hand and resentfully avoided my brother's gaze.

"What crime have I committed?" His cold stare chilled them all to the bone.

"Your class is your crime!"

"A man can't choose his class, but he *can* choose what path to follow. I'd like you to tell me where *you* stand on this question of class?" said my brother, loud and clear.

"We're for the saying—

  '*Heroes breed heroic sons,*
  Counters all hatch rotten ones!'*"

. . . A heated argument was in full swing, when another group of Red Guards came barging in.

"Yu Luoke, let's go. You're wanted at the factory!" So, they were from my brother's place of work.

"All right, let's take the joker away! He can finish his lecture somewhere else!" One of them came up and was about to twist my brother's arms behind his back.

"Not so fast!" my brother shouted sternly. Swinging his arms free from their grasp, he turned and walked proudly out. The Red Guards followed at his heels in a swarm and blew out through the door like a yellow whirlwind.

All of a sudden, the room was quiet and empty. . . . For a long time, my father and I sat hunched up on the floor, staring blankly at the door. . .

That was where my brother had stood. It seemed as though he was still there, standing firm, coldly surveying all those around him; his fiery, piercing eyes, his tightened lips, his calm, fearless countenance, all seemed still to be radiating a dazzling light from that very spot; his resonant voice, clear and composed, seemed still to be echoing in the room.

He was not physically tall, but somehow one had to look up to him. Whereas I was down on my knees, cringing subserviently on my knees!

Poor weaklings who accept this kind of humiliation to survive! They must examine themselves dispassionately if they are ever to know the truth about their own nature! Luoke, I had let you down....

Deep into the night, my father and I just sat on the floor in total silence, helpless, paralyzed by our sense of shame and humiliation, and by our admiration for Luoke. The clock struck two. Slowly we rose to our feet; and while the pain still racked our bodies, we started slowly and silently to tidy up the mess of things scattered across the floor.

⟨When I went out of the room in the pitch-dark to fetch the broom and sweep the floor, I did not dare to tread on that small spot by the door, which continued to radiate its light! I did not wish to sully it with the soles of my feet! I stepped carefully over it, and as I did so, how strangely my heart beat! I did not wish to sweep it, for fear that I might sweep away its brilliance. From time to time I turned back to look at it.⟩

We piled the debris in the middle of the room and lay down any old how. Father cleared a space for himself among the things strewn on the bed, and I just lay down on the big wooden chest which had already been ransacked and was quite empty. The only thing left intact was a full-length mirror. The reason it had been spared was because Father had pasted a large poster of one of Chairman Mao's quotations right over it. Could we too have been spared a beating if we'd pasted Chairman Mao's quotations all over ourselves!

The moon shed its peaceful light on that spot by the doorway, making it appear all the more beautiful. I lay quite still and stared at it. The soft light seemed to transport me to a time long-since gone, thousands of years ago, to a world which must have been filled with universal love... My brother's spirit floated before my eyes. Was I worthy to be his sister? Was I worthy? Why did I lack his courage? Tears of shame streamed down my face in the darkness; I tried not to make the slightest sound, and let my tears flow into the pillow...

⟨The soft moonlight shone down and caressed the window frame and that small magical spot, which seemed at that moment to be telling its deepest sorrow to the heavens...⟩ Where had they taken my brother? To the torture room in the factory, or to its underground place of detention? Were they beating him? No, surely not; he had such an air of righteousness about him, they would never dare touch him. It was my mother I ought to be worrying about: would she be driven to suicide while she was in prison?

And when I thought of my two younger brothers, my heart ached. There in the empty class-room on the desks, so many boys from "bad" families would be lying back to back, curled up, trying to keep out the night cold... Were they asleep? What were they dreaming about? ⟨The moonlight was shining tenderly down on them too. A hint of sweetness seemed to flicker across their lips—perhaps they were lost in some beautiful fantasy...⟩

...such an air of righteousness about him, they would never dare touch him. It was my mother I ought to be worrying about: would she be driven to suicide, like she was in prison.

And when I thought of my two younger brothers, my heart ached. There in the empty classroom on the desks, back to back, curled up, trying to keep out the night cold... Were they asleep? What were they dreaming about? The moonlight was shining tenderly down on them too. A hint of sweetness seemed to flicker across their lips—perhaps they were lost in some beautiful fantasy.

4. Memories: Labour Cure

The next day I was Strifed at the factory. I was now a Class Enemy, and to be kept under Masswatch* at all times. They went over every entry in my diary—more than twenty notebooks in all—with a fine tooth-comb, and managed to find six sentences to incriminate me as an "inveterate reactionary".

My mother and brother were by now shut away in their respective factories; and my two younger brothers had been made to join a Prolethought Class at school especially for Black children.

On December 21, I was marched off to the municipal headquarters of the Public Security Bureau* by a group of Red Guard students. The Cultrev fever was then at its height, and the Red Guards were in the process of "smashing up" the entire security and legal system. The PSB headquarters had been taken over by a group of students wearing red armbands which said Pol-Sci Commune—short for the Peking Institute of Political Science and Law—and the whole place was a shambles. People were constantly being marched in. My guards kept chanting hysterically: "Arrest Yu Luojin, or you're a bunch of Counters*!", and the Pol-Sci people eventually had to give in and arrest me. They then sent me off immediately to the Banbuqiao Detention Centre.*

Three months behind bars gave me a chance to get to know people from many different walks of life; it enriched my experience...

I had only one official interrogation there.

"Did you write this?" The interrogator handed me several small photographs of extracts from my diary and said, "Sign here."

I glanced at the photographs—there were six of them, all two-inches square. There was nothing the least bit reactionary about what I'd written. I hadn't attacked the Party leadership, or the socialist system; the extracts were just a few thoughts of mine on literature and art, some reflections on exterminating the Four Relics*, and a couple of remarks about ⟨ Chairman Mao's Red Guard armband, and ⟩ Lin Biao's treacherous appearance—was this reactionary thinking? What about everything else? The reams I'd written to spur myself on in my studies so that I could serve the people? Did that all count for nothing?

I stood there listening to the loud voice of the interrogator as he recited my ideological crimes; I stared at him in sheer amazement. I simply could not believe my ears! That wasn't me! I was being framed! Had I really managed to earn all those reactionary labels in such a short space of time? Was it really so easy to become an enemy? Yes, it had been much too easy! All I had done was fail to burn my diaries! The truth was that every Chinese person shared my thoughts; in which case they were actually all enemies ⟨ of the Party that led them! ⟩ I was an enemy! As from that moment, I was formally declared an Enemy of Society! I no longer had any freedom in life, I was only free to be the victim of Proledic! Three years of Labour Cure was what they'd given me! Three years! My heart sank. Three years of suffering, was that the price I would have to pay for simply failing to burn the diaries? Three long years! And there was no knowing what would come afterwards. At that moment I bitterly regretted not having burnt them. But it was too late.

"If you have any complaints, you can lodge an appeal within ten days."

I signed without a word.

The car sped along. I had no idea where they were taking me. I wasn't handcuffed, and my feet weren't chained—Labour Cure was a category of punishment for offenders who had not yet been totally cast out. I was still technically Incon*—within the ranks of the People.

I didn't understand. ⟨The Voicers of '57 were persecuted for speaking out. What they said was reckoned to be bad propaganda, to have a bad effect on public morale, just as later their confessions were reckoned to have a good effect. But what *effect* could a diary have?⟩

No one had any business reading a diary except the person who wrote it. And what a person wrote in a diary was only a thought of the moment—it didn't necessarily hold true for ever, and it didn't involve any form of action, so who did it harm? Surely people keep diaries for self-encouragement and self-improvement? Oh, what was the point! There wasn't anywhere you could go for justice! The thought of lodging an appeal was absurd—that much I'd already learnt. Some of the Voicers of '57 were sent off for Labour Cure just because they didn't admit their guilt with the necessary degree of penitence; any defiance, and it was Mould*! That had all happened when I was eleven and my brother was fifteen. We learnt some lessons early on.

And then I thought of all the others who were far more unjustly treated than I was—veterans who had been willing to lay down their lives for their country before Liberation, and who were now being persecuted and put to death—and the thought of their suffering made me see my own insignificance, and calmed me down a little. Compared to them, I wasn't too hard done by at all! ⟨My three years would go by very quickly; I should try to look on the bright side. What would my new universe be like? I should try to learn from it, treat it as an opportunity to acquire some wisdom and strength.⟩

The car took me to Liangxiang Camp* in the country south of Peking. Nearly all the prisoners there were women who'd been detained for illicit sexual relations; most of them were in their thirties and married. Their kind of labour detention was one of the lightest forms of punishment, ranging from only one month to a maximum of six.

When I look back on it, my three year period of Labour Cure was like a university degree, a rare opportunity to learn about society; and Liangxiang was my first course of study. I stayed there a year.

Once, during this period, I was interrogated by two men.

"What did your brother usually talk to you about? What influence did he have on your reactionary way of thinking?"

"My brother's ideas were progressive—he helped me a lot."

"What sort of thing did he say?"

"He often encouraged me to join the League. He wanted me to

Break* with the exploiting class and their whole way of thinking.''

"What?"

"He studied the works of Marx and Lenin very earnestly. He really believed in Communism. He was a true Marxist-Leninist.''

That was all I had to say. I refused to answer any more of their questions. My attitude made them very angry.

"This will get you nowhere!'' They concluded the interrogation on this threatening note.

⟨I had to say what I said, even if they put me in jail for it—because it was the truth.⟩

After a year, I was put on a train and sent under escort to Chadian Station, and from there to Qinghe Camp*.

*

. . .It was dusk, one evening after work, and yet another of their surprise searches was over at last. Three guards came to announce that our "reactionary group''—a dozen or so in all—could go back to its cell.

Throughout the entire machinery of Proledic, quarters were referred to as cell number such-and-such. In this respect, it made no difference whether you were doing Labour Cure or had actually been sentenced to a term of Mould—you were still just a number.

The cell, which several of us shared, had been turned completely upside-down. Only a short while before, during the search, the guards had taken the keys to all of our boxes and cases. The keys had been left in the locks. Some of the boxes were open and had clothes hanging out of them, and some had been moved from their usual places. On each bed-space, bedding and clothing had all been shaken out and dumped in a disorderly heap. We tidied it up without a word; none of us needed to say how wretched we felt. Perhaps because ten of the thirteen of us were Voicers from '57, and one (myself) was the writer of a "reactionary diary'', we were more liable to be subjected to this kind of surprise search.

"Oh no! That's done it!'' the woman who slept next to me

muttered despondently. She was an old Voicer and had already done twelve years of Labour Cure. She'd once been a reporter on the *Peking Daily*. "My diary's gone."

"Why didn't you put it somewhere safer?" And what was she doing writing a diary in a place like this anyway, I thought to myself?

"I hid it inside my mattress. They never found it on any of the previous searches." She sighed.

Sure enough, one end of her mattress had been ripped open.

"That's funny.... How could the guards have been so sure where to look?" I asked softly.

"Someone must have tipped them off."

She sat on the edge of the *kang*, staring vacantly.

"Anything subversive in it?" I asked her in a very low voice.

"I wouldn't dare! But it was gloomy enough... Oh no!"

It was true—if they found a single "reactionary" sentence in her diary, she'd be in trouble. I sympathized with her, but what could I do to help?

I glanced quickly at the mouth of the unused fire-place immediately below the space where I slept on the *kang*—I had two old pairs of shoes stuffed inside it, and under the shoes, buried in the dirt, was my own little notebook. The shoes had been moved, I could see that—but what about the book? I could hardly go and check there and then, in full view of the others. All I knew was that if someone had informed on me too, then my book would also be gone.

I looked over at the two Drossniks who'd been lumped in with our group of reactionaries. In a sense they were better off than we were, even though they were whores! When they'd done their time, they would be classified as Incon—conflicting elements within the ranks of the People. Any type of Drossnik or petty thief was guaranteed of Incon status; whereas reactionaries like us could never hope to be anything other than outcasts—we would never really be part of the People again! ⟨We would always be enemies for them to struggle against. These categories became quite the rage during the Cultrev!⟩

Oh, how I wished I could just reach into the hollow under the *kang* and see if my little book was still there! I stole another look. The floor outside the opening was very clean, and there was no trace of dirt having been stirred around. Had my little book gone undetected? I longed impatiently for the lights-out bell!

Everyone was busy eating supper, distributing hot water, washing their feet, going to the toilet; and then came Prolethought and roll call—there we were in the freezing courtyard with the north wind howling, all the inmates of the camp, reciting in unison the "three most read works of Chairman Mao*", and shouting "Long Live X . . ." and "Eternal Health to Y . . ." Endless rounds of Chairman Mao's quotations were chanted over and over again, ⟨ like lines from scripture. The singing was totally tuneless. I sincerely hope that one day, fifty years from now, our children and grandchildren will have a chance to listen to a recording of these songs; and that *their* verdict will be heard . . . ⟩

At last, the guard said "Dismissed!" It sounded like a general pardon! Our hands and feet were already frozen, and we ran back to our cells as fast as we could and laid out our bedding for the night. The deafening bell rang for lights-out. Seizing that moment of total darkness immediately after the lights were extinguished, I quickly took a pair of my cotton-padded shoes from inside the *kang* as if I was planning to wear them the next day, and then with a little darting motion that I hoped nobody would notice, I very swiftly and surely reached my hand under the soft bed of dirt—ah, my little book was still there in its plastic bag, safe and sound! My heart thumped for joy and relief . . .

Slipping back under my ice-cold quilt, I stole a glance at the journalist who slept on my left. Every time I saw her I couldn't help laughing to myself—she always slept flat on her back, facing the ceiling; what with her cotton-padded quilt and another layer of padded clothing weighing so heavily down on her body, it seemed quite impossible for her even to turn over. She wore a padded hat in bed which looked like a Buddhist nun's bonnet—people often made themselves hats like this in the camp because they were best at keeping out the wind; her face was grey with cold, and two cotton masks were drawn tightly over her nose and mouth. She lay there, as motionless as a corpse. Her husband, Cong Weixi*, another Voicer, was being held at a separate part of the camp, and their child was in Peking with his grandmother, leading a miserable and deprived existence by all accounts.

Before Liberation, this woman journalist had been willing to lay down her life for the revolution; she joined the Party when she was fifteen, and was always an excellent worker. In 1957, when the Party asked people to Speakheart*, her husband made a couple of remarks, and because of his landlord background, was Capped a Voicer. And then so was she, for not Breaking with him. Since both of them refused to admit to their guilt, they were relegated to Proledic, and their child was left with the father's unemployed mother, who had to support the two of them on a monthly allowance of nine *kuai* from the local police station. They were considered "big" Voicers. My parents were small fry by comparison. The majority of Voicers were well educated Krats* in government departments.

I lay awake for quite a while, thinking about my little notebook. I thought about all the times I'd taken it out or put it away, trying not to be seen by the others—what caution I'd had to exercise, and what a triumph it was to succeed! I thought about all those morning Prolethought sessions when I'd written in my notebook, hiding it behind another book, recording in it every last detail of the things my brother had said and done, from infancy right up to adulthood, in the belief that some day I'd be able to publish these memories—what confidence and pride I felt in what I was doing!

⟨Yes, alive or dead, he was and always will be hailed as a fine son of the Chinese people. He grew up with the young republic, he was in the vanguard of the fight against those fanatics who were doing such harm to our nation. He was a pioneer of intellectual progress, a model for Chinese youth!

Perhaps it had been foolish of me not to burn my diaries. But I tried to look on the positive side. Had they not served me as a little boat? How easy they had made it for me—had I not, without the slightest effort on my part, sailed on this little boat, with this constitutional passport, right into the heart of Proledic! If I were ever to write a book, and wanted to give in it a true account of daily life under Proledic, then my experience was a necessary prerequisite. The truth is that places like the one I was in are absolutely out of bounds. No writer, however famous, is ever allowed in, to taste what life is really like on the inside. And a person without firsthand experience of Proledic can never have a full understanding of our society. In the camp all the different sorts of humanity were gathered together, all of them typical in their different ways. It contained the most concentrated, the most intense, the most acute manifestation of our nation's ugliness and beauty, its evil and good, its falsehood and truth. It displayed the darker side of our society in telling detail. The people seemed so ordinary; but some of their crimes I had never even *heard* of before! When I first heard their stories, I was quite speechless with amazement.⟩

Looking back on my own past, I felt how ridiculously naive I'd been! I'd never even been aware of the existence of anyone outside my small circle of family and school friends! In my eyes the world had been full of beauty and light; I never dreamt that there was also an indescribably evil side to it! But now, I had come to know more about life, and about human relationships, and I was better prepared.

⟨Labour camp turned me from a spoilt young lady, afraid of suffering, afraid of toil, into a hardened warrior!⟩ For two years I was the person in charge of our group's manual labour. I really worked hard, making a conscious effort to toughen myself up. I found a great happiness in labour. After all, Mother Nature didn't look upon us as criminals. We dug fish ponds, we broke up the frozen soil in winter, we planted rice, we worked in the orchards and in the vegetable plots... all kind of things. We made demands on Nature, and at the same time we enjoyed the good things that Nature gave us—every sunrise or sunset, when the colours of the four seasons presented themselves before me in all their splendour, my heart would be filled with joy and an inexpressible sense of beauty. I made lots of sketches of outdoor scenes, hoping that someday I could send them to my brother and let him share in this pleasure...

It was the funniest thing, but even though we had no contact with the male prisoners, some of them tried every possible means of sending us little notes. I myself received two such letters asking me to be a "friend"—that is, a wife at some point in the future. Both of these men were from Red* families, old Red Guard hooligans from the early days of the Cultrev. They had both killed too many people, and had now been relegated to Proledic because they'd outlived their usefulness to the clique in power. Of course, the kind of letter I received deserved only a smile of contempt; and surely there was also something about it that made a total mockery of the whole preposterous theory of Class Pedigree.

In December '69, I reached the end of my period of Labour Cure. The camp authorities had already "sorted us out". Although I had behaved pretty well, I was still classified as Excon*, because of my "inability to place principle above family loyalty", and because of my "refusal to make a complete confession". By that time my brother had been in jail for nearly a year.

*

"It's hard to believe," Wei Ying said to me when I reached this point in my story; he was poring over my landscape-sketches with that reserved and intense expression of his. Then he looked up and said, "You did all this writing and drawing *there*... These pictures are really good!" He went on studying them for a long time.

"You'd probably never have believed it, if the ink and the paper hadn't faded. I suppose you think that in an environment like that, a person has to go around the whole time with a long face? I'm afraid it's not in my nature! On my first day in prison in December '66, a warder gave me two steamed buns and a bowl of meat and vegetable soup. I ate it all up, and then lay down in bed and instantly fell fast asleep. They didn't discover their mistake till the next day—they'd taken me for someone else, a Hikrat's* daughter who'd beaten some person to death! But afterwards I ate corn-cakes with just the same relish. And at the camp, the beauty of the countryside made me feel alive, I was still glad to be alive... It was really beautiful there. It was near the Gulf of Bohai. I wanted to capture it all in words and pictures—the clear sapphire sky, the fresh air, the beautiful clouds—it gave me such pleasure. And then part of me always wanted to send these creations of mine off to my brother. Supposing he'd already been sentenced, then these pictures and the youthful energy I'd put into them would surely help to revive his spirits while he was in prison. The funny thing was, in one of those surprise searches, a guard took away all my drawings; I was thinking I'd never get them back and I felt terrible, but much to my surprise, she returned them to me without a word, and not a single one was missing! So she too had a heart."

"Would you..." Wei Ying laughed and looked at me with admiration. "Would you let me take them home with me and copy them? I like them such a lot."

"Of course you can. Now let me go on with my story."

5. Memories: A Visit Home

The train was speeding along; my three years of labour were over. I couldn't tell whether the rumbling rhythm of the wheels made me feel happy or sad.

Outside the train window lay a harsh winter scene: the vast plain a patchwork of white and brown, the bare fields without the slightest sign of life, gray villages flashing past one after another. 1970—another frozen winter!

I was going home! Home! How I'd missed my family, how I'd missed my brother! I was longing, longing to be home, wherever that was! It had probably shifted several times during those three years!

*

... Was this it? Was this my home?

I looked at the envelope in my hand, then checked the number on the door, my heart thumping. There was nobody around, it was so quiet in the corridor. I was about to knock, but then leant forward, hoping to hear familiar voices inside. Who could tell whether pain or joy lay behind that closed door?

Knock, knock, knock. I rapped out this fateful sound to the beating of my heart.

Noiselessly, the door opened a crack, and then stopped—it was quite impossible to see who was behind it. In the darkness I could just faintly make out an eye opening wider and wider, and suddenly the door flew open and a joyful cry exploded into my ears:

"Sister!"

I stepped inside, and the elder of my younger brothers closed the door behind me.

"Dad! Luojin's come back!" My brother squeezed past me in the dark passageway and shouted towards the room where light shone out through a half-open door.

The sight of the old man in the room left me speechless. This senile old man, his bleary eyes gawping at me in bewilderment, could he really be my father?

"Dad!" I cried out, too distraught even to hear my little brother calling my name.

Father gazed at me in disbelief, his eyes wide open in astonishment; he'd been making flat-bread and still had a rolling-pin in one hand and a kitchen chopper in the other. All of a sudden, he burst out crying and collapsed sobbing onto the floor.

"Dad!"

"Dad!"

My two brothers and I went rushing over in alarm to help him up, but he just wailed and shook his head miserably:

"Let me cry...."

Tears poured down his wrinkled old face. The violence of his reaction shocked me out of my three years of nostalgia. We finally got him settled on a chair, and then I hurried straight over to my grandmother's bed; she was too ill and feeble to speak, and when at last she recognized me, she could only nod to me pathetically and then listlessly close her eyes.

"Child, you didn't even let us know you were coming back..." Father kept wiping away his tears.

"Luojin," my brothers said in a slightly scolding tone, "why didn't you send a letter or a telegram before you came?"

"I was too excited. You know, not many of us Free-workers* ever get permission to go home for a visit. And when *I* got leave, I was so happy I forgot about everything else."

"How many days have you got?"

"Ten, ten whole days! And the day after tomorrow it's Spring Festival!"

I took out the leave-certificate I'd got from the camp and put it on the table. It had only been Grandma's illness that induced them to let me go.

"Ah!" sighed my father. "This is all a dream!...."

"How's Mum? Hasn't she finished work yet?"

"She'll be back any minute. Hurry, Luojin, you'd better hide yourself in the back room or—"

"I know, I really should have let you know I was coming."

"Ah!" Father kept wiping away the tears from the corners of his eyes. "It really is a dream..."

"Anyway," the elder of my brothers broke out indignantly, "what did Luojin ever write in her diary but the truth? The policy *has* been fanatical these past few years. Literature and art *have* been reduced to set formulas. And the Red Guards *have* just been used! If Luojin's reactionary, then so is the whole of China!"

"Not so loud!" Father urged.

"Luojin, what's it like in the camp? Is it hard?"

"That's difficult to answer in just one word! How's Luoke? How *is* he?"

For three years this was the question I'd been burning to ask.

"I'm really worried...." Father's eyes were red from crying. He blinked and swallowed: "He was in the last batch of prisoners they brought to the stadium for public sentencing, and I don't understand why he was the only one they took away afterwards... His name wasn't on the list for the death sentence." He shook his head, his eyes staring dully at the floor: "Ah, I dream about him whenever I fall asleep... I'm so worried!"

"Did anyone in the family see him when he was taken to the stadium?"

"We weren't allowed to watch," the elder of my brothers said. "The two of us only got back from Shaanxi a few days ago. Luoke was one of a group of political prisoners who were Strifed the day before yesterday; but they were watching us to make sure none of the family went out."

"There's an old man who sweeps the streets with Dad," my little brother carried on: "He told Dad in private that he'd seen Luoke. ⟨All the prisoners were in handcuffs and fetters, and they were all tied up and gagged, so none of them could cry out. He said Luoke's face was yellow and swollen; two policemen were struggling to push him down, but he refused to bow his head and kept fighting back..."⟩

For a long while, nobody said a word. There was only the mechanical ticking of the old clock on the wall to accompany the beating of our numb hearts. It was as if our tongues were clamped down, and we would suffocate.

"I'm so worried..." Father sighed.

I glanced around the room. There was nothing left, except for a broken table and two old wooden chests. I'd only been away three years, and yet home had become a completely run-down and dilapidated place, it seemed totally without joy. There had been countless raids, and whatever could be taken away had been taken away; out of what remained, whatever could be sold had been sold. It must have been so hard just to survive.

Father emptied his pipe and slowly stood up to carry on with his bread-making. His back was more bent than before, making him look a whole head shorter. He slowly rolled out the dough, sighing and shaking his head gloomily. I felt unspeakably sad upon seeing this great change in him.

Suddenly, there was a faint knock at the door.

"Mum's back!" My two younger brothers both stood up at once. "Hurry, Luojin, go and wait in the other room!"

I ran in there straightaway, quickly shutting the door tight behind me; I pressed my right ear up against the ice-cold door and heard a sprightly step, unmistakably my mother's! In my mind's eye I could clearly see her striding vigorously into the room, her straight back swaying slightly from side to side. What hardship she must have experienced over the years! Ever since '57 when Father had lost his job, we had all depended on that firm stride of hers, and on that physical endurance, as she bustled and toiled to provide for us through all those years. And then Luoke and I had needlessly added our guilt to her burden! Had she aged? Had her hair turned white? Had her spirit remained unbroken? How I longed to set eyes on her!

Everything was silent again; not a sound could be heard. The chill air in the room made me shiver with cold. It was mid-winter, and yet there wasn't even a stove in the room; there was nothing but a home-made plank bed. Outside, the cold north wind was howling fiercely, rattling the window-panes. I looked outside—strange, I could see a woman, her rat-like face pressed up against the window, peering into the room; she ducked out of sight the minute she realized I'd seen her.

Why was there still no sign of anything happening in the other room? I couldn't restrain myself any longer, and opened the door just a crack. As I opened it further, these words, spoken in a tone of astonishment, came drifting out to me:

"Really? Luojin's back? Where is she?"

I burst out of the back room. ⟨I left that icy hole behind, and went rushing into a world of warmth and love crying,⟩ "Mum!"

"My child!" Mother gave me an anguished look, her eyes filling with tears, and then she covered her face with both hands and broke out sobbing. I just held her foolishly by the elbows while she stood there sobbing, her soft close-cropped hair nuzzling against my chin. I couldn't think of any words to comfort her...

*

That night, my two brothers slept in the freezing back room, and Father, Mother and I slept squashed together on one plank bed. The dim silvery light of the moon shone on my grandmother's face, deathly pale, on my father, dreaming his troubled dreams, and on my mother, her face swollen with dropsy, and her eyes closed; the lonely moon had swallowed all the stars in the sky... I couldn't get to sleep.

...I seemed to see my brother again on that overcast, gloomy day in Peking, three years before: "Does anyone dare argue this out with me?" He had leapt with one bound onto the stone steps outside the Craft shop in the middle of bustling Wanfujing Street, and was standing there eloquently demolishing the false theories of both opponents and would-be compromisers. His essay "On Class Background" had just appeared in the first issue of the *High School Cultrev Post* in January 1967. My younger brothers had been telling me earlier that day after

my mother got home, of the mad rush there'd been to buy this paper
every time it came out! And Luoke had gone on to write six or seven
major articles for it which always featured on the front page.

"The Peking Library always ordered ten copies of each issue,"
Luowen said. "They still have them."

"One day people will read them again . . ."

I turned over quietly, afraid of making a noise and waking my
mother. She lay facing me, apparently asleep, her swollen face green in
the moonlight; her close-cropped hair had been shaved more than once
and hadn't grown back to its normal length. But even though she lay
motionless, I didn't believe she was really asleep. As I gazed upon her,
I was drawn back once again into the past, to that terrible day.

. . . I was taking a few clothes and things to my mother under the
surveillance of some Red Guards armed with rifles. They brought me
to a scrappy piece of wasteland surrounded by a double barbed wire
fence. I looked about and saw no buildings and no sign of human life.

I was puzzling to myself, "What have they brought me here for?",
when suddenly, from out of the slightly elevated ground before me, a
person emerged! It was my mother! My heart was thumping hard.
"Mum!"

Her face was a deathly greyish-white and her hair was dishevelled,
but this wasn't what terrified me—it was rather her eyes, dull and
lifeless as I had never seen them before, her sluggish step, and her
feeble and fearful way of speaking:

"My child. . . I don't need anything now . . . Take it all back. I
wanted to see you to give you this watch . . ." She removed the watch
from her wrist.

I was just about to take it when all at once I came to my senses and
shook my head vehemently. "No, Mother, I won't take it!" I said
loudly. "You must be strong! I've just been to see Luoke, he's bearing
up well in his Prolethought group. He asked me to tell you—you must
be strong! Things won't always be as bad as this. They must get better.
Please Mum, don't do anything foolish! You must carry on!"

I couldn't say more. I swallowed hard and cast my eyes angrily over
the Red Guards all around us with their guns on their shoulders: "I'm

going straight to the Party Headquarters, Mum,'' I cried, ''to make an
appeal! What law have you broken? What right have they got to treat
you like this?''

''My child. . . .'' She started sobbing. It was the first sign of life she'd
shown. ''I can't see a thing. . .in that underground prison, I can't see
the fingers of my own hand right up in front of my eyes. . . It's dark
and damp. . . I sleep on two bundles of rice-straw. . . I can't see
anything. . . Here's the watch, go on, take it back home.''

''No, I won't.'' I put the watch firmly back on her wrist. She just
sobbed softly, and offered no resistance. I pressed all of the clothes and
the towelling coverlet up against her chest, wrapping one of her arms
around the bundle so that she had to hold on to it.

''Don't cry, Mother. I'm going to the Party Headquarters right
away!''

I'll never forget that Municipal Committee building. There was a
confused hubbub in the main hall, and all the political Freaks* who had
come to make their appeals were sitting squashed together on the floor;
you couldn't even *push* your way through the crowd. . . Everyone
came full of hope, but it was all futile. My mother, for instance, was
given extra Strife just because of my attempt to appeal on her behalf!
From that point on, except for my ailing grandmother, all six members
of our family were in the hands of Proledic—I was being Cured, Luoke
was under arrest, my two younger brothers were getting Prolethought
at school, my mother was locked up in her factory, and my father was
under Masswatch from the local Neicom*—for over three months, not
one of us was at home. . .

And that day, three years later, we were reunited, except for Luoke.
He'd always had such a weak constitution, but I knew his defiant
unshakeable spirit would battle on even in the face of death! Hot tears
streamed down my face—I was in for another sleepless night!

*

''What's this?''

It was around noon the next day, and a young policeman, about twenty years old, was sitting on a chair with one leg propped up across the other, pointing his finger emphatically at my leave-certificate: "So this is the 'urgent matter' that's brought you back to Peking, is it? Your grandmother's been ill for years! Ten days leave, for *that*? And the three of you just happen to turn up at the very moment when Yu Luoke is being given Strife and Crit* all over the city! Not thinking of getting him out, are you? Well, the girl can go straight back where she came from! And as for these two, it's back to their village in Shaanxi! What they need is a bit more good honest peasant education!"

At this point, Ratface, a neighbourhood Beaver, came swaggering in and settled herself on the bed to listen. Her brow raised, she looked coldly at us out of the corner of her eye, and then took two filter cigarettes from a cigarette case, handing one to the young policeman.

"But they've only been back four days." My mother gestured at my two brothers as they left the room, and then went on to explain to the policeman in a low voice: "All the Urblings in their village have come back to Peking to visit relatives. They don't even have firewood for the winter. How will they get through the winter if you send them back there now? Please, won't you let them stay until after the Spring Festival?"

"Spring Festival? That's a holiday for the People, not Counters! You're not like other people! I couldn't care less *how* they get through the winter!" The young policeman spoke harshly. "The peasants don't die of cold! They must go, all of them! By noon the day after tomorrow, at the very latest! We'll be back to make sure they've gone. And if they don't do what they're told, there'll be trouble!"

"Just look at your family," chimed in Ratface, making a great show of her importance. "You're all reactionaries, the whole lot of you! And what do you think you're up to, having the three of them come back at a time like this? You're the parents, it's your fault if your children have all got Counter ideas! And especially *you*!" She turned on my father and gave him a good dressing down: "You haven't had a proper job in ages. What kind of ideas have you been filling your children's heads with? Look at your son, and that anti-Party, anti-Socialist Poison* he's been writing! You know the trouble it stirred up in Peking, and now it's spreading all over the country! He's the very worst type of political offender, but he still thinks he can act all high and mighty, even in prison. You're his parents, you're directly to blame! We're holding a Neicom meeting the day after tomorrow in the afternoon, and we'll expect a proper Scrit* from you—your influence on your children, what you've been filling their heads with. You didn't go nearly far enough last time! We'll give you one more chance to turn over a new leaf. You'll have to do a lot better this time, if you want a clear from Revmass*!''

"Is that understood?" The young policeman repeated his warning: "If the three of them don't leave tomorrow, all five of you will be up on the platform the following day, for a Mass Strife and Crit!"

*

We had no choice. We resolved to take the train the following evening. But we didn't have any money at all in the house, and none of our friends or relatives wanted any more to do with us. My mother owed her factory money; she was still only on half-pay. So my brother and I decided to ride the train without a ticket.

The next day at noon, my mother gave me a one *kuai* note and said: "My child, we may not be able to afford to eat, but I must have a photo. Get a good one taken of the three of you today...."

"Mum, our train will already have left by the time you get back from work...."

"Then I won't be able to see you off. But don't whatever you do forget about the photo. There's no need to come out with me now. Stay inside. The Beavers might see us again."

Mother contained her grief and went off without once looking back.

We dashed out of the door to watch her from the first floor landing. To hell with Ratface! Let her snoop! We might never see our mother again! She had already reached the bottom of the stairs, so we turned and raced over to the balcony, gazing over the low balcony wall and following her into the distance with our eyes—ah, what suffering lay concealed beneath that slightly swaying walk of hers, that straight back, that thin, soft hair!

After supper, darkness fell at last.

"It's safe for you to go now." Father puffed at his pipe gloomily. "They won't be able to see you so easily in the dark. Don't go out together, go downstairs one at a time. If that Beaver spots you, we'll only be in for more trouble; even her children have learned her tricks."

My two brothers went out one after the other. I stared at the old clock on the wall, waiting... Those five minutes seemed like five years... Listening to the monotonous ticking of the old clock and Father's sorrowful sighs, I had an overwhelming sense of pain, of having been deprived of my right to live! I clutched the one *kuai* in my hand as if I was gripping hypocrisy and darkness by the throat; how I longed to tear the note into a thousand pieces and toss them all up into the dark and tormented sky; how I longed to howl my rage to the universe!

After sneaking downstairs one after another, just like in "The Thief of Baghdad", we met up again in the brightly lit street, in the shadow of a thick electricity pole, like underground party members in the old days. We then made our way to the photographers across the street.

When we were back home again, we got everything ready for the journey: each of our three worn bags contained patches for mending clothes, a water mug, a bar of soap, and enough flat-bread for three or four days.

And now it was time to leave this home, this joyless home, which we had yearned for all the same, and would go on yearning for, day and night!

My brothers and I each sat down on a stool, looking at Father and listening attentively to his repeated instructions:

"You won't forget now? If ever our family is broken up, on the first and fifteenth of the month you must go to the main streets, the big cross-roads, wherever there are lots of people, to check the Missing Persons notices; and while you're there, don't forget to put up your own notice. We'll use 'Xia' as a code-name for your brother. If anything should happen to him... I... I'll write in my letters to you, 'Xia has gone home'. You won't forget, will you?"

It was an effort for him to get this out, for he was haunted by the fear that one day he might actually have to write these words. The code was essential, since all the letters which my brothers and I received from home were opened by the authorities.

"We'll remember," we answered like clockwork.

"Be sure to keep the addresses of our old friends. Whatever else you lose, don't lose those. They may be keeping away from us now; I'm sure they're having a hard time themselves. But if our family should ever get split up, we may be able to find each other indirectly through them. You won't forget, will you?"

"We'll remember."

"And if for any reason I have to send you a telegram, and I use my *full* name, the words will mean the opposite of what they say; the Neicom or the PSB will have forced me to send it, or else it will be because I have something to tell you that I don't dare state openly. But if my surname *isn't* there, the words will mean what they say. You won't forget, will you?"

"We'll remember," we answered earnestly once again. Father could have gone on giving us an endless list of instructions, and we would never have tired of listening.

"If they throw you off the train," Father urged us again, "whatever you do, don't make a scene."

"We'll remember everything, Dad."

"Now, off you go." He was struggling with himself, and blinked away his tears.

Grandma had fallen fast asleep. We stood at the side of her bed stroking her hands and bidding her a silent good-bye.

Slinging our bags over our shoulders, we said softly, "Good-bye, Dad!" and crept stealthily down the dark corridor.

As we neared the stairs, Father went and stood at the waist-high wall of the balcony waiting for his children to appear downstairs.

What dim light there was in the street was obscured by the buildings, and our entire block, both upstairs and down, was shrouded in darkness. ⟨The tall buildings all around were like awesome monsters, towering over us.⟩

We looked up to wave good-bye to Father. He was leaning over,
trying to follow us with his eyes as far as he could, one hand clutching
the low wall and the other holding his glasses on... After a couple of
steps we turned round again to see him still in the same attitude, only
that his body was leaning even further outwards. We looked back every
few steps. Soon we would have to turn the corner and move into the
glare of the street. I deliberately trailed behind my brothers to get a last
look at Father. There, in the shadow of that dark building, his bent
body was straining to lean further and further forward, his back was
curved into an arch, he was still holding on to the top of the wall with
one hand and his glasses with the other; it was like a woodcut—a vivid
outline, a hazy texture—and it gripped tightly at my heart!

Three young people, with bulging bags and tattered old clothes,
strolling in the brilliant light of the street, like we'd just emerged from
some vale of tears, talking and laughing one moment, depressed and
preoccupied with memories the next... ⟨Even when we talked about
Luoke and his ordeal, it was with such intensity and animation! As if
our heartfelt cry of joy could somehow drift across the clear night air,
and reach him in his death cell!⟩

"Luojin, people are staring at us in a funny way," one of my
brothers remarked half-jokingly.

"Let them!" I replied ⟨defiantly. ⟪"Let the police and their plain-
clothes spies come and listen if they want to! If they're going to arrest
us for speaking out loud, then let them go ahead and do it!⟫ We're not
at home now. We've left that gloom behind, that vale of tears."⟩

Street lights were shining, star clusters studded the sky, the Milky
Way was a stretch of radiance. Gazing up at the beautiful western sky,
I wondered to myself whether anything like the grotesque absurdities
on earth occurred up there among the galaxies? Did they too use class
as a tool of oppression, way up there? Had any of them arrived at
communism? If so, what was *their* society like? How I wished I could
go up there in a space-ship to take a look! Great dense clouds massed
together like black swans, ready to soar away... I was lost in fantasy;
my body seemed to grow light and rise up into the sky, merging with
the dark clouds and becoming a swan. I beat my wings, and flew

straight towards the prison cells, towards death row.... Ah, wasn't
that my brother? His face was blue and swollen and spotted with blood
after a whole day of Strife; he was heavily shackled and stood there
behind the double row of iron bars like a bronze pagoda, gazing at the
night sky with eyes full of fierce sadness and longing.... ⟨I swooped
down from the sky and wrenched the bars out one by one with my
powerful beak.⟩

"Quick, climb up on my back, Luoke! I will carry you on my great
⟨ black ⟩ wings to the distant ends of the earth ⟨ to a land where there is
no oppression, to a land of freedom and joy!⟩

I had wrought a miracle! I had saved him!

*

It was already dark when I reached this part of my story. Wei Ying was
staring at me, motionless. He seemed plunged in a deep melancholy;
and yet there was warmth and affection mingled with his grief. He
certainly didn't seem to be thinking of leaving.

I got off the *kang* to turn on the light, but there was no electricity, so
I had to light the oil-lamp instead. The whole room was filled with a
golden, misty glow. How handsome Wei Ying looked in this warm
light!

"Is this the photo the three of you took that day?"

For a long time he stared down at the photo in his hand. His eyes
seemed riveted on one person. My heart trembled, partly in
excitement, partly in embarrassment. He went on staring, and didn't
take his eyes off the photo until I'd put out some dinner on the small
kang table.

After dinner I told him that I wanted to rest and that I'd carry on
with my story the next day. I invited him to stay the night, and said
that I'd go and stay with a neighbour.

I put on my scarf and my overcoat and went off to my closest
neighbour's, about fifty yards away to the west... It was a beautiful
night, the air cold but crisp; what would Wei Ying be doing in the
house at that moment? I could still picture in my mind the expressive

contours of his face under the light of the oil-lamp. How I hoped that
one day I could sketch him!

Little oil-lamp, shine a gentle light
On the dear face of my friend.
Let him be happy, like you,
And cast away sorrow, like you do.

Little oil-lamp, shine a kindly light
On the dear face of my friend.
Protect him from the jaws of black night,
And let your warmth enfold his heart.

I made up this poem in my head along the way and was at my girl-
friend Xu's place before I knew it.

*

⟨ "Had your dinner yet?"

My friend Xu greeted me with these words as soon as I came in the
door. She was feeding dry faggots into the stove. The whole room was
filled with the aroma of wine and meat.

"Why are you cooking so late?" I asked, taking off my scarf.

"My husband has only just got back from the commune. Go in and
sit down."

Mister Xu, her husband, was the Party secretary of our brigade. He
was sitting cross-legged on the *kang* to the left, against the northern
wall, drinking. On the *kang* table there was a big bowl of steaming
pork with pickled cabbage and bean starch noodles, a plate of sliced
preserved duck eggs with dark red yolks, and another plate of home-
made pickles. He was just popping a piece of pork into his mouth with
his chopsticks as I went in, and said to me affably:

"Eaten yet? Care for a bit more?"

A young man called Erbao, who lived at the west end of the village,
had also dropped by to visit the Xus, and was leaning back on the *kang*
cracking melon-seeds. The Xus' three children were lying asleep on
different parts of the *kang*.

"How long did the meeting last?" I asked.

"Three days. It didn't finish until today." Mister Xu sipped at his schnaps and added: "It was pretty heavy-going on the road. I had to get off and push my bike when the snow got too deep. I was dripping with sweat!"

"I'll have to sleep here tonight," I smiled, knowing there was no need to stand on ceremony with them. "I've got relatives staying."

"Sure," Xu smiled. She had sat down on the *kang* opposite, and was stitching a pair of cloth soles. "As long as you don't mind the dirt! There's room enough for three extra! You can sleep with my daughter tonight on that *kang*, all right? I used that stove this afternoon to cook up a big pot of pig food, so the *kang's* still warm."

"Tell me, Uncle Xu," Erbao was asking, "what kind of a meeting *was* it, that it went on for three days?" He was about twenty-four or five, and a distant relation of Mister Xu. He scooped up some melon-seeds in his cupped hands, put them beside me on the *kang*, and leaned back against the northern wall to carry on with his cracking. The speed with which the husks came flying out of his mouth reminded me of the melon-seed cracking contest a few Urblings and I once had with some of the locals. They'd completely thrashed us!

"The meeting?" Mister Xu drank some schnaps, wiped his mouth, and said: "The first day was for general business. The acting Party secretary gave a report—he's the head of the Commune Militia. There's another campaign on the way, to stop the old guard from making a come-back."

"How come he was standing in as secretary?" I asked. "What's happened to old Lü?"

"He and the other Party secretary both got the wind up!" sighed Mister Xu. "One headed off to the hot springs for a cure the day before yesterday—we won't be seeing him for at least three months. The other took long sick-leave and went to a sanatorium in Harbin. We all know they're just trying to lie low. There's no telling how big this latest campaign will be. As soon as the two of them had gone, up went the Wallscreeds: the fight will be on until this come-back is completely wiped out. And while it's on, there'll be plenty of people trying to get something out of it for themselves, you mark my words."

"You never know what's going to happen next these days," said Erbao with a mocking smile, shaking his round, ruddy face from side to side. "Those two had a hard time in '67. They were lucky to be released at all and get their old jobs back—you can't blame people like them for being scared of another campaign!"

"What do you mean a hard time?" I asked curiously.

"What does he mean?" Mister Xu got down from the *kang* and filled up his bowl with hot corn mash. "They were locked up underground and flogged every day until they were nothing but cuts and bruises. They were accused of being members of something called I.M.P.P."

"I.M.P.P.?"

"No one had any idea what this Imp really was," sighed my friend Xu.

"Impside, Outside!" muttered Mister Xu, shooting a glance at her. "They can put you on any side they like. Didn't you hear about Imp in Peking, Luojin?"

"No."

"Lots of our commune Krats were arrested, more than twenty altogether." Mister Xu was shovelling in big mouthfuls of corn mash. "They were supposed to belong to this Imp. I was the brigade deputy-secretary at the time, and nearly got nabbed myself! None of them knew what Imp was!"

"I thought it was short for the Inner-Mongolian People's Party. How could Chinese people have been involved?"

"Well, our commune deputy-secretary's Korean for a start, isn't he? And this is a minority region—a Daur Banner*—isn't it? It doesn't make any difference whether you're a Mongol or not, you're bound to rub up against the minorities one way or another. If the authorities want to blacken your name, that's all they need!"

"But what's this latest campaign got to do with Imp?" asked Erbao.

"Who said it had anything to do with Imp? But there's nothing to stop them settling old scores this time round, is there? If they want to say that you're part of the come-back, it's the easiest thing in the world! Now you see why the two secretaries got the wind up and scarpered!"

Erbao couldn't help laughing at the odd mixture of humour and distress on old Xu's face.

"What else did they say at the meeting?"

"Well, it looks like we'll have to forget about growing those ten thousand tobacco plants this year." Mister Xu had finished his supper, and burped as he pushed his bowl aside; then, drawing the tobacco basket at the end of the *kang* towards him, he slowly rolled a cigarette, struck a match to it, and took a long deep drag before going on: "Last autumn when they came from Peking to inspect our province, they criticized us and said we were too backward. They said we still had capitalist tendencies, and a soft attitude towards class struggle, and also that our ideological work in the commune was lazy and half-hearted. What it all boils down to is that we've got too much on three separate counts: one, too much Ownplot; two, too much garden; and three, too much grain being handed out to commune members. There'll be cutbacks this year. The whole team will be told about it tomorrow."

"What sort of cutbacks?"

"No garden is to be more than three *fen**."

"Three *fen*?" Xu stopped stitching the cloth sole and looked up. "But our garden's about three times that size. What do we do with the rest?"

"What do we do? We let it lie fallow! Better to let it go to waste than bother cultivating it! If we cultivate it, it'll be counted as Ownplot. So what's the point?"

"Ownplots will still be five *fen*, won't they?" Erbao sat up straight all of a sudden.

"Huh, the authorities think that's too much, but our commune wants to keep it at five. After all, there isn't a Krat in the commune without an Ownplot! It'll be a big loss of income for them every year if Ownplots are reduced—they can all work that out, whatever their 'views'! It's lucky for us this is a minority area! The minorities get special concessions, so we'll get them too. We'll still have our five *fen*!" He took a few puffs at his cigarette before stubbing it out on the edge of the *kang*. "But there are new regulations about what you can grow—only main crops are allowed on Ownplots. There's a general restriction on cash crops as well—two hundred tobacco plants per person for instance, and not a single one more. In May or June, an official Inspection Team will come here to pull up any extra plants. And growing crops just for profit is now definitely out.''

"Humph!" Xu poked her sewing awl into her hair. "The lengths they go to! We can't even *grow* what we want! What will they think of next!''

"Don't you grumble, Aunt Xu," Erbao put in. "I got a letter from my older sister in Liaoning Province the day before yesterday. She says they're even worse off there. A whole family is only allowed two hundred tobacco plants—hardly enough just for themselves! And each person only gets one *fen* of Ownplot for growing vegetables, and that has to be planted and harvested collectively, and the produce shared out. They have no garden at all. They can't even kill their own pigs without permission. They're a lot worse off than we are.''

"That's why so many of their Urbling girls try and settle somewhere else," my friend Xu complained.

Yes, girls like me, I thought to myself with a sigh.

We carried on chatting for a little while, and then Erbao got to his feet and brushed the melon husks off his clothes.

"Uncle Xu...about that job... Please do everything you can for me...''

"I won't forget," mumbled Mister Xu, rolling another cigarette and looking up at him. "Aren't you staying a bit longer?"

"No, I can't.''

"You can rest easy," Mister Xu added as Erbao was leaving. "I'll do my best.''

My friend Xu heaved up her sleeping twelve-year-old daughter and carried her over to the *kang* against the northern wall. Then she brought two quilts, one for her daughter and one for me, and drew the curtain. I took off my clothes and lay down.

But the fleas were biting so much I couldn't get to sleep. While I scratched and scratched, the girl was snoring away in a sound sleep. I couldn't help thinking they must have something in their blood, these people of the Great Northern Wilderness, making them immune to the fleas!

"Luojin?" A soft voice was calling me. It sounded like Xu. I opened my eyes a fraction.

"She's asleep." Her voice again. I still said nothing. The two of them began to whisper.

"Do you think Erbao might really get that teaching job?"

"Don't talk stupid! His father was a Kulak. So how could he ever get a job like that? Even if we put his application up to the commune, they'd only send it back."

"Then why did you promise him when you know it can't be done?"

"Well, I'll make sure he gets *something* for the two good meals and the quarter pig he gave me! I've got an idea."

"What?"

"There's a medical vacancy in the brigade—someone to make up prescriptions. Being a barefoot doctor wouldn't be bad, now would it?"

"Mm..."

"We don't need the commune's permission for that. Our brigade can make the decision itself."

"Yes... But don't you think we should still give Secretary Lü something for Spring Festival?"

"I heard he'll be coming back for a few days over Spring Festival anyway. Yes, he can have the pork Erbao gave us, and thirty pounds of tobacco as well."

"But that must be forty or fifty pounds of pork! It's rather a lot, isn't it?"

"You're missing the point! I need him behind me if I'm to get promoted to the commune... How much dried beancurd have we got left?"

"About forty pounds."

"We'll give him twenty. We can manage on the rest till the end of the year. And two bundles of bean starch noodles, five cartons of good cigarettes, and five litres of schnaps."

"All that!"

"And tomorrow I'll send him two cart-loads of kindling from the brigade..."

I fell asleep in the middle of this muffled whispering. I slept soundly, dreaming of Wei Ying's face in the pale yellow light of the little oil-lamp...⟩

*

The next day, I went on telling Wei Ying my story.

6. Memories: Hebei Province, in search of a husband

Not long after I returned to the camp from Peking, they embarked on an experiment. It was some new central policy—they selected a very small group of people, gave them each a settling-in allowance of a hundred and fifty *kuai*, and sent them back to the villages they'd come from. Those who didn't have a village (like me) were assigned one. This is how I came to be sent to a small village in Linxi County, in the southern part of Hebei Province.

I arrived there at noon, on a warm sunny day. It was already late March, but the fields were coated with white. Strange: could it have been snowing? Later I learned that this layer of "snow" was the commune members' yearly supply of salt. It could even be sold in the market for a bit of extra money.

My settling-in allowance of a hundred and fifty *kuai* was paid directly to the work-team, who welcomed it as a windfall, and used it to buy farm tools and seed—they were actually still in debt to the commune.

I asked the Party secretary of the village: "Now that the money's all gone, how can I build myself a house?"

"A house? It's only a matter of time before you'll get married and leave. Just stay with the Lis in their side room for the time being," he said with a casual laugh. "You're already twenty-three. It's time you had a husband. You'll find it very hard on your own."

A husband... I was getting on for twenty-four but still had no thoughts of getting married and settling down. Before I'd been in the village long, however, three match-makers approached me. The old customs still prevailed here. A marriage had first to be proposed by a match-maker; then the young couple met; then they got engaged. After the wedding, the woman usually didn't go off to work in the fields; she stayed at home spinning and weaving cloth, cooking, raising goats and rabbits, and that kind of thing.

They were a few middle-aged bachelors in the village, and two or three boys from landlord or Kulak families, who were nice enough despite their backgrounds. But none of these was proposed as a match for me. Instead, three other men were put forward, two from our village, and the third from some other village. They were nice enough young men, but there was no question of my feeling any love towards any of them.

I was nearly twenty-four. Had I ever really been fond of anyone, had I ever really been in love?

*

. . . When I was four I'd been fond of the little boy who sat beside me at nursery school. He had a girl's name—Shi Shuying—and was as clean and white as a little rabbit or lamb. He talked just like a little girl, and acted like one too, and he liked wearing flowery shirts. I never let other children borrow my coloured pencils or play with my toys, but I was always generous to him. Then once I forgot my rubber and asked him to lend me his, but he said no. I seemed to see him for the first time as he really was, and our ''love'' just fizzled out after that—which is why this incident has always stuck in my mind, I suppose.

Then at primary school, I was fond of a boy called Huaihuai. He sat right behind me. He was *all* boy—clever and mischievous, and very good at his lessons too. In class I didn't give him a moment's thought; but before school, or at break, or after school (especially during the last two years of primary school), I was always wanting him to take more notice of me and hoping to see him. After primary school, I was admitted to the No. 12 High School for Girls, and he went to another school. By the time I'd reached form two, I couldn't hold back any longer and wrote him a letter on the pretext that a teacher had asked after him. I didn't say anything about wanting to be his friend. But he seemed to understand straightaway, and wrote me back a long, enthusiastic letter, saying he hoped I would reply. You can imagine how excited I was! We corresponded for half a year before finally deciding to meet—we were in form three by then. But I hardly knew the person who stood in front of me. The clear and crisp tones of a child had deepened into the husky voice of a young man; the child's cheerful and animated face was coated with a soft black down; and the bouncing, grinning little thing I had known was now a strapping youth—how he had changed in the course of three years! He seemed so reserved and self-conscious. That beautiful apparition of childhood was completely gone. Gone! I felt so disappointed... It was all over between us!

After that I passed the entrance exam for a high school specializing in Applied Arts. At that time I was still a Young Pioneer. I fell in love with a student on the very first day of school. This at last was the real thing! I liked him for his honest face and his seriousness. He was a class monitor, in charge of schoolwork. But as soon as I knew for sure that I liked him, I started being deliberately cold to him and kept him at a distance; during four years of dormitory life, I spoke fewer than five sentences to him, though I was very familiar with people I didn't particularly like! Was I just being perverse? No. It was far more important to me to win his admiration than his love. I could see how like me he was—he wouldn't want to be fond of someone he didn't admire. And the only way to win his admiration was to excel in my work. So, I drove myself relentlessly. I worked hard at all my courses, and kept on practising at my painting; on one level I was trying to make myself useful to society, but on another level I was doing it for him.

There were plenty of opportunities for us to be alone together, but I avoided them all. I thought true love could wait. He had to love me as much as I loved him—only then would it be true love. I was nineteen when I finished my studies in 1965. We gave each other only a fleeting glance before silently parting. A year passed, but not a single day went by without my thinking of him. Once I was in Luoke's small room when he asked me casually if I had a boy-friend; he wanted to introduce me to one of his friends from high school days. I told him all about it.

"You should take the initiative and write him a letter," he said encouragingly.

"I'd be too embarrassed." I no longer had the nerve I'd had when I first went to high school.

"Don't be so feudal! Think of all the romantic women of the past—like Zhuo Wenjun, who eloped with her lover two thousand years ago! Just do it!"

Finally, I plucked up my courage and wrote a letter:

Dear X,

It is a year now since we left school, and it's such a pity that I exchanged fewer than five sentences with you during the four years we were at school together.

I have liked you since the very first day. The sparkle of your eyes seemed to mirror the light in your soul, and your beauty and goodness stood the test of those four years. I tried to win your love by doing exceptionally well in my studies. I never did as well as you, but that was my goal all the same. Whenever I was alone in the park sketching from nature, I so wanted you to be there just in front of me so I could draw a picture of you on my paper, to remember you by! Whenever I saw a beautiful landscape, I so wanted you to be there next to me so we could enjoy it and paint it, together! I often found myself daydreaming about all the things we could talk about and all the feelings we could share!

In the third and fourth years, I received various letters and notes from boy-students in our class and above, saying they'd like me as a friend, and I always felt disappointed: if only one of them could have been you! These are the words that have been in my heart every minute and every second for five years. Do you believe me?

Then I signed and dated it. I stood by the post-box for ages with the letter in my hand, my mind churning with doubt and indecision—if he were to reject me, I'd be too ashamed ever to show my face again! And how could I be sure he *wouldn't* reject me? But finally I took courage and posted it! My heart was thumping like I had a rabbit stuffed up my shirt. . .

Three days went by, and still no reply. It was all over. My whole being felt completely drained. Then suddenly, the man from the mailroom called to me:

"There's a letter for you!"

I raced to get it! I weighed it in my hand and held it up in the sunlight before finding a quiet place to open it in private—I was so afraid he had rejected me.

Dear Yu Luojin,

I have received your letter, and I want you to excuse me for not replying sooner. It *is* a pity, as you said, that we had so little contact during those four years. I hope that we can make up for it by getting to know and understand each other better.

I was moved by the deep feelings you expressed, and showed your letter to my parents. They would both very much like to meet you. When would be a good time for you? I think it would be better if we could arrange this face to face, but you could write instead if you like. I'll leave it to you to fix a time if you prefer to meet me and talk first.

Best wishes...

I still hadn't answered his letter and was just pondering over the best way of becoming more intimate with him and his family, when along came the trouble over the diaries, then the Raid, and then my surveillance as a Class Enemy. Immediately after that, I was marched off to the PSB, and to labour camp... And there I was, in my Hebei village. So our love was like a feeble spark ready to burst into flame, when a sudden hailstorm came and completely extinguished it. His father was a qualified engineer. If his family didn't suffer during the Cultrev, it must have been a very close thing. As for me, I very soon ruled out the possibility of continuing our romance, what with my various problems—my political problem, my residence problem, and my work problem. I couldn't ask him to burden himself with a "case" like me. Anyway, his parents would certainly no longer think of me as a "darling young girl", and he was a filial son, not likely to act against his parents' wishes.

So, I no longer had any illusions about our love, even though I'd loved him for five years.

And that was the extent of my love life up to the age of nearly twenty-four.

*

It was the day of the Grave Festival*. I was near the village, hoeing in the lush green wheatfields with some girls dressed in green and red. What a joy it was—the beautiful Hebei countryside, and the spontaneous laughter around me!

The postman came riding up behind us on his bicycle, along a raised path between the fields. He stopped and called out to me that I had a letter. I ran up to him happily. It was from Hunan. From my cousin. I opened it and read in great confusion:

... What's this about Luoke's death? What did he die of? Why couldn't he be saved? Your father didn't explain at all. He must be heart-broken, so I really didn't feel I could write and ask him...

What! Dead? Hadn't he been spared then?! Dead!!

"Luojin, come on over here, quick!" The girls were leaning on their hoes and had turned towards me, calling out gleefully.

I was standing there, stunned, gazing blankly at the word "death". I couldn't move.

"Come on, Luojin, quickly!"

"What's the good news from home? Go on, tell us!" Their shrill cries pierced me like needles.

I didn't want to move, but I had to. I had to try and be cheerful and act as if nothing had happened; otherwise there would be gossip in the village, maybe even a scandal, and then my sufferings as a Counter would be doubled...

"I bet your mum's sent you a postal order?" They watched me coming silently towards them, and chattered away nineteen to the dozen. A postal order for them must have seemed the height of happiness.

"No, she hasn't sent me a postal order." I forced a smile.

"Oh come on! You city people have all got money—not like us!" they said, curling their lips.

"If it's not a postal order, then it must be good news!" They looked at me closely—if they'd been able to read, they would have snatched the letter and read it for themselves by then. Perhaps it was this very handicap that left their lives as unrippled as water in a pond, forever peaceful and contented.

"Go on, tell us, Luojin!"

"Just everyday family news," I fobbed them off with a smile. "Nothing out of the ordinary."

I picked up my hoe and set to work quietly. To avoid any more of their pestering, I worked as fast as I could and kept well ahead of them...

*

Night-time, everyone asleep, everything still in the village...

I sat on the threshold leaning against the door, and gazed up at the pale moon.

Dead! Was he really dead? Tears streamed silently down my face... Was he really dead?

⟨No, he was not dead. He was there—in the vast wilderness of the excution ground near Marco Polo Bridge*. The night there was as black as it was here; the stars as few and remote; the same new moon hanging in the deep and desolate sky. Only a slight, cold tremor in the stifling air...

He was lying beneath the damp soil. It had not been firmly pressed down, and he was moving his fingers to loosen the earth. And then slowly he stood up... It was deathly still around him. He shook the earth from his body—in the light of the moon corpses could be seen lying scattered around his feet, the blood not yet dry on them... He stared at them. His whole body began to tremble violently! He stood there for a while plunged in thought, then he turned and walked slowly but steadily forwards, forwards...into the first grey glimmer of dawn breaking in the distance... His silhouette became smaller and smaller, and the east grew brighter and brighter—oh, that familiar silhouette, so dear to me!

He had vanished into the dawn!⟩

My brother! My beloved brother!

*

My beloved brother was no more; the object of my admiration and respect was gone. I thought I'd never get over it. I certainly didn't think I'd ever meet anyone who could have such a deep effect on me.

However, I had a more immediate problem to deal with—my financial situation. The payment for a working-day in our team was never more than ten cents, even in the best of years. The previous year it had been eight cents; women got a maximum of eighty percent of this, and since I was a newcomer, I only got seventy percent. $\frac{7}{10} \times 8 = 5.6 \ldots$ Enough to buy an ice-lolly and have ·6 of a cent left! That much money wasn't enough even for one meal a day. I had no alternative but to ask my mother for money. She sent me ten *kuai* for food every month just to keep me alive. With wages like ours, it was small wonder that even the strongest single male still owed a lot of money to the team after a year's hard work. And every year the team had to go begging to the State for grain.

My two younger brothers in Shaanxi were as poor as I was. Even in the best years, their payment for a working-day never exceeded fifteen cents, and they never saw any of this in the form of cash. My brothers often didn't even have the money to buy stamps. It caused me great anguish to think of my mother having to go off to work every day despite her illness; she still wasn't getting full pay, but she had to support my grandmother and my father, and on top of that, she had to send money to me and my two brothers. I kept wondering how I could make myself independent. After all, supposing Mother died, how would I cope then? And all the time, those three match-makers kept coming and pressing me: "That boy I spoke to you about, have you got your parents' consent yet?"

Yes, it was true, marriage would provide me with financial support.

And then, if Mother died, Father and Grandma could come to me rather than go begging in the streets. If I got married, I would no longer need to ask my mother for money! All I wanted was the bare necessities. The local people had ways and means of surviving, but I was quite incapable of managing on my own. No matter how hard I toiled every single day, I was still dependent on my mother. Things couldn't go on like this!

And love? For me, love had long been a "zero". I considered myself lucky just to be alive! What chance did I have of ever meeting someone I could love? To hell with love! And marriage? What was marriage after all? Peaceful co-existence with a man and his family. I could manage that—whatever they were like, they were bound to be easier to get along with than the people at the camp, and I'd never fallen out with anyone there. Who knows, I might even hit it off with the man's family. Why shouldn't I be a quiet docile little wife, just pumping the bellows, cooking food, sewing clothes, and stitching soles for cloth shoes?

Once my mind was made up, I wrote to my parents telling them about the marriage proposals that had been made in the village.

*

"Dad!" I stood in the cloud of dust at the bus door, stretching out my hands joyfully to help him down and to take the heavy bag he had on his back. His eyes were clouded and kept rolling distractedly from side to side. It frightened me—I wondered whether my brother's death had completely deranged him.

"Let's go."

I gave my father a long look—he had aged even more. Then I lifted the bag up onto my back and we headed off for the village several miles away.

The scorching noonday sun blazed relentlessly down on us and on the yellow earth of the road. Before we'd gone very far, we were sweating all over.

"Didn't the Neicom make any trouble over your journey?" I broke the unbearable silence.

"Oh, plenty of trouble! There's a new document being circulated in Peking about evacuation*. They say there may be a war. If I hadn't told you to send me a telegram saying you were seriously ill, they'd never have let me come!"

"Evacuation? But you didn't mention this in your letters."

"Let's sit down for a while under this locust tree and I'll tell you all about it..."

This was how it went: Party directives had been sent out, and a big campaign had been launched in Peking calling for a mass evacuation, all in the name of war preparations. A few days earlier, my mother's factory and the Neicom had asked for the addresses of my two brothers and me. They had put it quite bluntly:

"Once mass evacuation begins, you two will be the first to go, either to your daughter or your sons."

"...Ah!" Father sighed. "Your mother and I talked about it all night..."

"What did you decide?"

It seemed that another thought had struck him, and he didn't answer my question directly but asked instead:

"Are any of the three young men in the village to your liking?"

"No. I'll tell you how I honestly feel, Dad. If it wasn't for wanting to lighten Mother's load, I really wouldn't want to get married at all."

"I know..." He looked very gloomy and depressed. He seemed so miserable on my behalf, it only made me feel worse. I stood up, brushed the dust off my clothes, and urged him to carry on walking.

"In your letters you say that you never get cash bonuses here at the end of the year, and that you only get eight cents for a whole day's work, is that right?"

"Mm."

"Why doesn't your team set up a side-line of some sort?"

"The authorities wouldn't allow it. They say things like that are a capitalist cancer and must be cut out at once!"

"What if the villagers haven't got enought to eat?"

"Well, they trade their better cereals and millet for dried sweet potatoes and sorghum. They grind these into a flour to make a kind of steamed bread—sometimes they mix a bit of chaff in with it too."

"Is that all they eat?"

"Of course not! They have to fill up on slops. They eat a kind of gruel with every meal."

"What kind of gruel?"

"It's made from sorghum flour, and sometimes they stir in some dried sweet potato leaves."

"What vegetables do they eat?"

"They use salt from the fields to preserve a big vat of carrots. That has to last them the whole year."

"Do they have Ownplots?"

"They used to, but then later the plots were taken away. Everyone still has a quota of one *fen*, but it has to be used collectively for vegetable growing."

"Why don't they rear a few pigs and chickens, or sheep, or rabbits?"

"What would they feed them on when they don't have enough to eat themselves? The crops don't grow well in this salty soil, and even grass is hard to find. The chickens don't lay many eggs, unless they're kept by people living on the outskirts of the village."

"Then how do they manage to stay alive if they don't have any money all year round?"

"The villagers rely on selling their cloth coupons."

"Cloth coupons?"

"Everyone has a ration of six yards of cloth a year, see? When the coupons are first handed out, they're worth twenty-four cents a yard, but by the time Spring Festival comes round, you can sell a coupon for one *kuai* thirty-five. And another thing—if they have some ailment or other, they just stick it out. They don't buy medicine unless they're seriously ill, and since they usually eat liquid foods and never have meat, they seldom *get* seriously ill. They also manage to make a little extra money by selling the odd rabbit."

"What do they wear if they sell all their cloth coupons?"

"Homespun cloth. Even the men can weave."

"Do they get a decent quota of cotton?"

"No, not really. But when it's cotton-picking time, every woman wears her very baggiest trousers and ties up the bottom of her trouser legs, and the team leader just turns a blind eye to what goes on during those few days!"

"Can the cloth coupons be sold openly?"

"No. But on market day, they all know where to go and what secret signals to use. Then, when they've made contact, they'll choose a village some way off to clinch the deal. . . ."

It was exactly midday, and the boundless jade-green fields were as quiet as a sleeping baby. The midsummer wind kept on licking our hands, arms and faces with its hot dry breath. Our clothes were soaked through with sweat. Not a soul was anywhere to be seen in the lonely fields. The villages we passed, set against the azure blue of the sky, seemed lost in their peaceful reverie. My father and I walked in silence, our hearts tormented by the same unmentionable subject. Neither of us wanted to be the first to speak.

"Your brother. . . such a fine boy. . . ." My father finally choked out these words, and then began to sob loudly and bitterly. He was bent double, as if his old body could not sustain so much grief.

"Dad!. . . ." I held on to him with both hands, and told him he ought to stop and rest. But he shook his head and kept on walking ahead, groaning and sobbing all the while. . .

⟨"My child. . . You must keep the memory of your brother alive. . . You must try to write something about him!"

"Don't worry, Dad! I will! I promise I will write about him. . . ."⟩

The rustling wheatfield was whispering, as if in sympathy with the old man's pain, his immeasurable and incurable pain. . .

I supported him with one hand, and with the other I held tightly onto the heavy bag on my shoulder. On I trudged. Only one thought kept running through my mind:

"I must let Dad cry it all out!"

*

The moon shone through the paper window, casting a thin layer of

pale silvery grey light on the mud-walls of the house. My ears were still
ringing with the words Father had spoken to me in that room earlier in
the day:

"...The morning your brother was shot, I was at home cooking. A
policeman came in and started shouting at me. 'Your son's been shot.
Got anything to say? Sign here then, quick!' And with that, he threw
the document onto the table. It was some time before I could take in
what had happened. I sat on the floor and began to cry. I couldn't get
to my feet. He was very impatient; he wanted me to sign, to get the
whole business over and done with. I steeled myself to do it. What was
the point of crying! Why should I cry in front of *him*! I struggled to
my feet and signed, and then he strutted off... My son was dead, and
he asked me what I had to say! I couldn't carry on with the cooking,
not after that!

"I was still crying when your mother got back from work. She'd
heard about it at the factory. She wouldn't let me cry. Don't you think
that was hard of her? In fact she even scolded me and told me to go and
cry outside if I wanted to cry at all! She didn't shed a single tear
herself! I wasn't half as brave as she was!

"The next day, your mother and I helped each other along to the
prison to fetch your brother's things... That new waistcoat of his was
still neatly folded—he hadn't wanted to wear it because it was so
new. Apart from the waistcoat, there was just a bowl, a plastic belt, a
work-card, and a wallet with only a few canteen coupons and fifty
cents inside...and a fountain-pen...I've brought the pen for you,
my child. Keep it. I thought it was something you'd very much like to
have..."

I pressed that black pen to my cheek ⟨ and I kissed it ⟩ ... My
brother, I had to live to be worthy of the pen you left me! I had to
write down my love for you and my memories of you, even if what I
wrote was only something short. I had to write the truth, it had to be
real, even if it cost me my life! I would give everything for this! This
had been my goal since I was fifteen! Even then you seemed like an
eagle in my eyes! I'd written down everything I could remember about
you when I was under detention. I was confident that the people would

want to remember you! My brother, what need had I of a husband, or
children? What need had I of life itself? The only thing I needed and
could not do without was that pen of yours! It was your weapon, ⟨ it
was your soul, it was truth,⟩ it was all that I held dear!

Staring up at the smoke-blackened thatch of the roof, I thought
about the words Father had spoken to me earlier. They had
embarrassed me, and yet at the same time, they had made me see the
light:

"...Your mother and I talked this over all night... Life here is too
hard, child. You mustn't marry and settle here. And Luowen and
Luomian aren't any better off. If your mother and I have to go and live
with you or your brothers, we'll all be desperately poor—we don't
know how to survive the way the country people do here... You'll
get married eventually, so why not try and find a more prosperous
village? Then, if we ever have to take refuge somewhere, we can settle
there. It's easy to transfer a Domper directly from Peking to the
country. But suppose the whole family gets registered in this village,
and then you go and find a better one—you know how difficult it
would be to get us all transferred *then*..."

I turned to look at my father. He didn't seem to be asleep, even
though his eyes were closed.

"Dad..." I called softly.

Just as I thought, he opened his eyes immediately, waiting in the
moonlight to hear what I'd got to say.

"Dad, I've been thinking about what you said earlier. It's easier to
get one person transferred, like you said. And I'm going to get married
anyway, so I might as well try and find somewhere better. My brothers
often write to me saying how much they dream of moving to a place
that's more prosperous and where there are fewer people and fewer
restrictions. If we could make this move, it would solve all our
problems. Write those letters, Dad, write them tomorrow. Write to all
the relatives and friends you can think of, all of them, then we'll have
more places to choose from."

"My child... your mother and I really haven't any alternative..."

"Don't say another word, Dad. I understand."

That same night, my father took it upon himself to tell me the story of his life. I lay on the *kang* quietly listening, thinking to myself that what he was really trying to do was to prove to me his innocence and his kind-heartedness. But how could I ever have doubted my own father? That would have been like doubting myself.

I'd always considered myself a person of high principles, and it had never occurred to me that I'd end up deciding to marry whoever came along! Now I'd have worked in a brothel (if there'd been one) to provide for my family! Who would have thought that I could change so suddenly?

When the prospect of "marriage" first presented itself to me like this, all I felt was a sense of humiliation. Was I sad? Bitter? Full of pain? No. I was just numb. All I knew was that I *had* to do this, in order to stay alive. ⟨ The thought of our new marriage laws*, with all their assurances of freedom, only brought a wry smile to my face. ⟩

*

The next day I went off to work in the fields, and my father stayed at home to write the letter:

...I have a twenty-four year old daughter with a high school education. Her looks are passable, and she is in good health. We have received several marriage proposals, but cannot consider marrying her here in view of the poverty of this area. We would like to see her settled in a somewhat more prosperous village. Our only stipulation is that her husband should be a decent sort—as for his education, age, and so on, we leave it to your discretion. We can send a photograph, if you so wish...

I came back from work at lunch time and looked at the rough draft. My father was always a fluent letter-writer, but he'd only managed to produce this letter after a great many crossings-out and false starts. As I read it through, I felt a deep sense of pain.

But what else could he have written? Should he have demanded a high school education? Good looks and moral integrity? Intelligence and application? I had to tell my father he'd done a good job. There was nothing to find fault with!

I held out the letter, trying to appear as if nothing was the matter and assuming a cheerful air: "Why don't you write a few more just the same as this, Dad. It sounds fine to me. I've got some photos here we can send straightaway. You don't want to go to the bother of writing all over again."

"No." He took the letter from me, shaking his head sombrely. "It's not necessary to send the photos yet. I'd rather wait and write again."

Ah, those few words showed how much my father cared for each one of his children! I remember him lifting me up when I was five years old and kissing me and saying, "When my little girl grows up, I'll find her an engineer!" The wounded look he'd just given me pierced me to the quick! How I wished I could dispel that hurt and never see it again! If only they could exchange me for some happiness!

On market day, Father went to post about a dozen letters, all saying the same thing. He really gave me a shock when he got back at noon—his face was stained, traces of tears and sweat from his forehead merging into one . . . He said he'd been thinking of my brother when he was out in the quiet of the fields. But I was sure he'd been thinking of me too.

It was going to rain! Dark billowing clouds were rolling up . . . and then the heavy rain came pouring down in sheets. Lightning flashed overhead, thunderclaps shook the sky; a flash of lightning, rearing up like a silver dragon, suddenly struck down into our small front yard, only two yards away from our door! We quickly shut the door and hid ourselves inside the room.

The raging thunder roared angrily and reverberated outside the door . . .

"Love! Freedom! This is all mankind needs!"

In the surging sound of the rain and the violent peals of thunder, I thought I could hear my brother's voice, indignantly reproaching me . . .

Don't be hard on me, Luoke! Don't condemn me in the thunder! I'm not doing this for myself... Pain, anguish, despair, they all blended with the sound of thunder and rain.

Suddenly, the door was banged open by the wind, and the rain came whirling in. A blinding flash of lightning struck right in front of us—it was terrifying! An immense crash rent the sky, the wind raged, it seemed as if the whole world would be swallowed up.

"Come on, quick! The door!" shouted my father.

I rushed to fetch the piece of wood we used to prop against it.

Thunder, rain and wind whirled outside the door...

Luoke! What would *you* do now if you were in my place? Maybe you'd say: "Things aren't as bad as all that, and even if they were worse, you can't turn marriage into a means of livelihood!" Is that right? But I haven't got your courage! And anyway, what about the family?

The rain gradually abated...the rumbling of the thunder gradually faded into the distance...as if my brother didn't want to argue with us any more.

I pushed open the door. A gust of damp air blew against me, and the cool breeze seemed to pour new life into my depressed soul. There was a patch of blue in the sky; rain clouds like ink-splashes sped by overhead.

How quickly the clouds went racing by after the rain! How I longed to be like them and fly away into the distance!

The clouds were racing recklessly onwards, leaving everything behind... I suddenly had a sad feeling that it was my brother going away, leaving us in contempt!

*

A fortnight went by without any of our relatives or friends replying to the letter, and my father and I were running out of hope. We had almost reached a state of total despair, when a letter from my mother arrived and cheered us up considerably:

84 *A Chinese Winter's Tale*

I've been speaking of Luojin's problem to everyone I can think of, but I've had no luck yet. The situation in Peking is still the same as when you left. But yesterday, I bumped into Mrs. Zhao, quite by chance. We talked about Luojin and she mentioned that her son Zhiguo has settled in the Northeast. It's such a coincidence. She said that last year they were getting one *kuai* eighty-nine a day, and it hasn't fallen below one *kuai* seventy for years. She said she could ask Zhiguo to try and find Luojin a husband...

"Who's this Mrs. Zhao?" I asked my father.

"Oh, you don't know her. Your grandmother got acquainted with her after you left, at women's meetings in our neighbourhood, and at the market. But after we moved house, we lost touch with her."

"Have you ever met Zhiguo before?"

"None of us has. He left for the country before we got to know his family."

So every day after that, my father and I eagerly awaited another letter from my mother. It was our last hope.

Soon a letter came, telling us to go back to Peking. My mother said she had something to discuss with us. It turned out that Zhiguo had written her a letter, which read:

...People here get married very young. They're engaged at seventeen or eighteen, and by the time they're in their early twenties, they've already had two or three kids. At the moment there's no one suitable. But if Luojin wants to come, she's welcome to stay with us for a while. There are only three Urblings in our village and none of us can even cook properly! Luojin can then look around and find someone suitable for herself...

That seemed to be the only way open to me now—to go to the Great Northern Wilderness and try my luck. I should establish myself there first, and then get my Domper transferred as soon as possible.

How strangely Fate had worked it all out! I'd made up my mind—I'd venture up to the Great Northern Wilderness!

7. Memories:
Off to the Northeast
—and into a marriage!

"The travelling will be such an expense," my mother worried. "The train fare alone will come to twenty-six *kuai*, and then there's the bus fare, and your food on the train. And you'll need a few *kuai* in your pocket, won't you? You can't make do with less than thirty *kuai*."

My father and I just stared at her helplessly.

"We'll have to sell something!" Mother looked around the room gloomily.

We had by this time moved to a single-storey house consisting of two small rooms. Every time we moved, our new house and its surroundings were worse than before; and every time we moved, we had dreams of the new neighbourhood treating us better, not always as enemies—but they were only ever dreams! My father and I looked around the room as well: it was almost bare, what was there to sell?

"Come here, Luojin. Help me pull out this bedding." Mother walked over to the plank bed and lifted a corner of a thin cotton-padded mattress. "Take these two mattresses to the second-hand shop. They ought to fetch ten *kuai* at the very least."

"But what will you sleep on?"

Mother frowned impatiently. "You can see your grandmother hasn't got long now. There'll be a spare set of bedding when she dies! What are you dithering around for? Run along now!"

*

"Seven *kuai*." The shop-assistant turned his eyes disdainfully towards the window.

I hesitated for a few seconds, then hardened myself and handed him our Domper book. The whole transaction took less than three minutes to complete.

Mother was dismayed when she heard what the mattresses had fetched. What were we to do? Even for a one-way journey, we still needed another twenty-three *kuai*.

"Why don't I just get on the train without a ticket?"

"That's out of the question. They're very strict nowadays about Urblings jumping trains. They'll take you to the railway security if they catch you. You don't want to get picked up *again*, do you? You can't afford to take risks. Ah," she sighed, "if only we had a watch we could sell..." An idea seemed to occur to her, and she turned to my father, who was just sitting there silently smoking. "I was thinking... Couldn't you go to Sun's wife and ask to borrow ten *kuai*? Sun's your old friend, so it would look better if *you* went rather than me. This is the first time we've asked, so she's hardly going to refuse."

"I...ah!" My father never borrowed money from anybody, and hesitated for quite a while; but finally, he gritted his teeth, and got up and left.

I managed to slip out without my mother noticing, and went off to return a new pair of trousers my father had given me when he'd come to see me in Hebei Province—I thought they were too good to wear.

"We can't refund the money even if you have got the receipt," the shop-assistant grumbled. "It's too long since you bought them. Why didn't you come sooner if you didn't like the colour? Anyway, everybody wears this shade of blue."

"Please, have a heart. I'm not lying. I'm just a poor student who's settled in the Northeast, and I haven't got the money to get back."

"Well, why did you buy them if you're so poor? You can't go buying trousers and then just bring them back again! Do you think shops are run just for you?"

"It's my fault for not thinking it over carefully enough first, but please help me out... Surely you've got younger brothers or sisters, or relatives or friends, who've gone off to the country?..."

Not until the tears welled up in my eyes, and she'd turned the trousers inside out to examine them and had studied the receipt again and again, did she finally soften and refund the money.

"You needed something presentable to wear for the journey," scolded my mother, when she learnt that I'd taken back the trousers. "You're not going in those old rags?"

"What does it matter if I wear rags? It might even make things easier for me. Maybe they'll be more sympathetic."

I smiled bitterly to myself at the irony—what did new trousers matter, when I had thrown away all sense of shame?

*

The Great Northern Wilderness was more than a thousand miles away! With the supply of flat-bread my father had made me, enough for several days, I set out on my great adventure!

My parents went with me to the station. I felt so brave, so resolute, so fearless—a really heroic figure! I knew how much my parents would miss me and how worried they'd be on my behalf, so I did my utmost to appear happy; I prattled away to avoid any awkward silences.

"Listen, Mum and Dad!" I said in a loud and cheerful voice. "I've got this feeling that everything's going to turn out all right. Do you know why? No? Well then, I'll tell you. I specially stitched a piece of red cloth inside my padded shoes, to bring me good luck; who knows, maybe I *will* be lucky, maybe I will find a way of staying there straightaway. Don't worry, Mum and Dad. As soon as I've got myself registered there, I'll try and get my brothers transferred. Just wait for the good news. It won't be long before I'm back again!"

The woman attendant who was standing by the door of the carriage couldn't help laughing to see me looking so happy, though she couldn't have heard what I was saying. My mother turned to her and did her best to smile back. It was then I realized that there was really no need for me to worry about my mother; she'd actually always been better at acting than I had, at keeping a smile on her face. Her courage and self-control were quite exceptional. My brother admired her for

it, and so of course did I. By contrast, my father was too depressed
to utter a single word. He just watched us gloomily at our play-
acting—but what good would it have done to cry? As my mother put
it: "We'd all be crying, if crying could help us!"

The train was about to leave. Only when I heard the wheels begin to
turn did I finally let the "mask" fall from my face and clutch at the
train window to say a last good-bye. The old couple helped each other
along, tottering after the train as fast as they could go. My father's old
face was streaked with tears; my mother was neither crying nor
laughing; I had my face pressed up against the window, my eyes
blurred with tears...

Wooo!

A great cry rent the air, and roaring like a savage beast, the train
surged forward! This great cry was the howling of the wind, the
rumbling of the thunder! My heart beat to the wild rhythm of the
train, and I swore a solemn oath:

"Mother, Father—if I fail, I shall never come back! I'd rather be
a Blackbook* and live illegally in the northern mountains, I'd rather
be a beggar, than come back with nothing to show for it! I swear
it!"

For the whole of that train journey, two days and a night, I couldn't
bring myself to think about my brother or my boy-friend from art
school. It would have seemed like an insult to them if I had. I didn't
even deserve to allow them into my thoughts: I wasn't a human
being any longer, just a piece of merchandise!

I tensed my eyes, trying to fight back the tears... I recalled writing
to that boy-friend from school four years before. I never dreamed then
that the day would ever come when I'd be as brazenly shameless as
this. How could I call myself a human being, when I was openly
offering my services to the first comer, hawking myself in the Great
Northern Wilderness, crying to all and sundry:

"Who wants me! Here I am!"

Did I have any human dignity left?

No, not a scrap! I was just putting myself on sale!

That was a long and terrible night! I tried making up a story, to shut out the pain that kept welling up inside me... I was walking in this dense, virgin forest, and big soft snow-flakes were whirling all around me. I was treading the deep snow, on and on, my hands and feet frozen stiff, my empty stomach rumbling, and I had just about given up all hope when suddenly, just like in a fairy-tale, I spied a little house. A lamp cast a golden light, warm and hazy, through the window... I could almost feel the warmth on my face, and the kindliness of whoever it was that lived there; I could almost smell the delicious aroma of food, and picture the soft and comfortable little bed—what a lovely little house it was!

When I got down from the train, I immediately felt a piercingly cold bite in the air; this was my first autumn night in the Great Northern Wilderness! I squatted down in the station and huddled up there the whole night, waiting for daybreak, when I could continue my journey by bus.

*

Those rolling plains of the Great Northern Wilderness! I took the ferry over the wide Nen River and then travelled on by foot. The maize and soya beans were ready for harvesting but dwarfed by the lush weeds. I walked several miles without seeing a soul; the villages were spread out in the distance with stretches of wild grassland between them. This wasn't grazing country, so there was no livestock to be seen. There was so much land and so few people—that was probably what made the Great Northern Wilderness so prosperous.

Some small piles of charred things were scattered along the way—I wondered what they could be and squatted down to have a look. Roasted soya beans! Left-overs from the harvesters' meal. I poked in the ashes and picked out two big, round, charred soya beans and chewed them up; they were delicious... I was in another world altogether! The land here was so desolate and rough, but it was like a mighty giant drawing on some inexhaustible life-source. It was so totally different from the slender beauty, and incurable sickness, of Hebei Province.

*

Luckily, I was able to recognize Zhiguo straightaway, thanks to the description I'd been given—"extremely tall; dark shiny skin". This saved me the embarrassment (and probable scandal in the village) of trying to identify a complete stranger as my "relative".

Zhiguo arranged for me to stay with the Yans in the eastern part of the village.

"We're like family," Zhiguo said to me. "You can stay with them."

So, every day I went across the village to the house the three boy Urblings shared, and cooked their meals and ate with them; and every evening I went back to the Yans' place to sleep. A week went by in this way, and there was still no sign of my residence problem being sorted out. Every day seemed like a year to me... Zhiguo and I made out that our mothers were cousins and that we were therefore related. But before I'd even arrived, the whole village already knew about this distant cousin of Zhiguo's who was coming to the Northeast to look for a husband. I had long since put aside any considerations of face; I was fighting for survival, I couldn't afford to think about pride. I told Zhiguo all about my family's difficulties, in the hope that he and the Yans would help me. I also told the Yan family about the evacuation.

"Don't you worry," Mister Yan consoled me. "Tomorrow, Zhiguo will go and buy three bottles of schnaps, and my missus will knock up a few dishes, and we'll invite the team's committee members over for a drink and a bite to eat. Then we'll bring up the subject of you becoming permanent here."

"If only you'd come sooner," said Yan's wife. "Last year, my husband was a team leader. But this year we're not particularly friendly with any of the new committee. Anyway, you're here, and we'll think up some way of helping you. Your folks in Peking must be worrying themselves sick!''

The next day, I helped with the fire while she prepared several dishes. The committee members were meanwhile drinking at the Urblings' house along with Mister Yan, Zhiguo and the other two boys—this went on from noon till sunset.

''What a waste of breath!'' Mister Yan said angrily when he got back. ''I mentioned your problem three or four times during the day, but they all turned a deaf ear! The two lads listened, but a fat lot of use that is! The minute the drink was all gone, that Scab started playing the drunk and sent the table flying! Whether he really *was* drunk, who knows. But everything was such a mess by the time he'd finished, the others just packed up and went home. Look at this food and drink spattered all over my clothes!'' He took off his smeared jacket, cursing, ''Scab, the lousy bastard!''

''Who's this Scab?'' I asked curiously.

''He's a real good-for-nothing!'' Yan's wife answered. ''No one can afford to mess with him—his cousin's the brigade Party secretary. He broke his wife's arm about two years ago when he was giving her a beating, so she divorced him. She left him with a son who's nine this year. Scab just happened to have dropped by when we got that letter from you asking about a husband, and when he heard about it, he begged me for an introduction. I knew myself it was no good, and that Zhiguo would never hear of it! So you see, today he came to get his own back. It'll be hard for you to work things out if he decides to make trouble.''

In the middle of our conversation, Zhiguo shouted out from the gate:

''I gave that bastard a good thrashing!'' He came into the room looking furious. ''How dare he play the drunk with me, the fucking idiot, pissing around like that! He smashed a lot of our wine cups too, the lousy son of a bitch! I felt like killing him! I'll show him who he's up against!''

''Let me speak plainly, Zhiguo,'' put in old Grandpa Yan at this juncture. He'd been sitting cross-legged at the head of the *kang*, sucking at his long pipe, and now raised his eyelids and said in a steady voice:

"You haven't bothered to keep on good terms with them. And now you go asking them for help... Dear oh dear!"

He looked as if he had something more to say, but stopped at that.

"Don't you worry," Mister Yan consoled Zhiguo. "We'll see your cousin gets settled, come what may. I'll try and think of something else..."

So another banquet was held at the Yans, this time without Scab. Only the committee members and Mister Yan took part—even Zhiguo and the other two Urblings were excluded.

This time I watched it with my own eyes, Mister Yan and several Krats and the Party secretary drinking together for more than half the day. After the third round of schnaps, Mister Yan came to the point.

"I'm afraid I've lost my seal," said team leader No.1, staring into his wine cup. "I've turned all my boxes upside-down, I've looked all over the *kang*, but I just can't find it. I'll get a new one carved in a couple of days." He raised a pair of morose, lying eyes. "I really can't do a thing without my seal. I'll definitely be getting a new one, in a couple of days."

"I've lost mine too," said team leader No.2, staring into his wine cup as well.

How on earth had Zhiguo managed to offend these committee people? I tried asking Yan's father and his wife, but she evaded the question just like her husband had done:

"Zhiguo's a good guy. Only he always sides with the underdog, that's all—maybe that's the reason. Have you ever seen such a couple of no goods as those two team leaders! Lost their bloody seals, my foot!"

"Let me speak plainly," Grandpa Yan said to me, with some hesitation. "The trouble is that young people nowadays really don't know how to handle things! Maybe it would be better if *you* were to go."

The brigade and the commune had already given their verbal consent, but things really couldn't go any further without the team's agreement. My parents' hair must be turning gray with worry by now. My heart ached to think of them; a rash even broke out around my mouth. I was so gloomy I lost my appetite—what if Peking was to start the evacuation now?

"I've got an idea," said Mister Yan one day. "You and Zhiguo are distant cousins, aren't you."

"Yes."

"Well then, I think I know how you can get your Domper transferred."

I stared at him in bewilderment.

He went on with a smile, "First cousins can marry here, and it's considered quite proper. You two being distant cousins makes it even better. We only need Zhiguo to tell the Krats that you're *his* fiancée, and that he was just too embarrassed to say so before. The State actually encourages Urblings in the country to get married, so a piddling little work-team isn't going to dare stand in the way! And there'd be no need for the whole team to discuss the matter! It would really be a much quicker and easier way of doing it."

"But..." I was totally taken aback, and said in some embarrassment, "They'd know for sure it was all a pretence. And anyway, Zhiguo will never agree to go along with it."

"He will, I guarantee it," Mister Yan laughed. "You can rest assured, one word from me and he'll definitely go along with it!"

"But I'm four years older than him. People won't fall for it."

"Who won't?" he argued. "You look younger than him. Everyone says you look like his younger sister. And besides, there's nothing in the marriage law that says you can't be a few years older."

"But... If people jeer at Zhiguo afterwards, it'll all be my fault. He'd feel so ashamed!"

"Why should they jeer at him? He'd be doing it to help you find a home. What's wrong with that? Everyone would admire Zhiguo for having such a clever idea!"

To my complete amazement, when Mister Yan and his wife invited Zhiguo over and explained the plan to him, he merely blushed a little, and agreed to it at once.

*

I felt such relief when I finally got the permit from the commune authorizing the transfer of my Domper. Reading the word "fiancée" on that permit, I was reminded of how helpful and unselfish Zhiguo had been during my stay. He'd even bought me a train ticket home, which made me all the more grateful to him! Whatever his faults, I had to admit that he was a man of the greatest chivalry, and I resolved to repay his kindness in full.

The day after I received the permit, I set off early in the morning. Zhiguo came with me all the way to the bus station to see me off. I had stuck my hand out of the window to wave good-bye to him from the bus, when he suddenly said bashfully:

"There's a letter in your bag. Read it when you get on the train."

*

On the train. . . .

I took the letter out of my bag.

October 1970

Luojin,

You're leaving. Have a good time. Come back soon. I haven't looked after you properly, but please don't be angry with me. I hope you'll tell me how I can do things better. How I wish the reason for you getting your permit could be the truth! . . .

My best regards to your parents.

Safe journey.

Zhiguo

My happiness and gratitude actually diminished on reading this letter. . . No one, it seemed, helped anyone for nothing. I laughed at

my naivety and put the letter back into my bag with a heavy sigh...
My brother would never have behaved like Zhiguo! He would never
have written those words. But I suppose Zhiguo was one better than
men who refused to help you at all with a permit until *after* you'd
married them.

I discovered that in the Great Northern Wilderness "transfer
girls"* (as people like myself were called) were a common occurrence,
nothing out of the ordinary; but I was the first girl from the city to do
it. Most of the "transfer girls" were from Liaoning Province, because
that area was the most poverty-stricken. They would marry a man and
ask for nothing in the way of marriage gifts; their only condition was
that they might bring along their whole family. 《They were as
unfortunate as I was, but luckier in one respect: they didn't have a
brother like mine to measure their husbands against. And besides,
they were illiterate, and had no ideals, no goal in life. It was easier for
them to be content with their lot.》

Zhiguo's letter made me stop and think.... Was there any question
of my loving anyone at that point in time? Absolutely none. Even
though I'd already got my transfer-permit, I had no illusions about
suddenly finding the perfect husband, or indeed of ever falling in love
again! The issue at stake was how to get my brothers here, and I would
do whatever I could to help them. Once they were here, my parents
would definitely be able to come and join us when the evacuation took
place; but if my brothers had to stay where they were, my parents
would be forced to go and live with *them*. And then what would we
do? It would be extremely hard to try and move four people from one
village to another.

If I turned Zhiguo down, most probably my brothers wouldn't be
able to come. From my recent observations of Zhiguo, I knew that if I
did turn him down he would try and get back at me. But if I accepted
his offer, however much he might not like the idea of my brothers
coming, he would go along with it in order to please me. I was a
newcomer, and I needed his help. I decided to accept.

Should I tell my parents? If I told them how chivalrous he'd been
towards me, they'd be so grateful to him! But if I mentioned his letter,

then the gratitude in their eyes would turn to shame—and that was what I dreaded! I didn't want to watch them being humiliated all over again, I didn't want to listen to their sighs!

I was destined to shame. It had all begun when I was in Hebei Province. Must I make them share in my shame as well? I should taste the bitterness on my own. So long as I could get them all transferred, my task would be done.

There could be no happiness in a marriage such as the one Zhiguo proposed, so what was the point of asking my parents for their consent or their blessing? Hadn't they long before agreed to leave the decision to me? It was all so absurd!

*

"And that's how we came to get married!" I said to Wei Ying at last, in answer to his question. I was staring out of the window at the great expanse of snow stretching away into the distance, my chin cupped in my hands, and my mind lost in memories of the past. I went on at last: "It took a lot of effort to get my brothers transferred . . . and now here we all are! As it turned out, that evacuation business was all a storm in a teacup, it never came to anything. My father was digging air-raid shelters every day, and got nothing for his pains except constant abuse—not a cent! After my brothers came, he joined us. He raises chickens, geese, and pigs; he's pretty busy, but happy. My grandmother died while I was back in Hebei Province seeing to my transfer papers. My mother retired last month and she's written to say that she'll be coming to stay for a while. My brothers are now making more than a thousand *kuai* a year; they have their own house, and everything they need. One of them is the team accountant; the other's the team carpenter. They're both very happy. So you see, my task is done!"

It was quite a while before I realized how strangely quiet the room was. I turned towards Wei Ying: he was sitting there with his hands under his thighs, his head bowed and his mouth tightly closed. Tears were dripping onto the lenses of his glasses.

"What's the matter?" I asked, surprised but also greatly touched! Who could understand his feelings at that moment better than I could?

"Just look at you," I sighed. I got down from the *kang* to reach for a dry towel, and threw it over to him. "How can you be so soft? It's my own story I've been telling you, and I'm not crying over it, so why are you?"

He didn't answer, as if he was ashamed of his tears; he just took off his glasses and rubbed them silently with the hem of his jacket. I thought he wouldn't like me just staring at him, so I went out and fed the stove in the outer room with bits of firewood and straw. Then I slowly washed my hands walked back into the room as if nothing had happened and he'd not been crying. I casually tossed him a couple of sweets:

"Here, have these. Want me to pour you out a hot cup of tea?"

My manner helped him to relax a little, and presently he was his normal self again. He unwrapped a sweet, put it in his mouth and sucked it; his eyes were fixed on me for a while, and then turned to stare blankly out the window.

"Blast!" I suddenly remembered. "I forgot to feed the pigs and the chickens!"

It was two o'clock in the afternoon by the time I'd finished my chores and come back inside again—so I started making a fire to cook some lunch.

"Let me help you with the fire!" he said softly, coming out from the room.

"Here you are." I handed him the poker, and started peeling the potatoes.

He looked so handsome, squatting there with the firelight playing on his face.

"Do you and Zhiguo love each other?" he suddenly asked me gently and solemnly, raising his head and looking at me hard.

"What can I say?" I gave an off-hand smile. "He's a good enough bloke, but not someone I could love. Probably when I'm on my death-bed and looking back over my whole life, I'll have to say that I never loved anyone."

He kept on slowly feeding the stove with firewood, his head lowered, silent.

"But every time he comes to our place, he sings your praises. . ." he said, looking up at me.

"Does he? He praises me, and then he beats me! Great!"

"Does he beat you? Often?"

"Yeah."

"Why?"

I hesitated—should I tell him? I so wanted him to understand.

"Because we've only ever slept together once in three years—that was our wedding night, and the night I got pregnant. He reproaches me for not loving him. That's why."

The look in Wei Ying's eyes surprised me—it was a look of trust and understanding, the kind of look my brother might have given me! There was no suspicion in that look, no questions waiting to be asked; it was so frank and sincere, so friendly and trusting! Wei Ying's spirit seemed as all-pervading as the air; it was as if he already knew the story of my wedding night from beginning to end, the whole thing! That look touched me deeply.

I'll never forget it for the rest of my life.

"Isn't it all just like a fairy-tale, Wei Ying?" After lunch I poured him a hot cup of tea, and then I paced up and down the room with my hands behind my back, as if I was making a speech: "The way I see it, what happened is just like a fairy-tale. My brother has become a god, an immortal. I see him every day, I don't feel he's the slightest bit dead. He's there in Nature—in the blue sky, the sunshine, the pine forests, the evening clouds. . . he seems to be in all natural things. Can you feel it? I hope one day, Wei Ying, you will feel the same way, and love him as I do! I'm proud of loving him, and I think I love him better than anyone else in the world loves him, better than my father does, because *he* does nothing about it except moan and groan. But *I'm* going to do something. I'm going to write down all my memories of him, even if it takes fifty years, or a hundred years, to get it published. I'll pass it on to someone I can trust, and then it can be preserved for future generations. The day will surely come when it can be published!

It might even cost me my life; but I'm convinced that if I ever stand face to face with my executioner. I will say, 'I love you Luoke; please forgive me for all the stupid things I've done. . . .' The only thing that worries me is, I may not be able to make it a moving enough story.''

"Just write down what you've told me—that will be moving enough." He gazed at me with love and admiration, and his expression filled me with such warmth.

That night, I had a dream. I dreamed about something I could never bear to think about in my waking hours—my wedding night. . .

*

"Let's get to bed!" Zhiguo was already hurrying me like this, and it was barely nine o'clock.

There was something shifty about the slightly coy and bashful expression in his eyes—it made me uneasy. What was behind that look?

Right up to that day, we hadn't exchanged a single word about love; we hadn't even held hands! It was a perfect case of "marry first, love later"—typically Chinese! I myself was Chinese, and had nothing against Chinese customs in general. But that wasn't to say that I was happy about it either. I didn't love him at all.

Tonight, I would have my first lesson in marriage—what was to be the content of this lesson? What form would it take? What would it feel like? My mind was a complete blank on the subject. I'd never read medical books; my parents had never talked to me about it; I had never been taught anything about it at school; my friends were all like me, we'd never even discussed the topic.

It wasn't until I went to the labour camp that I got any inkling of what it was all about, from the foul language the Drossniks hurled at each other when they were fighting amongst themselves, hollering loud enough for the whole compound to hear. It was unfortunate that I'd received my first "sex education" from their dirty mouths! But even this didn't go very far. Our "reactionary" group didn't live with them or work with them; and the people in our group never talked about it. So that's why I was still a complete ignoramus in this respect, at the age of twenty-four.

And here I was, suddenly married. I was making the bed, when all at once the foul talk from the camp came flashing into my head. ⟨ Was it really like that? ⟩ But I quickly put a stop to this unpleasant train of thought. ⟨ Surely a decent person couldn't act like that? And Zhiguo wasn't a Drossnik, after all. ⟩

"Put the quilts together," Zhiguo ordered when I'd just finished making the bed—again he had that strange look in his eye.

I rearranged the bedding compliantly, feeling more and more uneasy. Zhiguo was washing his feet in the outer room. I took off my jacket and lay down without waiting for him.

This was the experience every young girl had to go through. Was it really my turn today? My heart was beating wildly.

Was there any joy?

. . . no.

Was I shy?

. . . no.

Happy?

No.

Content?

No.

Afraid?

Yes.

Worried?

Yes.

Was I in pain? Did I have any illusions? . . . I turned my face to one side, not wanting to see ⟪the lust in⟫ Zhiguo's eyes as he came in—it was so coarse! I closed my eyes, and quietly lost myself in fantasy. . .

⟪. . . We were sitting in bed in our pyjamas with our jackets draped over our shoulders, tucked up in the warm quilts, and locked in a tender embrace. . . I was expecting nothing, there were no thoughts in my head. I felt only happiness and contentment; I was as happy as an innocent child. All my past sufferings were going to be tenderly soothed away in this one night. . . ⟫

All my sufferings...

I had lost my job.

My four years training as a toy-maker had been wasted.

I'd been Capped a "reactionary".

I'd been put behind bars.

The spark of my first love had been quenched before it could break into flame.

My family had been deprived of its happiness.

My beloved brother had been shot.

And on top of all this, I had been compelled to abandon all sense of shame and sell myself in the Great Northern Wilderness—oh, after all this, after all this suffering, didn't I deserve some tenderness from my husband—from the man who'd "bought" me? Even though our union might look like some sort of deal, I wasn't a maidservant, or a whore! It had been humiliating for me to marry him to be sure, but still I cherished the hope that my humiliation would be dispelled by his tenderness, and that I would find even the slightest reason to love him.

...I imagined us lying under the quilt, holding hands in friendship—it was the first time we'd ever touched each other. He took me gently in his arms, stroked my hair and my face, and gazed at me fondly, treating me like a poor little child. It was right that he should comfort me like this, because he had suffered much less than I had. And I felt a deep contentment and a sweet happiness in this wordless expression of love. All the unhappiness and pain in my heart was melting away into nothing... The pleasant sound of his breathing was cleansing me of all my humiliation and pain... I was falling asleep in this tender embrace, dreaming sweet dreams the whole night through. And then the next day passed, and the day after, and many more days went by; and this person who'd "bought" me always treated me so tenderly that I came to love him more and more with each passing day, until the time came when I felt I must prove my love for him. And then, I said to him, "I want to have your child"—and after that, we would be truly married... How beautiful that would be! We just needed a bit of time, to fall in love...

...I imagined my gratitude and respect for him growing ever

stronger with all the tenderness and love he gave me; no matter how many faults I might find in him, I would excuse them all, if only for the memory of these first nights...

Suddenly, a large foot landed on the quilt beside me, and I opened my eyes, leaving my fantasies behind. It was a size 46 foot, enormously large! I looked up at him timidly, and there he was—a six foot giant standing on the *kang*, ⟨undressing himself.⟩ He was ⟪bending slightly to loosen his belt. The lustful glint in the corner of his eye when he glanced at me was⟫ a million miles from the gallant knight of my dreams!

⟪He sat down to take off his trousers, and proceeded to strip himself stark-naked, looking at me all the while.

What an ugly sight it was!⟫ I involuntarily closed my eyes, drew myself in, and clutched at my padded quilt, my heart cold as a sheet of iron.

I could feel his large hand lightly lifting up the quilt before he slid under it. ⟨His ice-cold feet and his hard bony legs hurt me.⟩ My beautiful dreams exploded into nothingness like fire-crackers. ⟪He began thrashing around with his arms and legs, roughly and clumsily stripping off my pyjamas and underwear and throwing them hurriedly aside;⟫ I just lay there like a terrified puppet, like a fish about to be killed, offering no resistance. Why did my life have to be so full of pain?

⟪Before I could gather my wits about me, the whole weight of his body was pressing down on top of me; two large rough hands were gripping my head. I closed my eyes. Oh God, his sticky tongue was frantically trying to push its way into my mouth! Oh God... I struggled with all my might to turn my face away, but I couldn't escape his "passion" however hard I tried. I felt a sudden pain in my crutch, as if I'd been brutally attacked... This indescribable agony only lasted about a minute, when suddenly he loosened his grip and collapsed onto the pillow, panting convulsively. I managed to get myself free of him and then sat up, my whole body a mass of pain. I leaned forward and spat on the ground over and over again—my mouth felt unspeakably dirty! I was about to put on my clothes and go and rinse out my mouth and wash myself, when I caught sight of a wet patch of blood on the bed—I was horrified!

"What's that?" I gasped in alarm.

Zhiguo raised his head. When his weary eyes alighted on the blood, he burst out triumphantly:

"You really don't know?" He suddenly became all excited again, and clutched me in his arms and pressed me down on the *kang*, murmuring in my ear:

"Haven't you heard the saying:

'The golden needle pierces the heart of the flowering peach.
The silent maiden puckers her brow to stifle a screech'

Ha-ha-ha!"

Even as he laughed, his wet tongue was coming at me again. God! I pushed him off with all the strength I could muster, and got down from the *kang*.

"You....!" I kept spitting on the floor, my face going white and then red with rage. "What are you saying! You filthy brute!"

I washed myself thoroughly with hot water, and found some clean pyjamas to change into. Zhiguo stared at me in bewilderment all the while, with his mouth open. I didn't want to look at him at all. One more look at him and my eyes would be blinded by filth.

But however much I might wash myself, I felt that I would never be clean again, as if an immeasurable poison was eating into my body. I could never be clean again! There was something inside my body no longer completely my own; there was something of him. And what did he represent for me? Love? No! Shame and vulgarity, meanness and filth were what he represented! I had hoped for love and tenderness that night, but what I'd ended up with was a double sense of shame and humiliation! Pain and disgust, foul language, repulsive kisses, those were his gifts to me!》 Was marriage really like this? Would every night from now on be like this? I would rather die, I would never give in! Just thinking about that cursed moment made all the blood in my body boil up inside! 《How I wished I could strangle him! I really couldn't bear the thought of his continued existence!》 In a flash, I opened the lid of the trunk and whipped out a pair of dress-making

scissors which I'd recently bought—the sharp blades flashed a
ferocious blue in the silvery moonlight. Grasping the scissors in my
right hand, I leapt onto the *kang* glaring fiercely at him, and spat out
these words one at a time:

"Now listen here, Zhiguo. If you dare lay a finger on me ever again,
I'll kill you—even if I have to pay for it with my own life! You'd better
watch out!"

His mouth opened wide with fear and astonishment, and he stared at
me dumbfounded as I pulled my bedding away from his side and put it
at the other end of the *kang*. He was silent for a long while, as though
he'd lost his breath; finally he mumbled in a baffled and choked voice:

". . . What have I done? . . . You're a strange one!"

I put the scissors under my pillow—from then on, I vowed that they
would never leave my side! I buried myself from head to foot under the
quilt ⟨but was constantly aware of the big black hairy ape sleeping at
the other end of the *kang*.⟩ I didn't even want to hear the sound of his
breathing. My mind was as confused as a tangled skein, I couldn't
think straight, I couldn't disentangle a single one of my thoughts. Sleep
just refused to come. . .

After a long time I began to grow calmer. The big ape seemed to be
sound asleep. I slowly lifted the quilt and sat up. Soft moonlight filled
the entire room. I looked at him with disgust: his mouth had fallen
slightly open, and the sight of it made me feel quite sick. Even sleeping,
he still wore that stunned and puzzled expression. I quickly turned my
face towards the window and looked out into space. . .

Oh, moon! Was this the happiness you had in store for me? What
did this man know of love? Absolutely nothing! ⟪This was all he'd
wanted out of me when he'd hurried me to bed—as if this was all the
love he had to give, as if he wanted me to know that this was how he
would be loving me for ever after.⟫ And in return, all I had for him
was the scissors—if I even chose to live after this! ⟨That cursed
moment was the sum total of our union; it was also the beginning of
our separation. . .⟩ I would never acknowledge him as my husband,
and I would never consider myself to be his wife. . . What about the

future? ⟨ Would I leave him the next day? Where would I go? My brothers still hadn't finished making their transfer arrangements; my father was having a hard time in Peking; my mother was struggling for survival just like I was, and having to work despite her illness and the pain of her son's death; and my grandmother was at death's door . . . my task wasn't yet finished, not yet! I must not lose sight of my reason for coming to the Great Northern Wilderness! . . . ⟩

《 Oh, more than a hundred years of bitterness and humiliation were contained in that cursed moment! How he had defiled the word "kiss"! 》

Ever since I first started nursery school at the tender age of three, the teachers were always telling us that the mouth was a breeding-place for infections and germs. I vividly remember when I was five, my father kissing my cheek and leaving some drops of saliva on my face. I immediately ran to the inner room to wipe at it again and again with a wet towel, feeling very angry but at the same time afraid that my father would be hurt if he saw what I was doing. . . So far as I was concerned, the mouth was for eating, for talking, and for singing. At the labour camp, I'd learned that it could also be used for swearing, for words you couldn't even find in *The World Dictionary*! I'd read in novels that the mouth could also be used for kissing, but I'd never imagined it could be like this!

《 I'd come across quite a few kissing-scenes in films and novels. They'd neither offended me, nor excited me particularly. But I simply didn't believe in the accuracy of the "burning hot lips" described in books—why should the body's heat be concentrated in the lips when someone was aroused? Had anyone ever measured them with a thermometer to prove that they were "burning hot"? This kind of cliché only reflected the personal feelings of those particular authors. (Of course, it is my personal feelings that I'm writing down now; but I'm not trying to impose my views on others.)

Quite apart from this question of heat, I'd never come across anything in a film or a novel to suggest that people had to kiss with their tongues! Where had Zhiguo got that from? Did some people go even further? Did something as sacred and as pure as love need to take place in a hotbed of germs? Was that what made it exciting? Ugh! Only the ignorant could love in such a crass fashion!》

〈 What was love in Zhiguo's case? For him, animal desire had taken the place of love, brutishness the place of tenderness, and coarseness the place of nobility. But the blame for all my bitterness could not really be laid at Zhiguo's door. I myself had chosen to come to the Great Northern Wilderness! I could only hate myself, be disgusted with myself. Who else could I blame?

Oh, moon! Surely our society ought to take some of the blame for all this? We were like simpletons as far as sex was concerned! Even mentally we were unprepared—so naive about sex for people of our age! Surely we should have been taught something about it, as part of our general knowledge?

I remembered my mother once telling me about these special colleges that were set up in Japan a long time ago, to teach young unmarried women a few basic facts about married life; and a girl wasn't allowed to marry without a certificate from one of these colleges—it wasn't such a bad idea! But we learned nothing about sex, either from our parents or from our schools. The very word was something shameful and immoral, to mention it was almost a crime. And yet all of us women would have to experience that night. So why should any understanding of it be kept hidden and secret from us? Why should a motley collection of men be left to initiate us instead, each in his own particular fashion?

Surely there was a more decent, a more pleasant way? Surely we should be able to talk about that first night with happy memories of tenderness and devotion? Surely we didn't have to feel ashamed and cheapened because of a man?

Since Liberation, there'd been no "sex education" whatsoever in China—we'd not even had enough of the most ordinary education, enough food for our most basic spiritual needs as human beings. 〉

《Those fanatics of the extreme left, their minds set on power, their heads full of one thought only—never-ending struggle...what had they given the people?!》

⟨I must return to my individual case. I must try and understand myself better.⟩

In Hebei Province, I had resolved to marry anyone as long as he'd support me. But now, after this incident with the scissors, I realized that my longing for a life of the spirit could not be denied. So why had I deceived myself in the first place? And why had I deceived others?

And what if Zhiguo wasn't frightened off by the scissors, what then? After it was all over, I was really scared . . .

*

And that was my dream.

8. A True Friend

From that time on, my relationship with Wei Ying was a source of great happiness to me. He used to come and see me at least once a week, sometimes twice. I told him he needn't be so attentive, and then he'd have more time for the other things he had to do. Once a week would be enough.

But he always used to say: "I couldn't help it, I just had to come!"

Sometimes when he arrived I'd be writing, and then he would read the paper quietly by my side, so as not to disturb me. Sometimes I'd be outside feeding the pigs, and could see him coming from a long way off. Then I would jump three feet in the air for joy, and the pigs would go running off in alarm, and Wei Ying would laugh...in those days, our laughter soared over the boundless grassland like beautiful music! Sometimes I'd be washing clothes, and he would give me a hand... In the lull of that lovely wintry time of year, I'd made a friend, I'd fallen in love, and nobody else even knew!

Our love was based on true friendship, it was a love between friends; if this friend had been a girl, I'd have loved her in just the same way, just as deeply, and it would have brought me just as much happiness—in fact, to tell the truth, I really wished he had been a girl! Then we might have been able to see each other more openly and more frequently. Whenever we met, we always had so much to say to each other; even our silences seemed a kind of communication—a language of harmony. And whenever we parted, it was as if we hadn't been able to say enough; we always longed for the next time—true friendship is really the greatest happiness in life!

I thought I could do perfectly well without a husband for the rest of my life. I had a real friend now, someone I could confide in. I could tell him all my thoughts and feelings, I could share with him all my sorrows and troubles, all my joys and pleasures. There was no trace of selfishness, no thought of gain in our friendship—only a sublime sense of happiness!

I seemed to have been born again. For the first time I felt alive, for the first time I felt like a human being of flesh and blood and emotion. The youthful gaiety of my art school days was rekindled. No, I was much happier now because *then* I'd always been suppressing my feelings, hiding behind a mask of indifference. When I looked back on it, it all seemed so stupid and foolish! What need was there for pretence? People should just be true to themselves! My heart was like a torrent bursting through the gates of a lock, surging forward and making me pour all my joys and dreams and yearnings for happiness into childish attempts at verse. I bought a notebook, and started writing a collection of poems to give to Wei Ying.

What should be my first poem in this bright blue notebook of mine? I decided to start by writing about my brother. I shouldn't forget him. So I wrote a ballad called "My Brother's Little Room", using his room to tell the story of his life. It ended like this:

> ... *On the day of his arrest,*
> *His treatise on wages was unfinished;*
> *His diary lay on the table, and on the open page*
> *Yesterday's pledge:*
>> If ever I deceive myself, or give myself up to anything other than
>> the quest for truth, it will be the saddest day of my life. I shall be a
>> true Marxist-Leninist, and dedicate my life to the communist cause!
>
> *He never came back alive,*
> *He refused to yield, he admitted no guilt;*
> *Two years of tribulation,*
> *Led to this, his day of death.*
>
> *Blue sky, white clouds,*
> *The stadium, the crowds.*

His day of—
Graduation.

A student quite exceptional,
To warrant such a spectacle!
His first thesis submitted,
A brilliant piece of work—
But the price to be paid,
His life.

Take it!
He laughed.
I'd rather pay this price
Than forfeit honour to survive.

A graduate of the School of Life.
Blue sky, white clouds,
The stadium, the crowds.
His day of graduation.

Has the lamp in his room been put out?
No, it still casts a misty light;
Has the lamp in his room been put out?
No, it is still a beacon in the night. . . .
Has the lamp in his room been put out?
No, it still shines in men's hearts;
The torch has not been quenched,
Its flame still burns, red and bright.

If I go into the courtyard,
In the still dark depths of night,
I always gaze with a deep emotion,
At the pale golden lamplight.

If I go into the courtyard,
In the still dark depths of night,

I always gaze with a deep emotion,
At the pale
  golden
      lamplight . . .

For the second poem, I still wanted to write about my brother. There were so many things welling up from the past, so many ballads waiting to tell his story. "My Brother's Eyes", "A Portrait" . . . who was it that gave me the melody of these poems? I never had any aspirations as a "poet", but Wei Ying always encouraged me and gave me strength.

After the poems about my brother, I wrote a long poem called "Mother"—about my mother's life and her unique personality. Whenever Wei Ying read these poems, he seemed completely lost in a great wave of emotion. It was almost as if he and I had shared the same experience!

Everything in life was a poem; my poems of the imagination were all written for Wei Ying. In my imagination I pictured the blossoming of the crab-apple trees in May and June . . .

May with its blossoming flowers,
Finest of the four seasons;
Trees thick with flowers,
Like longings for a friend.

In the vast fields,
Wild flowers a riot of colour;
Their clear scent wafting over me,
Like longings for a friend.

I run through the grassland,
Searching among the fragrant flowers,
Seeking the fairest of them all,
To offer my friend its scent.

Every time I went into the cave where I kept my beehive, I thought of how the bees would fly off in the spring to make honey, and how, come winter, they would have multiplied threefold; and again, poetry poured forth from my heart.

> *I always dream how one fine day,*
> *Bees will lead me to your paradise;*
> *Happily they buzz, as if to say,*
> *I am their long-awaited friend.*
>
> *The azure sky is my mirror,*
> *Soft clouds bathe my face;*
> *The sun greets me in the valley with a smile,*
> *The gentle spring breeze touches me with grace.*
>
> *Wild flowers in rainbow colours nod at me,*
> *I stoop to kiss their smiling faces;*
> *Green meadows wave at me,*
> *And ask will I comb their emerald tresses. . .*
>
> *You come running from the cottage, full of joy,*
> *The laughing streams are flowing just for us;*
> *You come running from your room, full of joy,*
> *The gift I bring, my two hard-working hands.*
>
> *We work happily together all the day,*
> *Like bees that have no care;*
> *We bask in the poetry of the night-sky,*
> *And the bright gaze of the moon and the stars. . .*

Wei Ying was very happy when he read this—and that was all that mattered. It was a dream-world, a poem, and we never thought of it coming true. We never once asked each other if it could. I even used to imagine his future wife reading these poems, and feeling as happy as we were now.

I went to visit him twice and found him to be a man who knew how to look after himself. The *kang* was warm and comfortable, the room was clean and tidy; in short, he'd made his "little nest" very snug. He was a man who could take care of himself.

One day, I noticed that his pillow-case was torn, so I went off to the shop to buy a yard of cream-coloured cotton and some silk thread, to embroider him a new one. I also made him a pair of corduroy padded mittens. They both turned out just the right size, the pillow-case and the mittens. I was so pleased that I wrote a poem:

Sleep soundly on this sweet pillow,
Ride the wings of Dream up into the clouds;
Fly on fresh winds, over clear streams,
To the side of the friend you have longed for.

I am here, thinking of you night and day,
I am here, impatient for the proud sun to rise;
The deep green woods send forth their heady scent,
Plants and birds sing their sweet melodies.

You come swooping down beside me,
Bringing me a mantle of morning mist,
Plucking me a scarf from coloured clouds of dawn,
Beaded with the shimmering morning dew.

When I went home that day, he walked with me a long way, almost three miles. There was a row of tall white poplars growing on each side of the dirt road. "How good it must be to walk here in summer," he sighed with emotion.

"You ought to go back now," I said for the second time.

"No, let me walk with you a little further." He suddenly laughed mischievously, "Anyway, you mind your own business! When I don't want to walk any more, I'll let you know!"

"OK," I smiled. "I'm happy for you to walk another ten miles with me!"

⟨ "Would you like to know something about my family?" he asked after a while.

"Yes, of course."

"I've never wanted to tell anybody else about it. None of the young people in our village know..." he said hesitantly.

I waited for him to continue, full of curiosity.

"Wei Li and I aren't actually brothers."

"Really?"

"We have the same father, but different mothers." Then he added, "His mother was my mother's sister."

"Why was your father shot? Was he a Counter?"

"No, he was a trafficker of white slaves, he specialized in innocent girls. He fell for my mother and my aunt as soon as he set eyes on them, and wanted to keep them all for himself. My mother lost her parents when she was ten, and had no other relatives. My father was shot in 1950. He got what he deserved."

"And do you all live together now?"

"Yes, we've always lived together. The two sisters depended on each other. Many of their friends advised them to marry again, and maybe they'd have been better off that way. But they were determined not to see us suffer at the hands of a step-father. My mother never had a job. She kept house, and we were all dependent on my aunt. My aunt was a senior primary school teacher, and made eighty *kuai* or so a month. But...in 1966, at the height of the Cultrev, she was Strifed and then beaten to death by her pupils..."

For a long while, neither of us spoke.

"My mother's hair has turned completely white, she hasn't got a single black hair left. Her constant depression has ruined her health..."

I thought a lot about what he'd said after he went back. His mother was a woman worthy of respect. She had worked so hard all her life, it had been such a struggle for her. He loved his mother. If she had become weak and timid in her old age, it was life's trials that had done this to her. I wrote a poem called "A Mother's White Hair" and gave it to him. He was delighted with it, and said he would send it to his mother and tell her who had written it.

"If you like," I answered with a smile. "And please send Wei Lan my regards. I often think of her."

A mother's white hair! Every mother has these white hairs!

White flowers deck the trees like balls of snow,
Clear fragrance drifting to the clouds;
Pear flowers in May, so white and fair,
But fairer still, a mother's white hair.

Lofty mountains with crystalline snow,
Endless chains of snow-covered peaks;
They breathe their coldness into the air,
But colder by far, a mother's white hair.

Gentle clouds soar in an azure sky,
Gracefully changing their dazzling gowns;
But in none of their dances can they compare,
With the silver strands of a mother's hair.

The sun endows all earth with life,
Vast wilderness stretching beyond the eye;
Snow-fields fill me with thoughts of home,
And my mother's white hair.

Ripples sparkle with silver light,
Like glittering fish-scales, flashing bright;
The little stream murmuring on its course,
A reminder of my mother's kind face.

Silver halo of the moon,
Caressing distant sleeping faces;
Bathing our loved ones in tranquil light,
Mother's hair with care worn white.

Pear flowers, icy snow,
White clouds, moon halo;
They have no soul,
No suffering.

Every strand of a mother's hair,
Has a deep emotion of its own;
Think of the stories locked up there,
In a mother's white hair. ⟩

Life poured its sweetness into my heart like honey. It was so beautiful! It was so good!

9. A Moonlit Night

At the end of March, Zhiguo came back from Peking. He wasn't at all happy to hear that I had got to know Wei Ying, but he didn't feel he could openly confront him about it. Wei Ying came as often as before, and Zhiguo was always very friendly. But the minute he left, Zhiguo would start running him down: "I can't stand seeing him eat our food!" or else, "What's he after anyway? Why doesn't he just stay at home like he ought to?"

I could hardly blame Zhiguo. He might have been more polite and less abusive, but he could never have been happy about it. Because he loved me! If I'd been in his shoes, I wouldn't have been happy about it either—who *would* be, to see the person he loved most in the world becoming closer to another than to himself? It wasn't jealousy, just a natural human reaction. Thinking about it, if Wei Ying *had* been married, his wife wouldn't have been happy either after reading my "childish verses". So I'd been deceiving myself all along.

I had spoken to Zhiguo of divorce before I'd got to know Wei Ying, but since Zhiguo insisted on keeping the child, and parting with the child was something I couldn't do, the whole subject of divorce had been shelved. And now I could only reflect sadly to myself what a pity it was that Wei Ying was a man! If I told him not to come, how I would miss him; but if I let him keep coming, Zhiguo would grow increasingly suspicious and unhappy. Even supposing we didn't have this child and had been divorced long ago, Wei Ying would probably get married sooner or later, and his wife might well resent our friendship like Zhiguo did. . . Ah! None of these problems would have existed if only he'd been a woman! There seemed to be no way out of my torment.

In mid-April, my two brothers and Zhiguo together with several other commune members, got permission from the work-team to go rafting logs on the rivers up in the northern mountains, and had signed a contract with the local Commodities Bureau of our Banner.

I insisted on going too. But with the exception of Zhiguo, they all said: "It's unheard of, a woman going logging in the mountains! What would you do up there?"

"I could cook and keep house!"

I begged them and begged them until finally, much to my surprise, they agreed. Their reason? It was my brothers who told me:

"It didn't seem such a bad idea in the end. If you and Zhiguo were apart for half a year, your relationship might suffer. But a change of scene might do it good—that's why we agreed."

How ridiculous!—they didn't understand me at all! Did they really think my love could be determined by considerations of distance and space? ⟨ Zhiguo and I shared the same *kang*, but my heart had not belonged to him for one single day. I wanted to go with them into the mountains so that I could write about it, and then give what I had written to the man I loved—to Wei Ying! ⟩

*

We were leaving in two days. I *had* to go and tell Wei Ying—he hadn't been for several days and still didn't know.

All along the way, my heart was singing in the spring breeze like a little bird. . . Every time I went to see him I felt happy, like it was a holiday. Had I ever thought about sharing my life with him? I'd written about it in my poems, but I'd never thought of it as a reality, because I didn't deserve him. He could always find someone much better than me. Did this thought make me sad? Only a little. He would be sure to get married one day. I'd often thought to myself that if he ever asked my opinion about a prospective girl-friend of his, I would tell him my honest impression of her and what I thought she was like; I would use all my experience of life to evaluate her strong and weak points. I wanted him to be happy, I didn't want his marriage to be a

tragedy like mine. I wanted always to be able to treat him as a true
friend, to conceal nothing from him, to tell him whatever I honestly
thought; he was a huge storehouse for my thoughts, where all my
happiness, worries, fantasies... everything, could be put for safe-
keeping. I hoped he could share in all my joy and pain. If he could only
preserve those thoughts of mine, and we could only respect each other,
trust each other, and uplift each other, I would be eternally grateful to
him!

How difficult it is in this world to have a true friend.

When I got to his village, my heart started to thump with
anxiety—what if he were out?

I was so overjoyed to see the clothes hanging in front of his door,
still dripping with water, and the cotton-padded quilt with its snow-
white stuffing airing in the sun. He was definitely at home!

"Wei Ying!"

I called to him from outside the window, but there was no answer; so
I pushed open the door and walked in.

I could see at once from his rolled-up sleeves that he'd only just done
the washing. He was now sitting on the edge of the *kang* with his back
leaning against the wall, leafing through my poems and the fragments
of my memoirs. At the sound of my footsteps, he turned his head and
looked so surprised and happy to see me:

"So it's you!"

"I was calling you—didn't you hear me?"

"I... I was too absorbed in my reading."

"Do you really like the book?"

"Yes I do."

"Then I didn't write it in vain," I laughed. "At least it's got one
devoted reader!"

He put the book into a chest and locked it up. Next he took some
chocolates and preserved fruit out of another small box, and then made
a cup of cocoa, setting it all out before me.

"This is far too extravagant," I reproached him. "Your family
can't afford it."

"There's nothing I can do about it!" He smiled gently. "I don't really want these things, but my mother just keeps on sending them.''

''You must paint a brighter picture when you write to her—there's no point in making her worry about you so much!''

''I got another letter from her only yesterday. She's still asking me to go back to Peking, even now. Read it for yourself and see.''

He handed me the letter with a smile. I opened it and read:

-/-/74

Ying: Why didn't you come back to Peking this winter? Li said when he was here it was because you didn't have money for the journey. So I sent you that thirty *kuai* and I was so looking forward to your coming. But now it's well past Spring Festival, and you still haven't come! I'm so afraid you'll fall sick in all that ice and snow. My nervous condition has recently been troubling me again worse than ever. I wake up every night at two or three o'clock, and every time I wake up I think about you, and then I can't ever get back to sleep again. It would make this mother so happy if her son could only understand how she feels! If you'd come back even for just a few days, it would set my mind at ease. Come home, stay till June or July—you won't have fresh vegetables to eat if you stay *there*.

By the way, our hydrangea is in bloom, and the pink flowers are so lovely. The bamboo has sprouted three new pale green shoots. Do come back for a few days! Have you received my last two letters?

Mum.

''Are her other two letters the same as this?''

''Even worse!''

''How different mothers are, the way they love their children!'' I sighed with emotion. ''My mother isn't at all like yours—but I'm grateful for her kind of love all the same. It's helped to toughen us up.''

''Do you imagine I like the way my mother pampers us?'' he said, laughing gently and shaking his head. ''At home, she doesn't even let us get our own tea; she's not happy unless she's doing everything for us. Sometimes we get really fed up with it. And every time we have to leave again for the Great Northern Wilderness, she cries her heart out. But what's the point? Will her tears save us from having to go?''

I couldn't help thinking to myself that he and his brother were rather like plants raised in a greenhouse...

"There's something I've got to tell you. I've come to say good-bye."

"Good-bye?"

"I'm going logging. I won't be back for six months."

"Six months?" He gazed at me with a startled look in his eyes.

"Yes, six months. Isn't it wonderful, Wei Ying!" I said in high spirits. "I'll bring you back a nice little book—my 'Logging Book'! What do you say? Do you think you'll want to read it?"

"Oh, yes!" he nodded, but totally at a loss.

"I'll be back in no time. Last night in bed, I even wrote the postscript. Here." I handed him a poem. "You can put it in my notebook."

But before he'd had a chance to look at it, I snatched it back again laughing, "Come on, I'll recite it for you, all right?"

"All right."

"It's called 'Going Logging'." I began to declaim it dramatically:

⟨ *I carry away my love with stealth,*
Racing to the distant north;
I hide my longing secretly,
Hastening to the vast forests.

Thorns and brambles, plenty the pitfalls,
Far away from heaven;
Dank cold air blows through my tent,
Comforts my weary heart.
Travelling on and on,
The power of love gives me strength;
I love nature, I yearn for the forests,
I can dally no more in the land of dream.

I shall feel the might of the forests,
Their hidden force;

The sound of the forests' silence,
A music no one hears.

I shall drift in the ocean of trees,
Drink the low chant of soughing pines;
Lose myself in the morning mist,
Wrapped in a mantle of thin white silk. . . .

I shall walk on soft fallen leaves,
Gambol among them, leap for joy;
Breathe in fresh sweet smelling air,
Breathe out weariness and care.

I love the colours of the sun,
Shining a rainbow on the forest;
I love to hear the sweet birdsong,
And see the wild flowers' smiling faces.
I love to hunt among the grasses,
For mushrooms with their velvet caps;
And on a day of rain and warmth,
Stumble upon a woodear clump.

I love a storm, when lightning
Cleaves the forest;
Howling mountain trees,
Shaking off arrows of rain.

I shall wander along a secluded forest path,
So far away, drawing me under its spell;
Gaze up at the full moon, calm and benign,
Pouring down its mystic silver light.

I love the rising of the sun,
Every green leaf tinged with red;
But most of all, the heart of night with spangled stars,
Kissing the tree-tops, the pines and the poplars.)

I listen while the forest whispers
Its plaintive song;
I tell the clouds the secret in my heart,
For them to carry to some distant land...

"What secret?" asked Wei Ying with a smile.

"Whether I miss you or not, that's the secret—and you'll be able to find out by looking at the clouds."

"What do you mean?"

"On a day when the clouds are particularly beautiful, you'll know that I'm missing you very much—"

"Then an overcast day will mean you're not missing me at all! My happiness will depend entirely on the weather!"

"Ha-ha-ha!" I was seized with a fit of laughter.

He insisted that I have dinner with him before I left.

"Let me give you a hand with the cooking." I was rolling up my sleeves to wash my hands, when I noticed that my nails needed cutting.

"Have you got a nail clipper?"

"I've got three." He pulled open a small drawer in the table and carefully selected the best one, saying, "I'd like to give this to you."

I took it from him gladly.

"Come, I'll do it for you." It seemed to take him a lot of courage to say this, but in the end he said it with resolution. Evidently he didn't think there was the slightest chance of my refusing him.

"Go ahead." I held out my hand happily—how could I possibly refuse!

⟨ We both sat down on the edge of the *kang*. He held my fingers gently and proceeded to cut my nails. The clock went on ticking away, and a sensation of happiness spread all over my body. I had never before felt so happy. How I wished that time would slow right down, so that he could carry on cutting my nails like this forever! His forehead was almost touching my hair; our breathing was gradually merging into one harmonious breath. I could tell from the tenderness of his expression and from his silence that he was feeling as happy, and yet as confused, as I was...

"Why are your hands so cold?" he asked softly. He had already finished cutting my nails, and was holding my hands in his.

I lowered my head, brooding. "I was thinking about my brother."

He couldn't help smiling, as if unconvinced by my explanation. In fact, my hands never used to get cold like this before I first had oedema; the oedema had been brought on by the interrogation (when I'd greatly enraged my interrogator), and by the anxiety I'd felt for my brother afterwards. But Wei Ying had no way of knowing all this.

"Here. Let me warm them up." He held my hands gently, as if he was wrapping his warmth around a piece of ice. This ice could feel and began to melt of its own free will... For the first time I knew what happiness was; for the first time I knew what tenderness felt like... But was this happiness real? No—I had a husband in the background, and a child too. They both seemed to be standing behind me in the darkness reproaching me, calling me a loose, unprincipled woman... Could this tenderness be lasting? No—I was another man's wife and I should not enjoy, and would never deserve, this kind of tenderness.

I stole a glance at him. He wasn't looking at me; his eyes were fixed on the table next to him. I couldn't tell what was flowing through his heart, and whether his face expressed happiness, nostalgia, love...or simply the desire to remain sitting like that for another three hours. If I had been his wife, I would have wanted to sit there for another *six* hours, and why not? And even then I might have said to him in a spoilt way, "That's not enough, my hands aren't warm yet!"

They were warm, though. His attentions had not been in vain. And even if they weren't, I still ought to have withdrawn my hands. Intimacy should follow understanding and not the other way round. It's no good carrying on in a loose way. You have to do things gradually, to avoid unnecessary heartache and anxiety and to build mutual understanding.

"That'a better," I said happily, withdrawing my hands. "They're warm now. Your hands are like a little stove!"

His only reply was a wry smile, as if to say he thought me incapable of sharing in his emotion. But I kept on acting like I was "tough", and just urged him to get on with the cooking.)

I had to leave after dinner, although really I couldn't bear to part from him!

"I'll walk with you a little," he said, putting on his padded hat straightaway.

We went outside. The sky was studded with stars, winking mischievously. What a beautiful night! It was early spring, and the evening breeze was brushing the tree-tops, making a soft rustling. Night, peaceful as a sleeping infant.

Everyone was having supper, and there wasn't a single person about in the village. From time to time one or two dogs barked in the distance, still keeping guard. Smoke from kitchen chimneys, mingled with the faint aroma of food, floated up into the solemn stillness of night. Somehow it evoked all the richness of life... How beautiful it was. I took a deep, invigorating breath.

"Isn't this wonderful, Wei Ying!" We walked along the dirt road in the moonlight. "Have you ever thought how one day we'll both be very old, we'll have white hair and you'll have a white beard, we'll be as old as your mother is now. Do you think we'll be able to remember what we're feeling tonight, before I went off logging? Will our feelings still be clear and fresh in our minds? ⟨ I'm not very intellectually minded, I'm not one for theories. I live by intuition—I'm like that now, I always have been, I always will be! I always rely on first impressions to understand life and society. What's good is good, what's bad is bad! Maybe I'm like a child. But I hope I'll always be as innocent as a child, always seeing society without prejudice, and viewing life with optimism!

"Take this logging trip. When we're all old, I wonder what we'll still remember about it—apart from the mosquitoes, the horseflies big as matchboxes, the forest damp and sultry, the bugs burrowing into our hair, and no fresh vegetables to eat? Will any of us still remember how we felt when we saw the first tree fall? Will we still remember what we talked about when we were pitching our tents and setting up camp? Will we still remember all the feelings we had as we struggled face to face with nature?

"Ah, this is the stuff of life! This is what writers should be writing about! This is real and alive! We shouldn't allow our literature to be cluttered up with garbage, with people writing just for the money and not even themselves believing the things they write! We should be telling people how to live. We should be telling them how beautiful, how precious, and how sacred this rich land of ours is! Then they will toil and sweat to create, they will yearn and aspire, they will live real lives, they will struggle—then there will be real progress!

"How wonderful it will be, Wei Ying, one day in the future when everything has been forgotten, to open my 'Logging Book' and see it all written down! It's bound to have been published by then. Don't you see? The written word never grows old! It stays eternally young!"〉In my enthusiasm, I suddenly clasped his arm.

Wei Ying was so completely carried away by my excitement that he took me tightly in his arms. It was only then that I realized the consequences of what I'd done just a moment before...

The thick padding of our jackets lay between us, but I could still feel the pounding of his heart. He held me so tight I could hardly breathe. And at the same time I was marvelling to myself that Wei Ying, who seemed so gentle and so fragile, could possess such tremendous strength.

"Come over here." The commanding but tender tone of his voice sounded so new and strange to me, and filled me with joy. He drew me gently after him to lean against a waist-high wall. It had been built by peasants from south of the Pass, who had come up to the Northeast in search of work. We'd already walked as far as the threshing ground at the far edge of the village.

〈We hugged each other tight, in complete silence. I buried my head inside the collar of his padded coat, and was aware of a warm scent that was quite new to me.〉

"Your body smells so good," I whispered blissfully, raising my head.

He just laughed softly. The sound of his laughter warmed my heart!

〈He held me close in his arms and gently kissed my forehead, my eyes, my eyebrows, and my mouth—his kisses were wonderful, they made me feel so good! His softly closed lips seemed to have the perfume of an orchid; they were moist, but not too moist; there was nothing dirty or vulgar about them. After those vile repulsive kisses I'd had forced upon me, these were perfect, they were everything I had ever dreamed of!⟩

"You've got such beautiful eyes, they're so beautiful!" He gazed deep into my eyes and kissed them with passion and tenderness.

I burst out laughing: this was the first time I'd noticed that he was a whole head taller than me. His slightly pale face seemed so precious with the soft moonlight shining down on it...

"You're wonderful," I said in all sincerity.

He just gently stroked my hair, and asked me with concern, "Are you cold?"

And without waiting for my reply, he unbuttoned his coat, though he only had a sweater and a padded waistcoat underneath. He kept saying insistently, "Come on in, come on in, come on in." His breathless whispers were like tiny beads dropping into a porcelain bowl, and quite captivating! I laughed:

"You've got such a lovely voice!"

He made no answer, but drew my hands close against his body and enfolded me in his coat.

"Now you must be cold," I fretted.

"No, I'm not." He reached up a hand to caress my cheek: "See, my hands are always warm."

The warmth from his body made me feel so good, like I was standing beside a stove...

⟨ The universe was still. Countless stars glinted their mystic light in the dark blue sea of the night. The gentle moon shone tenderly down on us, sometimes hiding itself behind the lotus-flower clouds as if afraid of disturbing our lovers' tryst... Dear kindly moon! How often I'd prayed to you to bring me happiness! And you'd remembered, you hadn't forgotten my prayers... Everything seemed to belong to us—the vault of heaven lost in silence, the earth, the world. The distant lamplights and the sea of stars borrowed radiance from one another—it was a solemn night, a night full of mystery!

In the stillness of the universe, I thought I could hear the song of the earth. It was as if a myriad voices were all humming a single song, a beautiful and poignant melody, from the bowels of the earth, and they were all my brother...it was as if they were giving me their blessing for having found my first love, for knowing true love. This faint and poignant song brought me infinite comfort; and yet at the same time, it plunged my heart into unutterable sorrow.

For even in that moment of rapture, I couldn't help asking myself: What did Wei Ying love in me? Did he really love me? Did I deserve his love? Was I worthy of him? Could this affection last for ever? Was he really thinking he would be with me for ever more?...⟩

"What is it you love about me?" I asked him softly, lifting my head. I gazed at him, as if by studying his expression I could see into his heart.

"Everything." It was so brief, so solemn, and so sincere, without the slightest trace of affectation.

"I'm not intellectually minded, I'm so stupid."

"I love your stupidity."

It was such a strange thing to say, and I couldn't help laughing.

⟨"I'm married, and I've got a child. This is against the law," I said gravely.

"You're wonderful." His face grew paler still, his innocence was tinged with sorrow, as though these words caused him great anguish. It seemed he didn't want me to look at him, for he embraced my neck and pressed my head against his shoulder. He didn't seem to know how to put his love into words.

"I'm not worthy of you." My heart was struggling in the midst of confusion and sorrow, longing to be forever united with him; and yet I had to say: "You can easily find someone better than me... Honestly, Wei Ying, I'm not worthy of you."

"There's no one to compare with you. I could never hope to meet another girl as good as you." These words were spoken from the heart and moved me deeply. Even though I knew full well I wasn't the best girl in the world, how I wished I could believe his words were true!⟩

"I suffer from oedema. I may not live very long." I wanted to bring all my defects out into the open.

"I can look after you until you die."

"I never want to have another child for the rest of my life. One is more than enough!"

"Then it'll be just the two of us."

I was silent. My hot tears fell on his warm neck... The tears kept on falling, but I didn't want to make the slightest noise and destroy this silence—this most beautiful song that my brother, Mother Earth, and Father Sky were singing for me. The only thing I wanted now was to pour out all my troubles, all my bitterness and pain, and let them flow away on the tide of my tears... Wei Ying seemed to understand me better than anyone could; he didn't try to cheer me up, he didn't say anything at all, he just rubbed his cheek tenderly against my hair and my forehead... When I'd cried it all out, I was calm and light-hearted, I felt a sense of relief I could not put into words. My tears were like a baptism of love. I, this creature of clay, who "would never be clean again", had been fully cleansed! It was he, my dear Wei Ying, who had done this for me. How could I ever love him enough to repay him for this! I gazed out in silence across the inky blackness of the earth, I gazed into the distance where the lamplights met the stars; and I listened quietly to my brother's song of benediction rising from the bowels of the earth. I leaned feebly in Wei Ying's arms, every fibre of my being filled with a boundless sensation of happiness and contentment.

"What are you thinking about?" he asked softly.

"Nothing," I murmured, without making the slightest movement. "I just feel so good."

I looked at him. He was gazing at me full of emotion, without a word... The misty moonlight illuminated his beautiful face, and made the frames of his glasses shine like crystal; it was so wonderful!

⟨ How I longed to stay with him like this until dawn broke in the sky! He too must have longed for it. But I couldn't. I was a married woman. If I wanted him to hold me like this every day, to drink in with me the intoxicating night air, to share the beauty of the moon and the stars, then I had to search for an honourable way of being with him! ⟩

Yes, I wanted to be his lawful wedded wife. But I didn't want to be an adulteress, and do things behind my husband's back. However pure and innocent our feelings for each other were today, however irreproachable our behaviour, ⟨however reasonable and necessary our love, still in the eyes of the law I had a husband and I had no right to be doing this. Strictly speaking, this whole scene tonight was illegal, something entirely underhand. We must stop while we still could. This must be the last time.⟩ I must divorce my husband first, and *then* we could enjoy numerous unforgettable moonlit nights such as this!

"I've got to go now." I heaved a deep sigh of regret, drew out my warm arms, and started doing up his coat.

"Stay a bit longer," he implored me, his head leaning to one side. "It's still early."

"No, it's late. I'll be in trouble if I get back too late."

"I hate to see you go," he said, grasping my hands as I was buttoning his coat.

"If you really love me, we're sure to have plenty more times like this. I'm just worried that maybe you won't love me any more by then."

"Nonsense," he gave a scornful smile, as if my words weren't even worth refuting. We left the low wall and walked back to the road.

"Go back now." I stood in his way.

"Are you telling me what to do!" His eyes were full of brazen mischief, such a delight to behold!

"All right, but don't come much further with me. I'm not a bit afraid of walking alone in the dark."

⟨"And what if you run into a wolf? You've still got seven miles to go!"

"A wolf? No problem! I'll break off a willow branch from the roadside, or I'll pick up a big stick, and I'll fight for my life!"

"And what if you bump into some nasty character or other?"

"Human beings are easier to handle than wolves. You can reason with them."

"You think it's that simple!" he said smiling.

"Perhaps because I *do* think it's that simple, I never run into nasty characters or wolves!"⟩

I ran ahead of him, bathed in the clear light of the moon, bounding and leaping for joy. I stopped to kiss him along the way. Then, in that dark wilderness, along that winding dirt-track, I began to sing, out of sheer joy. My antics set Wei Ying off into peals of uproarious laughter.

"Go back now," I said firmly, stopping once more.

"It's not far to the causeway. I'll walk with you as far as the causeway."

"No. In that case, I won't go." I gave him a challenging look.

He smiled at my contrariness. "All right then, I'll go back." He looked at me once, and then turned away....

"Luojin!"

I had gone quite a few steps when suddenly I heard from behind me his entreating cry. I turned round in surprise.

There he was, in the moonlight that bathed the night sky, stumbling towards me along the bumpy track. I found his dear face so moving, the clear frames of his glasses glittering like crystal, the ear-flaps of his padded hat, one pointing up and the other down, both bouncing along to the rhythm of his steps! There was something so endearing about the way he ran, he looked like an innocent and artless child.

"Let me take one last look at you!" He stood in front of me and placed his hands on my shoulders, his eyes lingering on my face like little birds clinging to a branch.

⟨"Look at you!" I chided him gently.

He hugged me tightly, kissing my eyes, forehead and eye-brows tenderly and passionately. This passion of emotion so completely overwhelmed me that I felt I was up in the clouds, happiness coursing throughout my entire being. How I wished he would pick me up in his arms like a little baby, and I wouldn't move, and he would carry me straight home with him to his warm bed! How I wished I could lie in his arms all night under his clean warm quilt, enjoying his tender caresses! ⟩

"Go back now, you're being naughty," I said, pretending to be cross.

⟨"I must have two last kisses. No, three. There, that's better." ⟩

He gazed at me intensely and then, as though it took great determination, he turned and walked quickly away. But after he'd gone only a few steps, he looked back at me again—I turned away instantly and marched off, resolved not to weaken. He must have thought I wouldn't look back again, but after I'd gone some way, I did furtively turn and follow him with my eyes as he disappeared into the distance, into the vast expanse of the night...

I carried on walking slowly home, going over in my mind along the way everything that had happened that night, and thinking about all the happiness he'd given me. But somehow, the warmth in my heart was turning imperceptibly into a feeling of unutterable anguish and desolation...

*

Zhiguo was sound asleep, but I couldn't sleep a wink. Just thinking about how happy Wei Ying had made me on this moonlit night only added to my anxiety. From this night on, Wei Ying and I were no longer just good friends. What should I do? Should I renounce anything between us that was beyond the realm of ordinary friendship? Could we go back to being just friends? No, that was impossible. What had happened was the result of a natural growth of feeling which would go on growing deeper and deeper. How could I bear to throw my happiness aside, and choose instead to lead a nun-like existence? I wanted to enjoy all that a human being could enjoy, and there was nothing wrong with that. Should I allow our feelings to grow? But they *couldn't* if I didn't get a divorce. I was still officially married, and I hated the thought of doing anything against the law.

It would be against my conscience. It would destroy my dignity as a human being. What I had to do now was to secure a divorce.

10. The Choice

That night, I tried to think things through... ⟨ I had for a long time been quite disgusted by the whole idea of "sleeping" with a man, so how would I respond if Wei Ying made demands of that nature? Before I'd ever met him, I'd always wanted to find a man like him. Sex had still not entered into our relationship, we were just very much in love. As far as I was concerned, embraces and chaste kisses had always been the very height of love. But a young man like Wei Ying would be sure to want more. Would I be able to satisfy him? And what if he wished to have children? I never wanted to give birth again. Could I bring myself to bear his child?

Since I loved him, I should be able to experience his joy as my own; I could learn to do it, I could learn to accept it, and eventually I could come to feel happy about it. I wasn't abnormal, after all. I wanted to be a good wife and a good mother. It was my experience with Zhiguo that had changed me! I had an infinite tenderness to give Wei Ying. I had such hopes that love would bring out once more the yielding young woman in me!

Should I ask Wei Ying to commit himself to me before I got divorced? He must want to be with me, judging by the way he'd behaved on that moonlit night. Any decent and honourable man would. Besides, he'd said it that night in so many words... ⟩

Supposing I were to ask him... But how could I? If I asked him to promise to marry me, then he would feel bad; he would feel he was wronging Zhiguo. No, I didn't want to see the guilt written on his face; he was such a good person, and I shouldn't press him into it. I believed that he loved me, and I loved him—wasn't that more than enough? What need was there of his promise? I knew his family might raise objections, but I was convinced that the power of love could surmount all obstacles. Even if his family didn't agree, they would come round sooner or later. I wanted to love his family too with all my heart; I believed in the power of love!

The most difficult thing to part with would not be the home I'd built up with the sweat of my brow; it would not be Zhiguo; it would be my own flesh and blood—my only son.

He may not have been the fruit of love, but what mother can help loving the "flesh of her flesh"?

The birth, and the nine months I was pregnant and went on working in the fields, were something I would never forget, right up to the day I died.

. . .It was the fourteenth of the eighth lunar month, and the day before the Mid-Autumn Festival*. I had been working that morning in our vegetable garden as usual, and had also filled up the large water-jar. After lunch I was washing some clothes when I felt spasms of pain in my stomach. The woman from next door came round as soon as she heard the news.

"It must be the baby coming," she said. "I'll go and tell Zhiguo to fetch the midwife."

Zhiguo came hurrying back from the main fields and immediately went off to get the only midwife in the village, who had formerly made her living as a sort of shamaness*.

There was no medical equipment whatsoever, and the hospital was ten miles away. It was too risky to ride there on the cart, and anyway we wouldn't have got there in time. So the two village women had to deliver the child in the only way they knew how.

I had become very weak, and didn't seem to have the strength to push the child into the world. Two hours went by and I didn't have a drop of energy left; I just wanted to die and be done with it. The old shamaness saw how bad things were and gave the child a mighty tug. Blood came gushing out all over the *kang*. My child was born!

In my semi-conscious state I heard the child's first cry—that affirmation of life—and I didn't feel one spark of joy, only disgust and fear.

But in the end my curiosity got the better of me, and I took a peep at him, still half in a daze—his head was all squashed like a bottle-gourd!

"Don't you worry," said the shamaness. "It's because it was a slow birth. It'll grow back to normal in a couple of weeks. We've seen plenty like this. You had quite an easy time of it really!"

I lay on the *kang* in a sort of dazed dream—I'd suffered so much to give birth to him, but for what? This little life, had it given me one bit of happiness since the first day of my pregnancy? If all the humiliation I'd suffered was invisible, then here was a visible reminder of it! And now I had been given this thing, to raise, to educate, to suffer for, to worry over... Could he bring me any happiness? I didn't think so! Had there ever been a mother so utterly dejected after childbirth as I was? Weren't a couple supposed to love each other more after they'd had a child? I had merely acquired a new burden to add to the miseries I already had. I would have to bring him up and see to all his little needs, whether he was the fruit of love or not! Ah! I heaved a deep sigh, and turned to look at the little life. He was asleep; everything about him made me feel he was such a stranger... Fate was so unjust; it must have me drink the cup of bitterness to the full, it would not spare me a single one of life's ordeals. I had not wanted *any* of this...

Two days passed. And to my amazement, the disgust I'd felt for him up to then just vanished into thin air the first time his little mouth sucked at my breast! His soft, nibbling little mouth, his serene, angelic expression as he lay in my arms, blew all the trouble and care out of my heart, like a balmy breeze... He could even *eat* straight after he'd been born. It was so touching to see his darling little mouth moving, I could have gone on watching it forever... I was proud of being a mother! When my milk sprayed onto his cheeks and eyes like a fountain, and he tried to jerk his head out of the way, I would burst out laughing—it was so comical! I knew now how a mother feels towards her own flesh and blood; and I could imagine what anguish my mother must have felt whenever she remembered Luoke sucking at her breast as a baby. How brave she must have been to hold back her tears! Now I could understand.

*

And this little life had grown—he was two and a half years old. His round head, his childish eyes, his fair skin, his perfect features, his tender little voice babbling away every morning, his attentive expression when he was listening to a story, his lovely movements when he was dancing. . . everything about him was so dear and lovable, and I was so close to throwing it all away! I had mentioned divorce to Zhiguo more than once, but he always said the same thing: "All right, but I'll keep the child." I'd thought about it over and over again, but could never bring myself to let go of the child. So why was I thinking of agreeing to his terms now? Why?

Simply because I knew Wei Ying could give me far more happiness than the child could. My happiness with him was more than the romance of that moonlit night; it was everything about him—his looks, his whole personality, even the way he walked, and the sound of his voice. The child could never give me this much joy.

⟨ I believe that the happiness of a small child is founded upon the parents' love for each other. If there is bad feeling between a husband and wife, then they will be willing to forsake their child, to abandon their own flesh and blood; but if there is love, they will be able to treat a child who is *not* theirs as their own offspring. Eventually the child grows up into a man, and then he has his own joy in life, and is no longer dependent on his parents. Surely I wouldn't have to wait for my child to grow up before I could seek my own personal happiness? How I longed to taste that happiness, more than anything else! ⟩ And besides, it was such a rare and wonderful thing to have met a man whom I loved, and who loved me in return. If I didn't cherish him, I might so easily lose him. It was not likely I'd be given a second chance like this—how often in one's life did one meet a true friend? And how often did one fall in love at first sight? I thought it was worth it, to exchange the child for Wei Ying.

At the same time, I had no choice. Firstly, these were Zhiguo's terms; secondly, the child had been staying in Peking since he was one year old and was doted on by Zhiguo's mother, brothers and sisters; and thirdly, my parents had said from the start that they would never look after any grandchildren—they thought they'd suffered more than enough in having us!

I would have to bear the pain and give him up. There was no other way, there was really no better way. I would just have to try and pretend I'd never had him, and hope that one day when he was grown up and had seen something of life, he would understand.

I would bring up the subject of divorce with Zhiguo when we got back from logging.

*

On the morning of the thirty-first, we set off on our logging trip on three big carts. All along the way, Zhiguo appeared to be in high spirits; he must have thought that I'd asked to go with him because I no longer wanted a separation. We'd already reached the Banner's main town when someone sent by the commune caught up with us and said: "The commune authorities heard about this trip of yours and have been looking into it. This kind of private enterprise is out. It's already been attacked at the highest level. It's a form of capitalism."

No matter how we argued and negotiated, no matter how angry the people from the Commodities Bureau were, we could not reverse the commune's decision. There was nothing we could do, except go back.

The next evening, I spoke my mind to Zhiguo:

"I want to have a talk with you."

"About what?"

"I think we should get divorced!"

"No!"

"Why not?"

"You came running to me for help when you needed a Domper. And now that your whole family's here and you think you can get by on your own, you want a divorce! Well, the answer's no!"

"You've driven me to it with all your beatings."

"Why don't you care for me? Why?"

"What's the point of trying to tell you? You never understand."

"There you go again! No, I'll never give you a divorce!"

"Perhaps the whole trouble is that I've never loved you."

"Then why did you agree to marry me if you didn't love me?"

"For the Domper. I had no choice."

"Hah! There's gratitude for you!"

"What's the point of abusing me? The question is: Can we or can't we carry on living together?"

"Ask yourself!"

"I think it's better if we separate."

"You think I don't know? You've found someone else, so of course you haven't got time for me any more!"

"It was bound to happen sooner or later; if it hadn't been him it would have been somebody else."

"I really don't understand! Haven't I been good to you?"

"I don't need to be reminded of all your good qualities."

"You're so ungrateful!"

"What have I got to be grateful for? You helped me get a permit, and I married you. Wasn't that a fair exchange?"

"Then why do you want to get divorced?"

"Because some day or other you're going to cripple me!"

"I won't beat you any more."

"You won't be able to stop yourself. Go on: you can have the child."

"What? Just like that! You've got no shame! How can you want to break up our family? I just don't understand it—won't you have any regrets?"

"No, I won't. I want some real feeling in my life."

"What right have you got to say that! For more than three years I haven't slept with you, not once since that first time, and I've put up with it. I've tried so hard to make you love me. But where's it got me?"

"Funny kind of trying!"

"I promise I'll never beat you again, Luojin!"

"I still won't love you. And I won't sleep with you again—ever! There, do you agree to that?" I paced the floor slowly, looking at him where he sat on the edge of the *kang*.

"Yes, I do!"

Oh, I never expected him to say that! His earnest gaze, like some adoring disciple, made my heart shrink. I felt sorry for him! I felt sorry for the three years he'd wasted trying to win my love, and failing! I felt sorry for his devotion! The entreaty in his eyes made me quite forget how satanic he looked when he was beating me. But I couldn't comfort him, I certainly couldn't cheer him up.

"You might agree to it, but *I* don't. I want some real feeling in my life."

"Hah!" He was suddenly shamed into anger. "I suppose you've already experienced it then, this feeling of yours? Or else where did you get hold of the idea? And how many men did you sleep with in the camp, I wonder!"

I couldn't help laughing sourly to myself at this.

"If I'm such a loose woman," I said in a mocking tone, "why don't you just let me go?"

A long silence fell between us.

⟨"Jin," he suddenly implored me, "don't leave me. You don't know how much you've helped me!"

"Helped you how?"

"You stopped me from stealing! Yes, I was a thief before I met you, but then I broke off with the scum I used to hang around with. They hate me for it. But as long as I've got you, I'll be all right. I don't see them any more. Jin, please don't leave me!"

I believed him. Maybe this was the whole basis of his love for me. But although I found his sudden revelation so moving and so painful, it still couldn't make me love him. To be moved and to love are two quite different things.⟩

"Let's part like good friends. If we miss each other when we're apart, we can always get married again. And I think if we do marry again, it will probably be forever."

. . . So our discussion was continued in a very sorrowful and dejected atmosphere, interspersed from time to time with outbursts of rage on Zhiguo's part. It took us a very long time to reach a final decision. In the end Zhiguo agreed, clinging to the faint hope of a remarriage. He would go through with the proceedings the following day—poor man! We didn't even cook a meal; neither of us had any appetite. We both felt as though we had a big lump of lead in our hearts.

Ah! I really hoped I'd never have to go through this a second time! It was too bitter—wounding and being wounded in this way. ⟨ Will the day ever come when divorce does not need to entail this kind of confrontation, when divorce will be possible without the agreement of both parties, and when it will be enough for one of the parties who no longer loves the other to make a statement to this effect at the police-station in order for the divorce to be granted? ⟩

*

That night, Zhiguo slept soundly; but on his forehead there was still a childlike entreaty. Poor man, he was only twenty-two; he shouldn't have had to experience the pain of divorce so young. I had inflicted it on him. But was it all my doing? No, I couldn't accept that I was entirely to blame.

I still remembered our wedding night, how I'd got up quietly in the middle of the night, thinking with pain of my own suffering, and how I'd looked at him in disgust. I'd never wanted to look at him again. But tonight, I found myself wanting to look at him, to study his face. . .

I was grateful to him. In all those three years he hadn't made another sexual demand. He sometimes sighed and groaned, he sometimes abused me under his breath, he beat me countless times during the daytime; but he had never once, in all that time, given me cause to grab hold of the scissors again. It might have been out of fear, or out of respect, or maybe it was just his pride standing in the way—maybe he felt ashamed of himself for having that kind of need. But whatever it was, I felt grateful to him for it!

I thought back to the time immediately after we got married, when we had practically nothing. We'd started totally from scratch, and had worked hard together to build our little nest. In the bitter cold of winter or the fierce heat of summer, rain or shine, we'd never spared ourselves; we'd bought a house, a bicycle, watches, a camera, a cupboard, a radio...and all the things that were necessary for a country existence. We ate well, we were properly clothed, and we were never short of money. This home had been built with the sweat of our labour, and now it was about to be dismantled, completely destroyed, all because of me; we would have to sell many of our things off cheap, and go our own separate ways. Our home would be no more!

I remembered how every time he went to the Banner's main town or to the local town, he would always come back with something nice for me to eat. Sometimes, even though he was hungry himself, he wouldn't touch it until he got back, so that we could eat it together... Every time he was about to go off on a long trip, he would say to me again and again:

"Jin, don't you go working too hard..."

When the child was born, he'd danced for joy. He was so happy to be a father, he'd hardly closed his eyes that whole night! And whenever the child cried at night, it was always Zhiguo who would get out of bed to pick him up.

I could never forget all these things! And yet this thriving little family of ours was to be shattered—by me! The child would lose his mother, the husband his wife, and the house would go to a new owner. It would all be over, everything would be broken... And all because I loved Wei Ying. No, that wasn't right—all because I *didn't* love Zhiguo.

My heart was not made of stone. I felt a great sense of guilt. I turned the decision over in my mind, again and again. It caused me such pain. But what else could I do? Did I have any other choice?

11. My Sacrifice, and its Reward

My mother stayed with me for a while, and then went back to Peking. The elder of my two brothers found a way of getting to the mountains to work as a carpenter, because it was easier to make money there. The younger had insisted on moving back to Peking, pleading family hardship as his official reason, and all the formalities had already been completed. My father, though afraid that he would suffer anew once he was back in Peking, still sold the house and family belongings and returned there with my little brother.

And now I was the only one left. All these upheavals made life seem just like a dream!

We settled our divorce in such a "civilized and amicable" manner that everybody believed it to be a pretence, and rumours to this effect spread quickly throughout the commune. I took it as a compliment to us both, and as evidence of the fact that the locals had only ever seen divorce conducted in a brawling fashion!

After our divorce, Zhiguo went back to Peking. He said he was going to try and get his Domper transferred back to Peking on the grounds of ill health, and he asked me to take care of the house until his return, when we would dispose of it. I agreed. Three months went by, and still he didn't come back. And Wei Ying didn't come to see me either, not once.

I didn't want to go to his place. He'd had plenty of time to hear the news of my divorce, and the Urblings who often went to visit him must have told him about Zhiguo going back to Peking—why then didn't he come and see me? It was so strange! I tried to be patient and wait a little longer. Finally, one morning, Wei Li came.

"Why haven't you been round to see us lately?" he asked as he came in the door.

"Oh, I've been busy looking after this place." I wanted so much to ask him about Wei Ying, but I was afraid he'd suspect something; so I could only wait, and hope he'd say something first.

At last he brought up the subject in the course of our conversation: "...A couple of months back, my brother was seriously ill. He's only just got better."

"Really?" I said in astonishment. So, I'd done him an injustice! I decided to go and see him at once, and went bicycling back with Wei Li.

He really had been ill! His cheeks were thin and drawn, his face looked very pale, and his eyes were sunken. He looked perplexed and uneasy to see me:

"Oh, so it's you," he said in a halting way. "I'll go and buy some fish from one of the villagers for lunch."

The whole morning went by, and still he didn't reappear. Wei Li went looking for him everywhere without managing to find him, and complained resentfully about it while he was making something for me to eat. I had no appetite. I scarcely touched my food, and then said good-bye.

I was so upset I hardly had the strength to ride my bike home...

I sent off a note to Wei Ying as soon as I got back:

Wei Ying, I really don't understand. Can you tell me what this is all about? Even just a few words?

A fortnight passed and still there was no reply.

*

Anguish! ⟨This was my first taste of real anguish!⟩ My feelings at that time could be summed up in just a few words—I wanted to die. I had no one to confide in. Alone with the empty house and the garden, I brooded over the two families in my life; one had left of its own accord, and the other I had myself rejected. I was like a withered leaf drifting on the ocean, not knowing when I'd go under and sink to the depths. Every day I just gazed up at the clouds, the sky, the sunset, and talked to myself. . . Life went crawling past me like a maggot. . . Everything made me sick at heart. If Wei Ying had once made me aware of the harmony and poetry in every blade of grass and every flower petal, then now that same grass, those same flowers, made me sick at heart! Now I knew the truth of Heine's poems, and saw that the feeling in them was not exaggerated. I remembered two lines in particular, and could finally understand what they meant:

"We must fall together into the mire
Before we find true friendship."

I knew now how plausible it was that Young Werther should have taken his own life for love! I really wanted to die! But I still hadn't heard a single word from Wei Ying, and I had to wait for his reply.
That day I got a letter from Zhiguo:

Jin—I know we're divorced, but I still want to call you this. Our son is so big now, and such a darling! My mother was shocked to hear about our divorce. She thinks maybe it's because our child wasn't with us that we grew so far apart. She wants me to come back to you with the child and for us to get married again. Have you thought things through yet? It can't really be all that good living on your own. Don't forget all that we've been through together! Don't let the child grow up without his mother! I hope you'll send me a telegram or a letter so that I know I'm to bring the child back with me. I've fixed up all the formalities at this end for my Domper, and I'll be leaving in a few days.

The letter didn't move me in the slightest, and I never replied. Even if Wei Ying never spoke to me again, even if I had to go through the rest of my life unmarried, I still wouldn't marry Zhiguo again—that wedding night had left too deep an impression on me, those beatings had affected me too deeply! Besides, we'd never really had anything in common. The child was innocent, but I would never be allowed to bring him up on my own. How could I possibly spend the rest of my life with this man who aroused no feeling in me other than the memory of my humiliation? No. All I wanted was to forget him for always and never see him again—with or without the child.

A few days later, he arrived. He came into the yard with a fierce look on his face. I could tell he was seething with rage at me for keeping him waiting all that time in Peking, for nothing.

"When's the buyer bringing the money for the house?" Those were his opening words.

"The day after tomorrow." I watched him nervously.

"Hah! You ungrateful bitch! You deceived me—marry again, you said! And I believed you! Now I understand! Well, here's your divorce!..."

He sprang upon me like a lion, with a terrible gnashing of his teeth. I can't find words to describe the horror of the beating he gave me. He beat me, he kicked me—all the resentment, and bitterness, and anger of those three years came pouring out. I struggled desperately to get out of the room, but he knocked me down and in the end I half stumbled, half fell into the yard. He went stomping off, muttering bitterly to himself.

I don't know how long it was before I came round. I heaved myself up and sat there propped up on my hands, my swollen eyes half closed... If at that moment Zhiguo had suddenly come striding up to finish me off, I would only have been able to surrender myself to my fate. Such beatings had been a common occurrence in the past. But we were divorced now; there were no longer any ties between us. He had no right to beat me like that! It was no use hoping to reason with him. If I'd still had a flicker of friendly feeling for him that night before our divorce when I'd looked at his sleeping face in the moonlight, then today he had completely destroyed it. So much the better; let me always remember him as he was today. This was the memory he insisted on leaving me with! And yet, it was I who'd first deceived him; it was I!

There was nobody around in the village; it was unusually quiet...

Wei Ying—if only he would come now, and I could weep in his arms!

⟨Wei Ying—the cause of all my suffering!⟩

I had sacrificed everything I had—Zhiguo, the child, my home. And I had endured as much as a person could—gossip and misunderstanding in the commune, jeers and insults... What was it all for, all this sacrifice and pain, this faith and hope? It was for Wei Ying's affection, it was to win his heart! ⟨And all I got in return was weakness and selfishness! Fear and distance! Heartlessness and indifference! A final rejection!

There was nothing more to be said!⟩

I struggled to sit upright, brushed the dust off my clothes, and with great difficulty got to my feet. I went into the room to find that Zhiguo had walked off with small items like the alarm clock and the thermometer. I picked up the broken mirror from the *kang* and looked into it. God! The whole right side of my face was badly swollen and bruised—I was a ghastly sight! Every joint in my body ached. I rolled up my trousers and saw that my legs were black and blue all over. I started rubbing my bruised shoulders and my wrists, which were numb from being twisted.

What could I do now? Commit suicide? But I still hadn't seen Wei Ying, and I had to have an explanation from him. There would be no peace for me in the grave without an answer. Was I to stay there and wait for Zhiguo to come back and give me another beating? He wouldn't dare kill me—he'd be too afraid of the consequences. But he might easily leave me a cripple! And then what good would it do me to sue him for it afterwards?

I had to leave. But where could I go? The only place that would take me in was the Youth Settlement*—they were on the look-out for new recruits.

The bruises on my face turned out to be a great asset. I made up a story: "My roof was leaking, so I climbed up by myself to mend it, and I fell off." And they sympathised: "It's very hard living on your own." So I managed to transfer there without any trouble.

It was well into autumn now, autumn had touched the fields and was blowing in the wind... During all this time, my heart was as bleak as an autumn day, the chill had penetrated the depths of my heart...

Oh Luojin, what a hopeless hotch-potch of experience your life had been! Could there be anything new in store? Could there be anything you hadn't already tasted?

I looked back over my life. The happiness of my golden childhood had been clouded by the oppression I began to feel as a teenager, because of my "class background". I had worked so hard at art school—for nothing; I had fallen in love for the first time—only to see my love destroyed before it could come to anything. Then came the Cultrev, and I'd been Capped a Class Enemy... I'd cherished the memory of my brother with such devotion; I'd sold my body so shamelessly; I'd endured the hardship of manual labour so bravely; I'd treasured love so highly and been willing to pay so high a price for it—but what had I gained from all of this?

I went to the Banner town and posted a letter:

Wei Ying,

As far as I am concerned, there is nothing more painful than not knowing. At least if you know the truth about something, however sad it may be, there can, and should, be an end to your torment. "Friends should be open, they should be understanding, they should know everything about each other"—can we abandon these three ancient principles of friendship so lightly? Is it so impossible for us to be open and frank with each other?

Perhaps I don't deserve to be your future wife. I've been married once, and I've had a child. I hate myself for having been so weak as to give in to the demands of my situation in the first place. But marriage is not the only relationship between a man and a woman; if there can't be marriage there can at least be friendship. I have no time for selfish people whose love turns to hate when they can't "own" someone. To hurt a person out of some selfish motive has nothing to do with love. If love is unselfish, then both people will hope only for the other's happiness and fulfilment. How I wish that all the love in the world—between parent and child, husband and wife, and between friends—were like this.

I hope you will give me a clear answer:

1) If you still want us to be friends, if you think this is a good thing for you and would make you happy, you and I can easily forget about that moonlit night, and not let it be a burden to us. You can still come and visit me

regularly at the Youth Settlement just like any ordinary friend. You can still keep that book, and I'd still like you to be the first to read whatever I write in the future.

2) If you want nothing more to do with me, I'd still like to know the reason why. Please don't leave me in the dark, in this torment. So long as I'm without an answer, I'll go on and on tormenting myself, and surely you don't want that? If we can't trust in each other any more, then please meet me the day after tomorrow (20 December)—we can both set off at one o'clock in the afternoon and walk towards each other along the causeway. When we meet, you can give me back my book. It is more precious than my life.

Wishing you all the best,

Luojin

18 December '74
The Youth Settlement

12. Tale End

Early afternoon, on the causeway...

There wasn't a single footprint in all the snow that had accumulated during the night, only the tracks of a horse-drawn cart winding away into the distance and meeting the bright blue of the sky.

I trudged along slowly through the thick snow at the foot of the causeway—I didn't want to walk along the top because I was trying to put off the moment of seeing him. How I prayed that he wouldn't come at all! Maybe he had changed his mind. Then my trip today would have been made for nothing, but at least there'd still be hope.

It didn't make sense to me. I tried to think why things had turned out like this. It couldn't have been anything I'd done. We'd been so happy on that moonlit night, and we hadn't even seen each other for eight months since then. Maybe he'd been introduced to a girl who wasn't married and he'd fallen for her. And did being unmarried make her better than me? What a wretched business! How shallow people are! ⟨It all happens in one night: a girl becomes a woman! And that one night, that first lesson in marriage, is experienced by different women in so many different ways. In the present age when there is supposed to be freedom in marriage, most women feel that their lives become sweeter, happier, and more beautiful after they are married. That is why there is so much literature singing the praises of conjugal affection, compassion, and devotion, singing the praises of unselfish love and of dedication towards children! At the same time, there is a minority of men and women for whom this lesson brings nothing but dismay. It reveals the boorishness and vulgarity of their partner, and leaves them with a deep sense of misfortune! But no one shows any understanding for these unfortunates. Their marriages may have failed, but no one ever says of them that this has been a rare education and that they will be able to lead better lives as a result. No one ever says that they have become wiser precisely because of the revelation of that first night. People should realize that this kind of knowledge is not to be found in books. But vulgar people understand nothing of all this; they simply believe that those whose marriages have failed have lost something, have somehow been tarnished. What is it they have lost? What is it these people set such great store by?⟩

If Wei Ying thought like this, that a happy marriage depended on that first act of possession, if this was in fact the cause of his rejection, then I despised him for it, and was only too glad to see him achieve his goal with some other woman.

Love was reciprocal, it couldn't be one-sided. Happiness was reciprocal too, and if one person wasn't happy, the other would never be happy either.

But these finer feelings of mine were short-lived; despite my efforts, they disappeared so suddenly! There was no escaping my pain and suffering!

What would this loss mean for me? Would I start taking life more seriously, or would I again treat marriage as a game? I really couldn't say with any certainty, I couldn't answer for myself...

The warm sunshine was powerless against the bitter cold of the endless snow...

I narrowed my eyes and gazed the length of the causeway: all along the top of the high and winding ridge, there wasn't a soul to be seen. I had walked about half-way, and decided to stop where I was in the snow, and wait for him.

There were no signs of human life in the vast snowy wilderness, other than my own deeply embedded footprints stretching away behind me to the horizon. The Youth Settlement and other neighbouring villages were obscured from view by a dense willow copse.

Now, in the distance along the causeway, I could clearly make out a small black dot, growing bigger and bigger.

It was a young man. He stood out against the blue sky and the silver snake-like causeway, and his dark blue clothes contrasted with the paleness of his face. He had an old yellow bag slung over his shoulder, and he came walking along with his head slightly raised, as if looking for something.

Could that firm stride possibly belong to such a weak person? It was hard to believe! That slight raising of his head, that white shining of his glasses, and that way he was walking, reminded me again of my brother...

He suddenly caught sight of me and came running down the slope of the causeway.

I stood there with grief in my heart to see him coming through the thick snow towards me, one step after another, his hand pressing the bag tightly to his body. His head hung low, and his face was pale, as though he was suffering intense pain. He didn't even dare look up.

He stopped in front of me, his head hanging lower still. We were both silent.

"Have you got the book?"

That was the only thing I could think of saying; I couldn't remember any of the things I'd meant to say to him.

"Yes, I have," he faltered.

"Then give it to me." I felt such pain.

"Do you really want it?...." He put his hand over his bag and looked at me sadly, as though he was reluctant to open it.

"Yes, I do." I couldn't think of anything more to say.

He finally opened the bag in a dejected way and handed me the thick book. His hand was visibly trembling. How I longed to take hold of that hand and cry out my tears!

"Tell me why, Wei Ying? I don't understand!" Pain and sorrow came welling up from my heart. I tried hard to keep control, and not make an exhibition of myself by starting to cry.

"I...." He kept his head lowered; he seemed to have so much grief bottled up inside.

"Have you got a girl-friend now?"

"Who told you that?" He threw me an anxious look with his sunken eyes, and hurriedly denied it: "No, of course I haven't...."

"I don't understand! I can't think of any other reason!"

He hung his head even lower. He looked as wretched as a criminal.

"Surely you know I wanted to be a good wife and a good mother?" I couldn't hold back my pain and bitterness, and the tears flooded down my face. I stumbled forward and he followed me as meekly as a lamb.

"I've been married, and I've had a child—I'm not worthy of you." I wiped away my tears and stood still, and then turned to look at him and said, "If you've got a girl-friend, or you just don't want me as a friend any more, I won't hold it against you. It wouldn't say much for my love for you if I did."

"No, no—it's not like that!"

"Then why, Wei Ying?"

I so badly wanted to know his answer!

"I spoke to my mother about it." He was nervously fiddling with the corner of his bag. "She..."

"Your mother was against it?"

He lowered his head, saying nothing.

"So it's all over between us then?" How I longed for him to tell me I was wrong!

Hesitation. Silence. The suffocating silence, the suffocating wilderness!

I waited; I waited for an answer—if only he would say that he and I could just be ordinary friends! I had no intention of standing in the way of his future happiness, but I knew I never wanted to marry again, never in my whole life: he was the only one who would ever understand me.

Suddenly, he lifted his head, his face deathly pale, his eyes fired with a desperate determination.

"I'm going now," he said distinctly.

The words were hardly out, and he was going away without turning his head. He hurriedly climbed to the top of the causeway and walked off, not once looking back.

Oh, was this his reply? Was this all he had to say, in answer to all my passion? I felt I knew him for the first time. All my blood seemed to drain from my head down into the ground; I felt a coldness in my body, I was powerless to move my feet.

I turned round in a numbed state and tried moving a few steps, but in the end I just stood there, not knowing what I was thinking or doing...

It seemed like a long while before I turned to look after him—I felt I must wait and not look round until he'd gone some distance off so that he wouldn't see the tears all over my face.

He was standing there on the causeway, in the distance, gazing towards me.

I turned away again, choked with sobs. My tears rained down like pearls falling from a broken string. I could scarcely walk...

I stopped. I looked back at him once more as he walked listlessly away into the distance, silhouetted against the snow... But when he next stopped to turn, I quickly looked away.

However many times he might turn his head and look round at me, he never came running back and asked me to forgive him! He still kept on walking away, in the opposite direction.

I didn't want him to look at me any longer, so just before he next turned round, I dived into the willow copse in front of me where the thickset willows screened my whole body from view. And now at last he couldn't see me any more!

I staggered blindly through the dense thicket. The withered snow-laden branches cut into my face but I didn't take any notice, I didn't even feel them.

Suddenly, before I knew what had happened, I found myself standing paralyzed in the heart of the copse, by a frozen pond. One step more, and I would have gone plunging through the thin layer of snow-covered ice!

Death? Death? Could death liberate me from my suffering?

I felt nothing, my mind was empty; I only stared blankly at that pond where I knew others must have drowned!

Without thinking, I was clutching the book tightly with my fingers; a grim thought entered my mind—should I leave the book on the bank or take it with me to its end?

The book was unfinished. Who would finish it? I remembered Luoke's lines:

"The cause I bequeathe you requires all your might...
The world is so heavy, and I am so light."

My heart was about to break with pain. Helplessly I sank down onto the snow and began to weep pitifully.

⟨Oh my brother!... Luoke! Will I never see you again, Luoke?...⟩

The sound of my sobbing shook the wilderness ⟨and rocked the boundless silver world around me...⟩

Let me cry, Luoke! I haven't cried so much since your death! Let my tears fly from this clean expanse of snow to Marco Polo Bridge, the place of your heroic death, and let them sink down into the earth that is soaked crimson with fresh blood! Let that blood rise up into the sky and be transformed into the glowing glory of dawn and sunset, so that I can see it every day, gaze upon it every day! Let me cry out all the tears in my heart, till I can cry no more! Never say to me again, Luoke, that crying is a sign of weakness!... Will I really never see you again?

⟨My tears gushed up like a spring, and the sound of my crying shook the heavens; it was a sad and poignant music floating far up into the blue sky...⟩

I looked up at that clear blue sky. There was not a cloud to be seen. I buried my face between my knees, and hugged the book to my chest, sobbing my heart out.

The wilderness of snow was completely silent; ⟨it listened in stillness to this call from deep in my heart.⟩ It seemed that the earth already knew my heart's desire, and was carrying my grief and remorse to my brother far away...

My happiness was dead, forever dead. If I ever loved again, it would never be with the freshness, the beauty, the intensity, I had felt for Wei Ying. Yes, I mourned the death of that happiness, that freshness and beauty I'd never know again; I felt the pain of all the wounds that still scarred my heart; but most of all, I lamented my own weakness! In my place, my brother would never have acted like me! If he were still alive, what shame and pain he would have felt on my account!

It was true that at one time I had thought my story could never be revealed; I was too ashamed of what had happened. But it was Wei Ying's affection that had first given me the idea of writing it all down.

Even then I'd still wanted to keep some things back. What was I afraid of? Was I afraid that other people would reproach me and despise me for it?

But now all I wanted was to bring the whole thing out into the open—I wanted nine hundred million people to understand me. ⟨Even if it was no more than an insignificant love story, there was still much food for thought in it. I believed I could finish putting my memories of my brother into words, and at the same time write my own story.⟩ All I wanted was to be cleansed, to be baptised by the impartial judgement of nine hundred million people; all I wanted was to find peace of mind through honesty and courage.

It was a long time before I grew calm. I wiped the frozen tears from my face and stared at the pond, lost in thought...

⟨I seemed to become someone else. I was running fast and wild, and then I stopped suddenly at the edge of a precipice. I raised both arms in defiance towards the heavens, and cried out in a rough and terrifying voice:

"I want to live! I want to be happy! I want my brother!"

The words kept on echoing, over and over again... It was a terrible, sinister sound, vibrating through the universe, piercing through the coldness and indifference with the force of an X-ray... All creation awoke with a start, tense and trembling, and listened with bated breath, frightened and shamed into silence...

It seemed that the whole of mankind was dead, and that I was the only person left on earth. And now I was resting on the bosom of my Mother Earth, listening attentively while she and Father Sky wept sadly, telling me of their remorse, beseeching me to forgive them for the excess of suffering they had caused me... In solemn silence I listened to them, I listened closely; but even if I believed them to be sincere, and even if I could feel their warmth as I sat in their embrace, I could not begin to forgive them.

Whatever warmth there was left in my heart, it was for telling the whole truth, and for earning my brother's forgiveness; and in that

forgiveness I hoped to discover a source of energy to last me to
eternity!⟩

My tears fell silently as I thought back over the past, trying to judge
myself...

To sort out the muddle of my thoughts, I rubbed a handful of snow
onto my face, and felt much better.

Why had Wei Ying cast me off? What had driven him to his final
decision? He later told me that it was indeed his mother who had
forced him to change his mind, and these were her reasons:

One—I'd been married. This alone was enough to make her
disapprove. Many people saw a fundamental difference between those
who'd been married and those who had not, and she was no exception.
She was afraid of being laughed at by her friends and relatives.

And two—I had political problems, and so did my family. I had
thought that since both he and I came from a bad class background,
there was every reason for us to be ideologically compatible. But as it
turned out, this was precisely what had led to our separation! For
twenty years, his mother had suffered so much because of his father!
She had scrimped and saved to support her children, all the time
hoping that when they grew up they at least would not meet with
misfortune. She had already interfered with her daughter's marriage,
so why shouldn't she interfere with her son's? She simply wanted to
make sure that her own painful experience wasn't repeated in the
second and third generations. Class background! Class! ⟨How deeply
that feudal brand was burned into people's hearts and minds!⟩

I wasn't sure at the time why he had left me, ⟨but there was one
thing I was quite sure of—I couldn't forgive him. The gulf between us
was too great.

Take his whole attitude towards loving me. He had embraced me, a
married woman, without thinking about the realities of us living
together. And while I had been trying to be honest with myself and
serious towards him, he had just been a helpless coward.⟩

Maybe he really did love me but just couldn't hold out against his
family's tears and threats—in which case he didn't love me as much as
he loved himself. For the first time, doubt clouded my mind—what was

really so good about him? And what was there about him deserving of admiration and emulation? If we *had* lived together, would we have been happy? I'd never considered this before, I'd never doubted it for a moment. I was shocked by my new-found doubt. Then, was it love I had been looking for in him? Or what *was* it? . . . What did the future hold? I had no idea. I didn't have any faith whatsoever in future happiness. There was only one thought in my head—to carry on living, for my brother, for my book!

⟨Forgive me my weakness, Luoke, forgive me for contemplating suicide. I still haven't done anything for our people. I want to live, I want to strive! Although we have been discriminated against from the day we first learned to strive, your death has finally awoken me. Forgive me my foolishness, forgive me my abject way of life.

Oh, I wanted to look up into the western sky and see if my brother had appeared there. . .

I struggled to my feet and stood upright at the edge of the stagnant pond like some great giant.

I made my way through the willow copse to the foot of the causeway, and gazed in the direction of the Youth Settlement—I gazed at the western sky and the boundless snowy wilderness, lost in thought. . .

If I could strive again, if I could once more hold my head high, if I could think of my brother every day, then surely I would find a new will and a new purpose in life!

I took a mouthful of snow and ate it. It was so fresh and cool—the sweet melted snow trickling down into my heart.

Yes, as long as there was still breath in my body, I would face life with optimism. The book I was writing was unfinished. I must finish it: it was the truth! I hated myself for ever having been so irresponsible as to think of casting it away. My brother would never have done such a thing.⟩

Forgive me, Luoke!

I gazed at the darkening western sky, and a silent plea echoed in my heart.

Forgive me, Luoke!

⟨My voice seemed to echo to infinity. Its solemn, heart-rending resonance brought tears to my eyes...

The air seemed to grow exceptionally warm and fragrant, as if an invisible old man somewhere in the universe was tenderly caressing my black hair with a warm, ethereal hand. I was deeply touched by this silent love...⟩

The evening sun was setting in the west...

The glow of sunset rose up into the sky like a flame and gazed down upon the earth...

Ah, I thought I could see my brother in those brightly coloured layers of petal-like cloud. He was smiling at me softly, as if he had been watching me all this while... I looked at him in astonishment, mesmerized... ⟨That great love touched me and calmed me,⟩ it filled me with strength! I so wanted to call to him over and over again, and to pore over his face, as beautiful and as inspiring as the sunset!... Luoke!

I clambered straight to the top of the causeway, to see him more clearly. The cold snow kept stealing down inside my boots, making me tingle with cold; but my heart was like fire, burning with faith!

⟨The glowing sunset stained the vast snowy wilderness crimson, and swathed the great white earth in a mantle of gorgeous red. There wasn't a soul to be seen on the untrodden snow of the causeway. I watched my brother's joyful and forgiving face as I strode through the snow towards the Youth Settlement, not once turning back.⟩

I found myself thinking of a poem he had written:

The vast expanse of snow bathed in evening glow,
Destiny and Will are lost in infinite mist.
No path lies ahead, save the one you tread;
And that path winds on, and the night is long.

Night was falling once again, but no matter how long the night, day would dawn.

And another spring would come. Luoke. My most beloved brother.

Photographs

My mother, Peking 1938.

My father, 1952.

Luoke(7) and myself(3), with our
grandmother(53) in 1948.

The four of us on Children's Day
(June 1) 1953.

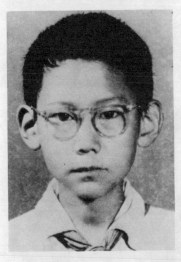

Luoke on leaving primary school,
July 1954.

Myself, Peking 1956.

Luoke and myself, June 14, 1954.

The four of us, with our mother, Spring Festival 1960.

The six of us, 1961.

Luoke, on first entering High
School, 1956.

Luoke, while working as an
apprentice in a factory, June 1966.

Luoke shortly before his arrest in January 1968.

Luomian(L), Luowen(R) and myself, taken before our hasty departure from Peking, early 1970.

Luomian, c.1971.   Luowen, c.1971.

Zhiguo.

Working outside, with the baby
on my back.

Zhiguo and the baby.

With the baby.

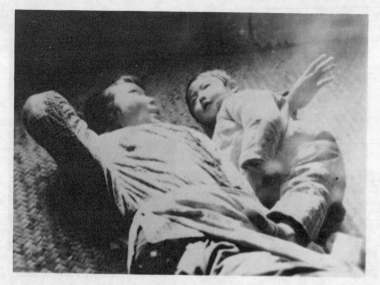

Telling the baby a story.

Father with the baby.

My parents shortly after Luoke's death, March 1970.

Taken after my official "rehabilitation" in 1979.

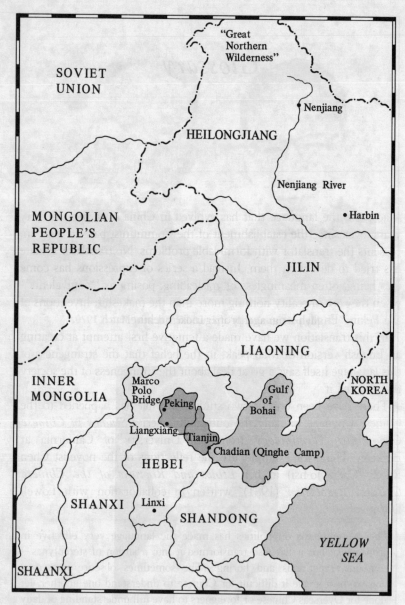

Sketch Map of North and Northeast China showing places mentioned in
A Chinese Winter's Tale

Glossary

Maospeak, the language that has evolved in China over the past fifty years, ever since the establishment of the Communist base in Yan'an, presents the translator with formidable problems. No translator to date has tried to deal with them. Instead a series of expressions has come into being, often meaningless or misleading, posing as "equivalents" when they are in reality nothing more than the makeshift inventions of the Peking English-language propaganda machine.

In this translation we have made a tentative first attempt at creating an English version of Maospeak, in the belief that the strangeness of this language itself says a great deal about the strangeness of the society that formed it.

There have been one or two studies of what has happened to the Chinese language, notably the outstanding series *Studies in Chinese Communist Terminology* from the University of California at Berkeley. Here, for example, are the reflections of the novelist Chen Ruoxi (Chen Jo-hsi) in her *Ethics and Rhetoric of the Chinese Cultural Revolution* (1981), written in collaboration with Lowell Dittmer:

> The overemphasis on politics has made the language very effective in propaganda; but it has also transformed it into a jargon of stereotypes—pompous, repetitive and boring. (The sometimes obscure numerical slogans) have made it difficult for Chinese to understand one another, let alone for Overseas Chinese or foreigners to have full understanding of daily expressions . . .
>
> Mao Zedong lorded it over the Party for nearly half a century and ruled the whole country for half that long, and the Chinese language held no

exemption from his dictatorship. Hailed as the saviour of the people, whatever he said or wrote was looked upon as an imperial decree, to be studied and eventually copied. Thus, the language is full of his personal expressions and literary style.

H.C. Chuang, in his *The Little Red Book and Current Chinese Language* (1968), had earlier written:

Mao knows only too well the importance of "terms and phrases". Ever since the Communists came to power 19 years ago, every political campaign in China has been simultaneously a semantic campaign as well, introducing or reviving a plethora of shibboleths and slogans with such determination and concentration that it sometimes borders on verbomania or graphomania. Mao strikes one as a true believer in word-magic...

T.A. Hsia, in yet another book from this series, his *A Terminological Study of the Hsia-fang Movement* (1963), sums the whole thing up very powerfully:

Anyone who has not lived through a mass movement in Communist China can hardly feel the power of words when backed up by the power of the party-state. For it is words that incite the people to action; it is slogans uttered by the men on top and echoed by the propaganda machine that start what is often described in the Communist press as the "tidal waves" or the "conflagration that reaches the sky". When a mass movement is in full swing, a small word group, such as *t'u-kai*(land reform), *san-fan*(three-anti) or *wu-fan*(five-anti)—what Miss Li Chi rightly designates as the "king-size term"—becomes a magic phrase, surrounded by an aura of sanctity and inspiring awe. It embodies the Party's will and represents an undertaking to which the whole nation is for the time being dedicated. It carries with it a tone of emergency, as if to misunderstand its meaning or to fail to put it into effect with full force would constitute a national calamity. Acting in the name of history, the "king-size term" reorganizes the people's life, unifies their will, and generates a mass strength to reach certain goals or to destroy certain enemies.

*

The language is a self-contained system, just as the society is. This accounts for the peculiar density of the abbreviation "q.v." in this glossary. Ultimately none of these terms make sense without reference to all the others.

In coining equivalents for Maospeak, and in compiling this glossary (which also includes certain place-names and other unfamiliar expressions), we have made use of the following invaluable reference books:

1. Humphrey Evans, *The Adventures of Li Chi*, Dutton, New York 1967.
2. Lai Ying, *The Thirty-sixth Way*, Doubleday, New York 1969.
3. Bao Ruo-wang (Jean Pasqualini) and Rudolph Chelminski, *Prisoner of Mao*, Penguin, Harmondsworth 1976.
4. Gordon White, *The Politics of Class and Class Origin*, Australian National University, Canberra 1976.
5. *Glossary of Chinese Political Phrases*, Union Research Institute, Hong Kong 1977.
6. Simon Leys, *The Chairman's New Clothes*, Allison & Busby, London, 1977.
7. *Political Imprisonment in the People's Republic of China*, Amnesty International, London 1978.
8. The introduction to the French translation of *A Chinese Winter's Tale*, *Le Nouveau Conte d'Hiver*, Paris 1982, unpublished translation from the French of Huang San and Miguel Mandarès, by Jean and David Hawkes.
9. *China Rights Annals*, ed. James O. Seymour, M. E. Sharpe, New York 1985.

J. M. & R. M.

BANBUQIAO DETENTION CENTRE

"When the jeep stopped after an hour, I found myself outside a gate in a very high wall topped by barbed wire. The street name was Half-Step Bridge [Banbuqiao] and the plaque by the gate read: Detention House for Corrective Education Through Labour [= Labour Cure, q.v.], which I later learned was part of the Peking Municipal Prison."

Wu Ningkun, *Cambridge Review*, June 1986.

Banbuqiao is one of three detention centres run by the Peking PSB (q.v.). Theoretically these centres are for the temporary detention (maximum three months) of prisoners while their cases are being examined, but in practice some "offenders" stay on in detention centres for years.

> I could write a book about China's gulag, just based on my experiences at Banbuqiao. The people of Peking are scared to death at the mere mention of the place, in part because the street number is 44—which in Chinese sounds like "double death".
>
> Fang Dan, in *China Rights Annals*, New York 1985.

BEAVER (*jiji fenzi*, literally "positive element" or "activist")

Beavers in general are eager to carry out Party policy, and can always be relied upon in political campaigns to struggle "actively" against Class Enemies (q.v.). The term implies positive commitment, optimism and constructive effort.

A Neicom (q.v.) Beaver is often female, and usually not a Party member. She belongs to Revmass (q.v.), and has a good Red (q.v.) Class Background (q.v.).

It should be noted that this term can also be used ironically, especially by those to whom this kind of "dedication" is suspect. One might hear someone say, for example: "So-and-so is altogether too much of a Beaver for my liking." Or: "They tried to turn me into a Beaver, but I simply couldn't work up the enthusiasm."

BLACKBOOK (*heihukou*)

A Blackbook is someone living illegally without a proper Domper (q.v.).

> You probably don't realize that outside our normal society there is a "black" society, made up of all sorts of people: those who work on their

own [people without a 'work-unit'], the unemployed, people who have
been driven out of the mainstream for all sorts of reasons but who still have
to live.

Dai Houying, *Stones of the Wall*, London 1985, p.39.

BLACKS (*heiwulei*, literally "five black categories")

These were the various categories of Class Enemies (q.v.), constituting
(according to the "official quota") roughly 5% of China's population
(i.e. 50 million). There was never an authoritative definition of these
categories, and popular usage was not uniform.

Before the Cultrev there were five categories of Blacks. These were:
landlords, Kulaks (q.v.), Counters (q.v.), bad elements and Voicers
(q.v.). The first three categories were the targets of the various
campaigns between 1950 and 1955. The fourth referred to common-
law criminals and petty offenders; it designated people regarded as
exhibiting improper social behaviour (e.g. laxity in sexual relations,
shenghuo zuofeng wenti, larceny, *daoqie xingwei*, etc.). The fifth
category—Voicers—appeared in 1957.

During the Cultrev, as the regime grew harsher, several more
categories were added to the list. These were: Kroads (q.v.), black
gangsters, renegades and special agents, and Lecks (q.v., so-called
"intellectuals", the "stinking ninth" category).

The Black categories were officially abolished in 1978.

BLOOMS AND VOICES (*baihua qifang, baijia zhengming,*
literally "let the hundred flowers bloom and the hundred schools of
thought contend")

This was the slogan, what Miss Li Chi (see the quotation from T.A.
Hsia above) would have called the "king-size term", that dominated
the period from the summer of 1956 to the summer of 1957, when the
Party invited outspoken and fearless criticism of the regime and its

policies—and got it, in a measure they obviously had not bargained for. This was the period of the so-called Hundred Flowers. So many individuals Bloomed and Voiced that they were very soon suppressed and persecuted, in a backlash starting in June 1957, and leading directly into the notorious purge of Voicers (q.v.). This purge is often referred to as the Anti-Rightist Campaign.

BREAK (*huaqing jiexian*, literally "draw a clear line of demarcation")

Breaking is the process by which a person dissociates himself from people or ideas or things considered politically undesirable, thereby demonstrating that political considerations are of prime importance and come above love, friendship, belief, etc. If a member of a family is pronounced a Voicer (q.v.), or Black (q.v.), etc., other family members must Break with him or her. Children must Break with parents; husbands with wives or vice-versa (divorce being the cleanest form of Break); friends with friends; Krats (q.v.) with Class Enemies (q.v.), etc.

If young people of "bad" Class Background (q.v.) are prepared to "turn their backs on their families" (*beipan jiating*) by Breaking, then they too can join the ranks of the proletariat—theoretically at any rate. In practice such people can never qualify for high-security posts, in the air force or diplomatic service, for example, however many family bonds they may have Broken.

CAP (*kou maozi*, literally "put a hat on someone")

The practice of sticking a label on people, or branding them, by denouncing them as reactionary in one way or another. A man can be Capped in a matter of minutes, at a Strife (q.v.) session. To be Decapped, or officially "rehabilitated", can take decades. In most cases the Cap is an immovable stigma, and stays with the person concerned to the grave.

CLASS BACKGROUND AND CLASS PEDIGREE (*jiating chushen*, literally "family background and origin" and *xuetong*, literally "blood lineage")

From a strictly Marxist point of view, economic status should be the only criterion by which members of society are divided into social classes. This was how "class" was defined in China in the pre- and post-Liberation period. A man's Class Background was his officially registered class history, which depended on the main income source of his family when he was a child.

But Mao gradually revised this concept of class status in the late fifties and early sixties and expanded the criteria to include political beliefs, social connections and blood lineage. Mao's new definition of class blended a Marxist-Leninist concept of class status with a traditional Chinese feudalistic notion of family origin, and gave birth to the theory of Class Pedigree. This monstrous theory said in practice, for example, that the descendants of a landlord family would *always* be landlords, even though they might never have owned an inch of land.

Reactionary, exploiting-class ways of thinking are presumably transmitted from one generation of a family to another genetically!

CLASS ENEMY (*jieji diren*)

Maoist doctrine divided China into two sections: one (the great majority—95%) consisted of the People, or Revmass (q.v.); the other 5% (actually about 50 million individuals) consisted of a "handful" of Class Enemies.

All of the Blacks (q.v.) were considered to be Class Enemies, but petty criminals etc. could still rank among the People—they were only considered Incon (q.v.). It was much easier to be demoted from People to Enemy, than to rejoin the ranks of Revmass once you were marked as an Enemy.

In the incessant class struggle and inner-Party struggle that characterized Mao's rule, this opposition of People and Enemy provided the theoretical basis for the singling out of identifiable groups of victims or scapegoats to be crushed by an overwhelming majority (see Proledic). This stratagem was applied not only at the grass-roots level, but also within the Party's politburo. It was particularly intensely applied during the Cultrev (q.v.).

COUNTER (*fangeming fenzi*, literally "counter-revolutionary element")

Counters are officially defined as "those who sabotage and resist the revolutionary system and persist in the counter-revolutionary system". They are divided into "historical" Counters (i.e. those whose crimes were committed before 1949); and "active" or "current" Counters, a term which covers a multitude of evils, from simple expression of dissent to politically motivated common-law offences.

CULTREV (*wenhua dageming*, "the Great Cultural Revolution")

The Cultrev initially had little to do with "culture", and much to do with an inner-party struggle for power.

Mao had begun to lose both popularity and power as result of the disastrous Great Leap Forward (1958) and the subsequent three years of "natural disaster" (the accepted euphemism for a famine which was in fact brought about by political errors, not nature). He had been forced to give up his position as Head of State to Liu Shaoqi, who, with Deng Xiaoping as General Party Secretary, proceeded to implement a more pragmatic policy, attempting to improve the Chinese economy by re-introducing certain material incentives. By 1965 the economy was on the mend. Mao, however, interpreted this as a capitulation to bourgeois revisionism, and wanted to re-engage the nation in the struggle for a more egalitarian society. His simple but subtle way of ousting his opponents was to appeal to Chinese youth. Young people all over China were exhorted to "bombard the headquarters", and on

August 18 1966 Mao himself attended a mass rally of a million Red Guards (q.v.) in Tiananmen Square.

What in fact ensued was a ten-year period of anarchy, sometimes verging on civil war, and of widespread persecutions and executions, particularly during 1966-8, when rival Red Guard factions fought amongst themselves and terrorized those in authority, and anyone considered to be a Black (q.v.).

CULTURE PALACE (*wenhuagong*)

These "palaces" are large centres (often ugly neo-Soviet buildings) for the dispensation of culture to the masses, sometimes including under one roof theatre, cinema, exhibition hall, library etc.

DAUR BANNER

The people of the Daur Minority, numbering about 78,000, live mainly in Inner Mongolia, and in Xinjiang and Heilongjiang provinces. They practise agriculture. Some are nomadic herdsmen. Their language is closely related to Mongolian.

The Banner was originally a military unit used by the Mongols and Manchus, and is now used as a geographical and administrative unit in that part of China, roughly equivalent to a County.

DECAP (*zhai maozi*)

See Cap.

DOMPER (*hukouben*, literally "domicile-permit registration book")

A Domper is a combination of residence card, work permit and ration book. It is a very effective means of control which can be used to prevent the exodus of rural population to the towns, and to limit the movement of population into the richer provinces. It reduces people to the status of immigrants in their own country, somewhat like the notorious South African passbooks.

If a person wants to move from one area to another, from one house to another, from one job to another, he must get permission at both ends before making the relevant transfer arrangements.

DROSSNIK (*liumang*, literally "layabout, hoodlum")

A Drossnik is a person whose life-style and behaviour mark him (or her) as a social outcast. It is an old and very widely used catch-all phrase for undesirables—petty thieves, prostitutes, perverts, black-marketeers, people to be "kept off the streets". "Drossnik behaviour" is most often simply a euphemism for sexual misconduct.

The Drossnik, like the Urbling (q.v.), has also become a symbol of alienation in Chinese society, the Chinese Outsider. He represents defiance and rejection of the system. He is Kerouac's hobo. See for example the vividly portrayed Drossnik character Bai Hua, in Zhao Zhenkai's novel *Waves* (Hong Kong, Chinese University Press, 1985).

EVACUATION (*zhanbei shusan*, literally "evacuation in preparation for war")

In 1970, at the time of the border conflict with the Soviet Union over "Treasure Island" in the Heilongjiang River, Lin Biao ordered national mobilization and mass evacuation of people from the cities to the countryside. In the city of Tianjin alone, 100,000 people were sent to the outlying counties. This was a convenient way of disposing of "undesirables" and removing Lecks (q.v.) to the country.

EXCON (*di-wo maodun*, literally "contradictions between the enemy and us")

See Incon.

FEN

A Chinese land-measure. There are 10 *fen* in one *mu* (q.v.).

FLOATER (*mangliu*, literally "blind flow")

This refers to the large numbers of peasants who, either because of poverty, actual famine or political harassment, moved "blindly", originally to the cities from the countryside.

They had no Dompers (q.v.)—they were Blackbooks (q.v.). Or they had "pocket" Dompers (*koudai hukou*), which meant that they had been given permission to leave one place, but hadn't yet got permission to remain in another.

In Chapter 1, Yu Luojin and the Wei brothers speak of the great numbers of peasants (probably from Shandong and Hebei provinces) who have Floated up to the Northeast in search of a new life. The extreme policies of the Cultrev (q.v.) had driven them to it. The attraction of the Northeast was its small population and fertile land, and the fact that eventually these Floaters had a better chance of getting a Domper there.

FOUR RELICS (*sijiu*, literally "four olds"—old ideas, old culture, old customs, and old habits)

During the Cultrev, the Four Relics were among the main targets of the Red Guards, who made Raids (q.v.) on countless households to "root them out". One of the most graphic ways of doing this was to burn "old" books, clothes, paintings etc. In their place, they were to establish the Four News.

FREAKS (*niugui sheshen*, literally "cow-ghosts and snake-spirits")

In 1967, Mao adopted this old expression to indicate people who were socially and politically undesirable, i.e. Class Enemies (q.v.). All of the Black (q.v.) categories were referred to collectively as Freaks.

During the Cultrev, Freaks were often arbitrarily arrested by one faction or another and confined (sometimes for long periods and without any legal process) in a work unit's improvised place of detention, known as a "cow-shed" (*niupeng*).

FREE-WORKER (*xingman liuyong renyuan*, literally "personnel kept on after the expiry of their term")

This is the euphemism used for various categories of ex-convicts "retained" after the expiration of their term, either at their original camp or nearby. Although they have more freedom of movement than prisoners, they are not allowed to leave their designated area and cannot go looking for employment elsewhere. It is a way of extending a person's sentence indefinitely, and of creating a huge labour-force to work in the underdeveloped parts of the countryside.

GRAVE FESTIVAL (*qingming jie*, literally "Clear Brightness Festival")

The Festival falling on the 5th April, at the beginning of the fifth of the twenty-four solar periods of the year in the Chinese calendar. It was traditionally a time for cleaning family graves.

GREAT NORTHERN WILDERNESS (*beidahuang*)

The vast undeveloped area of northern Heilongjiang Province, so called because of its harsh climate and sparse population.

"HEROES BREED HEROIC SONS, COUNTERS ALL HATCH ROTTEN ONES!"

This was a slogan made up by an extreme and violent group of Red Guards in Peking. They were all the children of Hikrats (q.v.). The slogan became widespread in July and August 1966, as the catch-phrase of the theory of Class Pedigree (q.v.)—the inheritability of political characteristics from one generation to the next. These Hikrat Kids (*gaogan zidi*) were therefore automatically Red (q.v.).

In his essay "On Class Background" (q.v.), Yu Luoke quoted and then refuted this slogan as reactionary. He claimed (and many shared his view) that Class Background (q.v.) should merely be "referred to" in evaluating family influence, and that social influence far outweighed family influence.

The message of the slogan was similar to that of a traditional popular saying:

"A dragon gives birth to a dragon; a phoenix gives birth to a phoenix; but the son of a rat can only burrow holes."

HIGH SCHOOL CULTREV POST (*zhongxue wenge bao*)

A Peking "rebel" newspaper that printed Yu Luoke's essay "On Class Background" (q.v.) in its special issue for February 1967. The publishers' full name was "Propaganda Department of the High School Students Revolutionary Rebel Headquarters".

HIKRAT (*gaogan, or gaoji ganbu*, literally "high-level cadre")

Krats (q.v.) are graded on a 24-point national scale. Any Krat from points 1 to 14 on this scale (it used to be point 13) is classified as a Hikrat, and is entitled to all the privileges of China's "new ruling class".

The children of this elite, Hikrat Kids, form an important unofficial stratum in China's social hierarchy.

INCON (*renmin neibu maodun*, literally "contradictions within the ranks of the people")

Mao's 1957 speech, "On the Correct Handling of Contradictions Among the People", distinguished between two types of contradiction: that "within the ranks of the People" (Incon), and that between the Enemy and the People (Excon). Incon was of an ideological nature, and could be resolved by "criticism, persuasion and education" and by "administrative regulations"; but Excon was antagonistic in nature and must therefore be dealt with more severely, by submitting the Enemy to the Dictatorship. (See Proledic, Labour Cure, Labour Mould)

All of this can only be understood in terms of the Maoist doctrine of "permanent class struggle". The People are those who "support and work for socialist construction", whereas the Enemy are those who "resist the socialist revolution and are hostile to or sabotage socialist construction". Mao's talk was inspired by the failure of the Blooms and Voices (q.v.), and it would seem that the definition of these two types of "contradiction" was a way of rationalizing the persecution of dissenting elements—mostly Voicers (q.v.).

Mao went on to say that a certain type of Incon could transform gradually into Excon; and that a certain type of Excon, if handled properly, could transform into Incon.

This theoretical elasticity (compounded by the absence of legality) makes it extremely difficult to draw a clear line of demarcation between the two types of contradiction, and therefore easy for a miscarriage of justice to occur.

Yu Luojin's case illustrates this. As an offender undergoing Labour Cure (q.v.), she is technically still within the ranks or on the periphery of the People; but she is actually an Enemy because she is in the category of Counter (q.v.).

KANG

A raised mud-brick structure heated from below, used in Northern China, for sitting on in the daytime and sleeping on at night.

KRAT (*ganbu*)

A bureaucrat holding an administrative or similar position of responsibility and power, usually but not always a member of the Communist Party. Traditionally translated as "cadre".

KROAD (*zouzipai*, literally "capitalist roader")

This term was introduced in 1965 to describe the politicians (especially Liu Shaoqi and Deng Xiaoping) who were adopting Soviet-style reforms, and who were therefore considered guilty of taking the "capitalist road" away from socialism—by introducing material incentives to boost the economy (profits and bonuses in industry), and Ownplots (q.v.) on the communes. Such policies are currently (1986) back in favour.

KUAI

A more colloquial word for *yuan*, the basic Chinese unit of currency, made up of 100 cents (*fen*), and now roughly equivalent to 20 pence sterling.

KULAK (*funong*, literally "rich peasant")

The Chinese Kulak, in the days before "liberation", owned land and had some working capital and means of production. He may have worked on the land himself, but he "exploited" others by hiring farmhands, renting out land, or lending money at high rates of interest.

Kulaks were one of the 5 categories of Blacks (q.v.).

For a moving story of the fate of a typical Chinese Kulak in the early fifties, during the period of Land Reform, see Eileen Chang's novel, *Naked Earth* (English version, 1956).

LABOUR CURE (*laodong jiaoyang*, literally "re-education through labour")

This is an "administrative", as opposed to a criminal, punishment, and does not require a judicial sentence—whereas Labour Mould (q.v.) does. It is meted out to persons considered guilty of "mistakes" rather than "crimes", although the distinction between the two is not clearly defined by law, and much is left to the "discretion" of the courts, the police and the Party—especially in the case of political offenders.

The 1957 "Decision on Labour Cure" was drawn up primarily to deal with vagrants, minor offenders and troublemakers of various sorts. But because of the Anti-Voicer campaign of that year, it also included a paragraph directly relating to political offenders.

Labour Cure can take place in a special labour camp (euphemistically known as a "farm") for Labour Cure offenders, or in penal institutions (prison-factories, camps, farms) holding other categories of offenders. According to the law, Labour Cure offenders retain their civic rights, and have more privileges and a better diet than Labour Mould offenders, from whom they are theoretically supposed to be segregated. But there is overwhelming evidence that the two categories are treated equally badly.

Labour Cure is normally for a term of three years, but this can be extended.

LABOUR MOULD (*laodong gaizao*, literally "reform through labour")

Labour Mould is a criminal penalty, involving a proper judicial sentencing to a term of imprisonment (*panxing*) ranging from 2 to 30 years. The term can be extended.

The 1954 "Act for Labour Mould" is one of the most detailed Chinese laws. Its purpose is defined in its first Article as being "to punish all counter-revolutionary and other criminal offenders and to compel them to reform themselves through labour and become new persons". Labour Mould offenders are in fact used as a mobile, unpaid labour force; they are transferred from one camp to another according to "economic need", and are liable to be sent off to remote and sparsely populated areas to do "pioneer work".

There is a simple, basic truth about the labour camps that seems to be unknown in the West. For all but a handful of exceptional cases (such as myself) the prison experience is total and permanent. The men and women sentenced to Reform Through Labour spend the remainder of their lives in the camps, as prisoners first and then as "free workers" after their terms have expired.

Labour camps in China are a lifetime contract. They are far too important to the national economy to be run with transient personnel.

Jean Pasqualini, Prisoner of Mao, p.11.

LECKS (*zhishi fenzi*, literally "educated elements")

Anyone with a high school education qualifies as a Leck. From this one can see how inadequate the existing translation—"intellectual"—is. The Lecks were known during the Cultrev as the Stinking Ninth category of Blacks (q.v.), and were always prime targets. One of Mao's favourite slogans was: "The more you know, the more stupid you become!"

The demoralization and alienation of the Chinese Lecks since "liberation" is a basic fact about Chinese society little understood in the West.

LIANGXIANG CAMP

Labour camp south of Peking, primarily for women offenders.

MARCO POLO BRIDGE (*Lugouqiao*)

Famous bridge over the Sangkan River, to the southwest of Peking. Here in 1937 the Sino-Japanese war began.

The site of the execution ground where Yu Luoke was shot.

MARRIAGE LAWS

Despite the various laws passed since 1949, including one in 1980, many feudal attitudes toward marriage and divorce still persist in China. Yu Luojin was to encounter these attitudes directly with her second divorce and the publication of her second novel *Spring Tale*.

In 1980, at the time when *A Chinese Winter's Tale* was published, Yu Luojin's second marriage was going through a crisis. She had married Cai Zhongpei (an electrician living in Peking) some two years earlier largely as a means of acquiring resident status in Peking and achieving independence from her parents (shades of Zhao Zhiguo . . .). She filed for a divorce, justifying her stand on the grounds that the marriage had failed to fulfil her emotional requirements. At the initial hearing the divorce was granted, but Cai appealed against the decision, and the ensuing debate made the case nationally famous. Yu Luojin found herself in the middle of a national controversy on the ethics of marriage and love.

> In China, especially in the countryside, marriage is often thought of as an investment, the dowry which the young man contributes being currently the equivalent of several years' pay. There are even cases of two families, in each of which there is a boy and a girl, arranging to have a double wedding in order to save themselves these expenses. Such forced marriages often end in tragedy.
>
> But marriage is not just a matter of money, it is a matter of status. It perpetuates the social hierarchy. Until the Black categories were officially abolished in 1978, Blacks seldom mixed with Reds (the ruling class). Even today, such class distinctions, particularly where marriage is concerned, remain very rigid. The Krats go to great lengths to preserve and

strengthen their little universe. [Interestingly enough, the grandchildren and great-grandchildren of some of the Blackest families—the descendants of the great warlords and capitalists of the twenties and thirties—still intermarry on the Mainland even today, in the late 1980s!]

Marriage is also a political tool, since the authorities are free to favour certain unions and forbid others, by virtue of the control they exercise.

By contrast, divorce is held to be immoral, especially when it is the woman who asks for it. This state of affairs, which the novelist Ding Ling denounced in the Yan'an days, has scarcely changed. A divorced woman is no longer considered a complete person, especially in the countryside. Separations of a political nature are, however, an exception. If one or other of the couple becomes obnoxious to the Party, divorce is not merely encouraged, it is practically enforced. It is necessary to Break with a Class Enemy, on pain of being regarded as an accomplice.

Major changes in the Party line have thus had many repercussions on married life. Immediately following the Cultrev, the "rehabilitation" of the 1957 Voicers and other disgraced Krats resulted in a spate of remarriages between couples who had been forced to divorce for political reasons. On the other hand, Blacks who had married Reds in order to try and clear themselves with the Party now asked for divorces.

But the general run of marital disagreement is the result of an arranged marriage. Since divorce is rarely granted, this sort of conflict often ends in tragedy. According to a survey carried out in Shaanxi Province, 43% of women murdered in the province met their deaths as a result of forced marriages, failure to obtain divorce, and extramarital affairs. (*Zhengming*, Hong Kong, no.42, p.18)

Judicial practice is thus closely linked with the extreme puritanism of the society at large, which became more pronounced after the Blooms and Voices. With the Cultrev, a simple flirtation was an example of bourgeois decadence, and love, that most extreme manifestation of petit-bourgeois individualism, had to be banished from art and literature. Sex itself was not even discussed, since it remained, as it always had been, a crime. It is in this context that we have to place the ignorance and sexual naivety of Yu Luojin.

These taboos were not, however, shared by the people who imposed them. Hikrats had no difficulty in obtaining the services of young nurses or devoted secretaries...

based on the introduction to *Le Nouveau Conte d'Hiver*

MASSWATCH (*qunzhong jiandu*, literally "supervision by the masses")

A term for the less formal mode of Proledic (q.v.), in which surveillance is exercised not directly by one of the "organs of security", but through the work-unit or Neicom (q.v.) of the offender.

MID-AUTUMN FESTIVAL (*zhongqiu jie*)

Held on the fifteenth of the eighth lunar month (night of the full harvest moon), this festival is normally a time for family reunions.

MU

A Chinese land-measure, equivalent to about one sixth of an acre.

NEICOM (*jiedao jumin weiyuanhui*, literally "neighbourhood committee")

The Committee is theoretically under the supervision of the Party, but in fact it works hand in glove with the local police station. It issues ration cards and is supposed to look after the welfare of those living in the area of its jurisdiction—usually just a few streets—but it is above all an invaluable police adjunct: it reports to the police on strangers in the area, on unfamiliar comings and goings, on suspicious gatherings in people's homes. Its members also call on people, unannounced, seemingly just to pass the time of day but really in order to test out political enthusiasm and reliability.

Lai Ying, *The Thirty-sixth Way*, p.156.

Neicoms rely heavily on their Beavers (q.v.) for information.

"ON CLASS BACKGROUND" (*chushenlun*)

A long essay written by Yu Luoke, completed in September 1966, repudiating the theory of Class Pedigree (q.v.), and objectively analysing the influence of the family on an individual.

He concludes that the influence of the family is insignificant compared to the influence of society, and points out the dangers of the Class Pedigree theory.

The essay was first circulated in a duplicated version and subsequently printed in the *High School Cultrev Post* (q.v.) in February 1967, in an edition of 100,000 copies.

The context in which Yu Luoke wrote this important treatise is well described by Huang San and Miguel Mandarès in the introduction to their French translation of *A Chinese Winter's Tale*:

> The fanatical proponents of the theory of Class Pedigree attributed the sum of social ills to the continued existence of the Black categories, much as, at other times and in other places, all social ills were attributed to the Jews. In their eyes the elimination of these harmful elements would be sufficient to bring the country to communism.
>
> This was how it came about that in August of 1966 China experienced a series of outright massacres. In one Peking suburb the Blacks, including children two months old and old Party veterans, were rounded up for execution. Several wells were filled with their bodies (see *Zhengming*, no.24, p.22). Soon communes and even whole districts were boasting of having cleaned up all their Blacks. Xie Fuzhi, who was at that time Mayor of Peking, calmed the ardour of the activists by explaining, with perfect seriousness, that the absence of Blacks might bring the class struggle to a premature end, and pave the way for "revisionists" like Liu Shaoqi. As an immediate measure, he took the unheard of decision to release a series of political detainees and hand them over as gun-fodder to those brigades that had run out of Blacks—thereby ensuring the protraction of class struggle for a little longer. Orwell's *1984* became a reality. The August massacres left at least 50,000 dead in the Peking suburbs alone, according to one contemporary witness (Lin Heng in *Huanghe* no.2, pp.15-22—the journal of the Chinese League of Human Rights, published in Hong Kong). The

Reds treated their victims with savage vindictiveness, beating them, torturing them, shaving the women's hair off, making people eat excrement, etc.

It was in this context that Yu Luoke wrote his essay. In his view, the influence of the family was considerably less than that of society—beginning with the influence of education. The system of collective responsibility and social control caused by the division into Red and Black categories was essentially feudal. It could go on reproducing itself generation after generation, relegating the ultimate goal of a classless society to an ever more remote future. The partisans of Class Pedigree were victims of an idealist illusion, since thought is a product not of one's parentage but of one's experience.

In support of his hypothesis, he first evaluated the extent of the repression and described its methods, and then proceeded to exhort other young outcasts like himself to rise up and claim their rights.

The success of his treatise was such that it became a sort of platform for the new Red Guards who came from Black backgrounds. The matter was brought before the central group of the Cultrev, which reacted violently through the agency of Qi Benyu and Yao Wenyuan. In April 1967 the *Post* was banned and Yu Luoke was placed under the surveillance of the secret police until his arrest on January 5 1968.

OWNPLOT (*ziliudi*, literally "land reserved for private use")

A quota of land allotted by the commune to each commune member for his own cultivation. It was also possible for the produce to be privately sold for individual profit. The existence of Ownplot has depended on the fluctuations in official policy.

THE PASS (*Shanhaiguan*, literally "Mountain Sea Pass")

This is a famous town situated close to the Gulf of Bohai, at the extreme eastern end of the Great Wall. It is the point of access to the Northeast.

The Chinese speak of being "within" or "without" the Pass.

PLUM BLOSSOM DRUMSONG

A Drumsong is an old form of story-telling in which the story is usually sung, to the accompaniment of a drum-beat. The "Plum Blossom" is just one of many different varieties of Drumsong.

Yu Luoke wrote new words, about Jiao Yulu (q.v.), to the original tune and drum rhythm. This would have been just one solo item in the Story-telling Troupe's programme.

POISON (*ducao*, literally "poisonous weed")

A term used for writings, films, paintings, etc. considered to be anti-Party, anti-Mao, anti-socialist—often the work of Voicers (q.v.). Mao listed the six criteria for distinguishing "fragrant flowers" from "poisonous weeds" in his famous article "On the Correct Handling of Contradictions Among the People" (February 1957).

PROLEDIC (*wuchan jieji zhuanzheng*, literally "dictatorship of the proletariat")

Proledic refers to the use of political violence, rather than of democratic procedures, against Class Enemies. Since the proletariat is actually represented by the Party, Proledic can more accurately be defined as the dictatorship of the Communist Party over its enemies. Proledic was at its most forceful during the Cultrev.

The Chinese term "organs of Proledic" (*zhuanzheng jiguan*) denotes the whole state apparatus involved in exercising Proledic—the Public Security Bureau (q.v.), police stations, prisons, camps for Labour Cure or Labour Mould (qq.v.), the Army and the Courts.

If a Class Enemy is to be "subjected to Proledic", he can be dealt with in five main ways:—

1. he can be publicly denounced, or "Proledicked" (it can even be used as a verb), at a Strife (q.v.) session, on a large or small scale.

2. he can be placed under Masswatch (q.v.)—either in his work-unit, or in his village, or in his urban neighbourhood (see Neicom).
3. he can "receive" a term of Labour Cure.
4. he can be sentenced to a term of Labour Mould.
5. he can be sentenced to imprisonment or death.

In *Winter's Tale*, to simplify matters, "Proledic" is used to cover proletarian dictatorship, "organs of proletarian dictatorship" and sometimes even "mass dictatorship", since these are all part of the same elaborate system of control.

PROLETHOUGHT (*xuexi*, literally "study")

Prolethought, and the Prolethought Class (*xuexiban*) were among the major ideological "remoulding" techniques of Maoist China.

The organization of a Prolethought Class was generally an indication that some or all of the participants were in trouble 'and had to "remould" their way of thinking. The practice was derived from one of Mao's sayings: that "reactionaries" must "sit in socialist classrooms" in order to change their viewpoint. These "reactionaries" were primarily to study "Mao Zedong thought", and while their viewpoint was being remoulded, a thorough investigation of their cases was being carried out. A final judgment would then be made.

Bao Ruowang (Jean Pasqualini) writes in *Prisoner of Mao* of the similar type of sessions he underwent in a Peking interrogation centre:

> One of the prisoners, appointed cell clerk, would note each man's words and then make up the resumés that would be placed in the individual dossiers. If a prisoner says something unusual or criminal, his words enter the dossier in full and later he pays: a stretch of solitary, years added to his sentence or perhaps a Struggle [= a dose of Strife—q.v.].

PUBLIC SECURITY BUREAU (PSB)

In the years preceeding the Cultrev and again after 1978, the whole system of law enforcement in China has been carried out by Proledic's three main "organs of dictatorship". These are the Public Security, the Procuratorates, and the Courts. Between them they deal with the complete judicial process, from arrest to trial.

The PSB apparatus is responsible for the detention and the investigation of suspects and offenders in "society at large". (There are special internal organizations in charge of controlling civil servants, Party members, and the military.) It controls all police and security operations—uniformed police (including traffic police) and plain-clothes security officers. Penal institutions also come under its jurisdiction.

Branches of the PSB exist at all administrative levels in urban and rural areas. Under the Central Ministry come the Provincial PS Departments; within a province, each city has its Municipal PSB; the city is then divided up into districts, each with its own Sub-Bureau; the district is further subdivided into "administrative streets" (or neighbourhoods), each with its own PS station.

(China's three largest cities—Peking, Shanghai and Tianjin—are an exception to the above in that they come directly under the authority of the Central Government, not of their province.)

The same structural arrangement exists in the countryside: the Provincial PS Departments have branches in counties and districts; at the level of communes and production brigades, one or several Krats are generally responsible for public security.

Within this vast network, the basic units of the PS structure are the "police stations" which exist in small county towns, villages, and city neighbourhoods.

In provinces and large cities, the PS Bureaux are split up into a number of divisions, each having a particular area of responsibility—one division will be in charge of criminal cases, another handles the investigation of political offenders or suspects, another is in charge of prisons and labour camps, and so on.

During the Cultrev, Mao thought that this system of law enforcement was revisionist and needed revolutionizing. The three arms of the legal system—the PSB, the Procuratorates, and the Courts—were "smashed" and a new form of Proledic was created, in which the state apparatus and "mass organizations", such as the Red Guard groups, and Neicoms (q.v.), were supposed to work in close collaboration. This is the situation in Chapter 4 of *Winter's Tale*. The outcome of this "revolutionizing" process can best be described as an extended period of lawlessness.

QINGHE CAMP

Large labour camp, near the Gulf of Bohai, north of the city of Tianjin. This camp was under the jurisdiction of the Peking PSB. A full account of it is given in Pasqualini's *Prisoner of Mao*.

RAID (*chaojia*)

During the early part of the Cultrev, the Red Guards carried out Raids (usually at night), particularly on the homes of those considered to be Class Enemies. The Sixteen Point Circular (q.v.) of 1966 had, among other things, called for the destruction of the Four Relics (q.v.), and the Red Guards were supposedly on the lookout for anything which fell into this category. But the Red Guards also used the Raids as an excuse to steal or wilfully destroy property, and to physically intimidate and beat (sometimes to the point of death) the occupants of the house.

RED GUARDS (*hongweibing*)

This term was borrowed from the Russians. These Little Soldiers (*xiaojiang*) were "received" by Chairman Mao for the first time on August 18 1966, in Tiananmen Square. They were Reds (q.v.), theoretically guarding Mao, the Party and the motherland. In fact they went around attacking Krats and Lecks (qq.v.) and eventually one another. Despite their initial idealism, they soon became pawns in local power struggles, and were often no more than vandals and hooligans.

REDS (*hongwulei*, literally "five red categories")

Officially the five Red categories were: revolutionary Krats, revolutionary soldiers, martyrs of the revolution, workers, and poor/lower-middle peasants (those who had worked for someone else for low wages up to the time of Land Reform Movements of the early fifties).

In actual fact there were only three Red categories. Peasants and workers enjoyed none of the material privileges which went with political power. They were used simply as a justification for the Party's policies and had to submit to its authority on pain of being demoted to one of the Black (q.v.) categories.

Children of Red family background are supposed, according to the theory of Class Pedigree (q.v.), to be "dyed" Red. Ideologically, and perhaps even biologically too! "Heroes breed heroic sons!" (q.v.) Because of their Red roots, they are presumed to develop healthily into strong seedlings. Initially, Red Guards were all from Red families. Party leaders recruited Party members, Youth Leaguers (q.v.), and Beavers (q.v.) from people of Red family background. Armed with this belief in their innate superiority, some Hikrat (q.v.) Kids developed into monstrosities of human depravity.

Although 5% of China's population was said to be Black, it does not follow that the other 95% was Red. In between the two principal layers of Red and Black came the large intermediate groups of middle peasants, artisans, business employees, and "intellectual workers", all of whom were regarded with suspicion.

REFERENCE NEWS (*cankao xiaoxi*)

A digest containing summaries of news not appearing in the public media, including translations from the foreign press. Previously restricted to Party members and Krats, this paper gradually became more widely available.

REVMASS (*geming qunzhong*, literally "revolutionary masses")

A broad term for the "95%" of the masses that were supposedly in "support of the revolution".

SCRIT (*ziwo piping*, literally "self-criticism")

A key confessional stage in the Maoist process of thought reform. The making or writing of a Scrit set the seal on a person's acknowledgement of guilt.

SHAMANESS

Shamanism has a long history in China. It was common both in the South, and in the northern areas inhabited by Manchu tribes. In some remote parts of the countryside it has survived into recent times.

SIXTEEN POINT CIRCULAR

This was adopted by Party Central on August 8 1966 and became widely accepted as the most authoritative statement on the aims of the Cultrev.

It consisted of sixteen short articles, the first of which described the main objective of the Cultrev as a process of *doupigai*—literally, Strife, Crit (qq.v.), and Transformation: to *Strife* Kroads (q.v.); to *criticize* and repudiate reactionary bourgeois ideology; to *transform* education, literature, art and "all other parts of the superstructure not in correspondence with the socialist economic base".

SPEAKHEART (*jiaoxin*, literally "offer heart")

In the Speakheart Campaign of the early months of 1958, Voicers (q.v.) were called upon by the Party to make a clean breast of their bourgeois thoughts and crimes, and thereby accelerate their process of self-transformation.

SPRING FESTIVAL (*chunjie*)

The Chinese Lunar New Year Festival.

SQUAD (*gongzuodui*, literally "work team")

A Squad is a group of Krats (q.v.) or other political personnel sent to a particular place by a Party Committee or organization, basically to ensure that things are in line with higher policy, to mobilize people and to explain official policy to the locals.

When the specific objective is completed, the Squad disbands, and the Squad members either return to their original posts or are given another assignment.

STRIFE (*douzheng*, literally "struggle")

Strife as a technique of political pressure, persecution and indoctrination, is a Chinese invention dating from the thirties, and still in existence. It is used in prisons and camps, and also in ordinary civilian life, against "political offenders" (people with incorrect political attitudes).

Pasqualini describes Strife as a combination of "... intimidation, humiliation and sheer exhaustion. Briefly described, it is an intellectual gang-beating of one man by many, sometimes even thousands, in which the victim has no defence, even the truth."

Physical violence was also very much a part of the Strife session, though this is no longer the case.

Strife has several functions:

—to denounce the accused publicly.

—to punish him for improper attitudes.

—to extract a confession. The accused must be made to confess before he is punished, even if his punishment has been decided beforehand. Even if he confesses at once, Strife is likely to continue regardless.

—to act as a deterrent and to use the accused as a negative example to others.

Strife can go on indefinitely—it has no time limit. It can take place on a small scale (within a prison-cell, within a work-unit), or on a large scale (e.g. at mass meetings or rallies, especially against political offenders who are considered to have admitted their crimes with insufficient thoroughness, or to have shown an inadequate degree of repentance).

Mao once made the famous remark: "In a nation of eight hundred million, Strife is a necessary part of life." (*Bayi ren budou xing ma?*)

STRIFE AND CRIT (*pidou*, literally "criticism and struggle")

The intensified and often violent form of Strife that became common during the Cultrev.

THREE-ANTIS CAMPAIGN (*sanfan yundong*)

A nation-wide campaign launched in early 1952 to oppose corruption, waste and bureaucracy within the Party and within the State apparatus.

THREE MOST READ WORKS (*lao san pian*, literally "three old essays")

The three most widely read essays written by Mao, which were:
  1. Serve the People

2. In Memory of Norman Bethune
3. The Foolish Old Man Who Removed the Mountains.
The study of these became *de rigueur* in the People's Liberation Army
from 1964.

TRANSFER GIRLS (*luohu guniang*, literally "settling girls")

Girls and young women like Yu Luojin who sought to escape extreme
poverty by settling in a relatively well-off area, often giving themselves
in marriage in order to obtain the necessary transfer-permit.

URBLINGS (*zhishi qingnian*, literally "educated youths")

Urblings are young school-leavers from urban areas.

In the late fifties and early sixties, when the Chinese economy failed
to create sufficient job opportunities for them, Urblings were strongly
encouraged to go to the countryside ("up mountain or down country") supposedly to learn from their country cousins. In the early years
of the Cultrev, this "rustication" of Urblings became compulsory.

Several factors, such as the young people's own urban background
and the reluctance of the peasants to share their far from ample arable
land with these none too co-operative outsiders, made it extremely
difficult for Urblings to acclimatize themselves in their appointed places
of resettlement.

After Mao's death and the fall of the Gang of Four, a large
proportion of these rusticated Urblings managed to return to their
places of origin, where they became Jobblers, *daiye qingnian*, literally
"job-waiting youth". "Job-waiting" is an obvious euphemism for
"jobless", and the actual process of waiting has in many cases
outlasted the youth.

Some of the less fortunate of these Jobblers, who for understandable
reasons were involved in various forms of delinquency or Drossnik

(q.v.) behaviour, became known as Slippers, *shizu qingnian*, literally "youth who had slipped in their footsteps".

VOICERS (*youpai fenzi*, literally "rightist elements")

Voicers were among the five Black categories. The term first appeared in 1957 to designate those people (particularly members of the intelligentsia) who had voiced criticism of the Party during the Blooms and Voices Movement (q.v.).

The Blooms and Voices Movement was launched in 1957 on Mao's initiative, actively and openly inviting political criticism of all kinds. The response over the following few weeks was overwhelming, ranging from the trivial to the profound. The Party apparently did not expect that the fundamental principles of its policy would be questioned, and retaliated in June 1957 with the Anti-Voicer campaign as a means of suppressing this new category of "enemies". Voicers were seen as "bourgeois reactionaries who opposed communism, opposed the people, and opposed socialism", and their writings and speeches were referred to as Poison (q.v.).

As Class Enemies, the majority of Voicers were severely dealt with and sent off to camps for Labour Cure or Labour Mould (qq.v.).

WALLSCREEDS (*dazibao*, literally "big-character posters")

Wallscreeds were propaganda posters written in large characters, usually with Chinese brushes, and pasted high-up on walls or boards. They were widely used during the 1957 Anti-Voicer campaign and the 1958 Commune Movement, and even more extensively during the Cultrev. Mao called them "an extremely useful new weapon" — especially useful for the purpose of denouncing people, or as a means for one group to attack another.

They could also be written in the form of letters, memos, cartoons, poems and songs.

They are now illegal in China.

WORK-TEAM (*shengchandui*)

The commune was divided into brigades, and the brigades were further divided into work-teams (e.g., First Team, Second Team). The "team" can thus refer either to the geographical division, or to the people living within that area.

THE WORLD IS WIDE...

These were the much reprinted words of Mao's exhortation to Urblings (q.v.), as they set off to "build socialism in the countryside".

YOUNG PIONEERS (*shaoxiandui*)

The junior branch of the Communist Youth League (q.v.). Roughly 95% of children aged 9-15 are Young Pioneers, and wear a red cotton scarf round their necks to indicate the fact.

YOUTH LEAGUE (*qingniantuan*)

Formed in the twenties along the lines of the Soviet Komsomol. The Party organization for youths from approximately 15 to 25 years old. Entry to it is seen as a first step towards entry into the Party itself.

YOUTH SETTLEMENT (*qingniandui*)

According to some accounts (e.g. Amnesty International), these rural settlements of young people consisted of children of Free-workers (q.v.), who had graduated from junior high school and were encouraged to set up on their own away from the corrupting influence of their ex-convict parents.

Biographical Notes

Chen Boda (1904-)
Mao's secretary from 1937, and closely associated with Mao from early Yan'an days. An unoriginal and hard-working Party theoretician who wrote numerous propaganda works expounding and extolling the thought of Mao Zedong. Mao's mouth-piece for over 30 years.

Chen Boda was appointed the head of the Cultrev Group in 1966, but was later disgraced. Now in prison.

Cong Weixi (1933-)
Writer of fiction and prose. Capped (q.v.) as a Voicer in 1957 for his writings and sentenced to labour. Finally released after twenty years, and allowed to return to Peking in 1979.

Jiao Yulu
Jiao Yulu, Party Secretary of Lankao County, Henan Province, was a national hero of the early 1960s. He had cancer of the liver, but did many "good deeds" for his county before his death.

Lin Biao (1907-1971)
Minister of Defence in 1959, and responsible for the ideological reorganization of the army. Before he died he became Vice-Chairman of the Party and Mao's "closest comrade-in-arms".

He was officially reported to have died in an airplane crash as he was fleeing toward the Soviet Union, having failed in a coup d'état and assassination attempt on Mao in September 1971. (What actually happened is unclear.)

Although many people secretly rejoiced at Lin's disappearance, public denunciation was postponed for more than two years.

Yao Wenyuan (1931-)

Yao Wenyuan began his career as an obscure literary critic in Shanghai, and eventually became a specialist in the denunciation of writers and intellectuals. He was much hated in literary circles.

In 1965, Mao commissioned him to write an article for the Shanghai paper *Wenhui Bao* that was instrumental in helping spark off the Cultrev. He was publicly named in 1966 as one of the 17 members of the Cultrev Group, and later became a Vice-Premier and one of the Gang of Four. Now in prison.

Yu Luojin

Yu Luojin was born in 1946. Her father was a qualified engineer who had studied in Japan, while her mother owned a small factory which she later handed over to the State. Her parents suffered during the Anti-Voicer Campaign of 1957, and subsequently her father lost his job.

Yu Luojin attended the No. 12 High School for Girls in Peking, and afterwards studied at Art School (she graduated in 1965). She then worked as a trainee in the carpentry workshop of a toy factory.

In 1966, in the early weeks of the Cultrev, she was detained in connection with the discovery of diaries belonging to herself and to her elder brother Yu Luoke, and was sent for three years of Labour Cure — first at Liangxiang Camp south of Peking, then at Qinghe Camp near the Gulf of Bohai. In 1970 she was sent to the poor and remote rural area of Linxi in southern Hebei Province, from which she managed to transfer later that year to the richer (though wilder) province of Heilongjiang (the so-called Great Northern Wilderness). There she married Zhao Zhiguo, a young Urbling from Peking. Their marriage and separation (in 1974) form the background of *A Chinese Winter's Tale*, the first draft of which was written in 1974.

By 1976 she was back in Peking, where she soon found it impossible to continue living with her family. Her parents were living in very cramped quarters. Her father still had no proper job, her mother had started drinking, and of her two surviving brothers (Yu Luoke had been executed in 1970), one was unemployed and the other was in jail.

She found temporary employment as a nurse, and later married again—this time to an electrician called Cai Zhongpei.

In 1979 she was officially "rehabilitated", and received 678 *kuai* as compensation, and her old job at the toy factory. In the autumn of 1980, the first expurgated edition of *Winter's Tale* came out in the magazine *Dangdai*.

Meanwhile, Yu Luojin was seeking a divorce from her second husband. Her outspoken stand on the issue of divorce, together with the banning of her second autobiographical work, *Spring Tale*, and the "scandal" surrounding her relationship with Ma Paiwen, literary editor of the major national daily *Guangming ribao*, made her a celebrity. She became notorious as the "fallen woman" on the Chinese literary scene.

Finally, in May 1981, the divorce was granted. But *Winter's Tale* had meanwhile been prevented from receiving the prestigious literary award for which it had been recommended by the famous older writer Ba Jin.

In July 1982 she was married for the third time to Wu Fanjun, a teacher at the Peking Institute of Metallurgy.

In late 1985, she left for a privately sponsored visit to West Germany. Early in 1986 she applied for political asylum, and is still (November 1986) awaiting the decision of the German authorities.

Yu Luoke

Born in 1942. Graduated in 1960 from Peking No. 65 High School. In 1962 he was assigned to work in Manyuan Hongxing Commune.

In November 1965, Yu Luoke submitted to the Shanghai paper *Wenhui Bao* a rebuttal of Yao Wenyuan's (q.v.) attack on Wu Han. He later attracted the attention of the authorities with his essay "On Class Background" (q.v.). He was arrested on January 5 1968, and executed on March 5 1970.

> Even in prison, handcuffed and in chains, Yu Luoke did not abandon his optimism. He organized classes in philosophy and foreign languages for the other detainees, amused himself at the expense of the interrogators, and won the respect of the criminals and delinquents among the common

prisoners who saw in him a spokesman of the under-privileged. He had only to write a Scrit (q.v.) to save his neck, but he refused, sustained by an idealism which he now used as a weapon against authority. He was subjected to several mock-executions to make him recant, and when he was finally stood up against the wall and given two minutes to reflect, he calmly asked...to be given a tube of toothpaste!

(Huang San and Miguel Mandarès)

In 1977 he was officially (and posthumously) "rehabilitated".

C